The Grave House Guest

Henrietta F. Ford

PublishAmerica
Baltimore

ISBN: 978-1-4489-5627-2
PUBLISHED BY PUBLISHAMERICA, LLLP
www.publishamerica.com
Baltimore

Printed in the United States of America

Other Books by Henrietta F. Ford

Angels in the Snow
When Sleeping Dogs Lie
Murder on the OBX
The Hessian Link

To

Brian Thomas Maus

Acknowledgements

There is some danger in acknowledgements in that an author might inadvertently omit the name of a person who has been helpful. However, there are those whose support was so valuable in the writing of this book that it makes the risk worthwhile. To them I express my deepest appreciation below:

To my husband, Jim Maus, without whose help and encouragement I could never write mysteries. Thank you, Jim. You are my faithful advocate and my best friend.

To my sister-in-law, Ann Ford, who gathered information for me about Seaboard and Northampton County. I thank you, Ann, for being such a determined sleuth.

To Linda Eccleston who read and offered suggestions for this book. You are a true scholar and a dear friend.

To the Northampton County, NC Bicentennial Committee congratulations on your superb publication, "Footprints in Northampton". I found the book to be most useful in researching this mystery.

Characters

Sophie Singletary—recent divorcee
Andrew T. Temple—Sophie's ex-husband
Jan Ewing—Sophie's closest friend
Julie Hinson—Sophie's oldest friend
Jeff Sands—United States Marshal and Sophie's high school love interest
Gladys Spencer—Sophie's housekeeper
Melvin Brinks—Sophie's handyman and Gladys's love interest
Eileen Brown—librarian
Josie Clark—assistant librarian
Mrs. Carrie Hendricks—local genealogical authority
Buddy Turner—young, untested Deputy United States Marshal
Jesse Ray—United States Marshal on-site office coordinator
Arlis Bryant—Jeff's Superior from Raleigh
Dillon—Seaboard policeman
Frank, William, Robert—Dillon's deputies

Friendship

Oh, the comfort—the inexpressible comfort
     of feeling safe with a person.
Having neither to weigh thoughts,
Nor measure words—but pouring them
All right out—just as they are—
Chaff and grain together—
Certain that a faithful hand will
Take and sift them—
Keep what is worth keeping—
And with the breath of kindness
Blow the rest away.

Dinah Maria Mulock Craik
(1826-1887)

Prologue

A silver Lexus pulled into the deserted parking lot, cut its lights, and a driver stepped out. He was a tall man with a muscular build and was dressed in an expensive gray suit. The top button of his blue shirt was unfastened, and an unknotted red striped tie hung loosely around his neck. The driver stretched widely and kneaded his lower back. A heavy haze rose from the Potomac River and drifted across the Washington skyline like a misty shroud. The driver narrowed his eyes, peered into the mist, and then began walking slowly down the path along the riverbank.

Suddenly a man stepped out of the shadows and spoke softly.

"You are late," said the intruder.

The driver looked around guardedly and said, "I wanted to make sure I wasn't being followed. Walk over here."

The two men stepped into the shadows of a stand of birch trees. The intruder was a tall, dark man with piercing black eyes and black hair, and he spoke with a Mid-Eastern accent, "The terms have been agreed upon. The contract is made. This provides you with information about the one you must kill."

He handed the assassin a small envelope. The assassin took the envelope, opened it, and looked inside. He saw a small black rectangular object about the size of a quarter with seven copper tabs attached. It was enclosed in a plastic casing.

"A secure digital memory card," said the man with the thick accent.

"I know," said the assassin.

"The card reveals the target's calendar of scheduled appearances for

13

the next nine months. Changes will occur, of course, but as you will see there are many opportunities and much time for preparations." The intruder hesitated and looked intently at the assassin. "If you did not come with impeccable recommendations, we would be concerned. Under the circumstances, however, we shall rely upon you to make all arrangements."

The assassin simply sneered. "What about the money?"

"Half of the agreed upon amount has been deposited to the numbered account. The other half will be deposited to that same account the day after we determine your target is indeed dead."

"Good. Then we have completed this part of our business." The assassin pocketed the envelope and walked toward the path. He did not look back as he disappeared into the fog.

The intruder sighed, spread his hands in a gesture of resignation, and stepped into the shadows.

Chapter 1

He was very cold. The late afternoon sky was dark and leaden with unshed snow. The man in a bulky parka with the hood pulled up round his face stood in the shadows of the parking lot at the Tex-Mex Restaurant in Roanoke Rapids, North Carolina. His eyes were fixed on the goings-on inside. Steam from the kitchen accumulated around the edges of the restaurant window and framed a scene inside that stirred memories the man had suppressed for years.

The restaurant was empty except for a few cocktail-hour customers and five women engaged in lively conversation at a window table. He would have known her anywhere. The years had not changed her that much. Of course, she no longer wore a long auburn pony tail. Instead her hair sprinkled with silver was pinned up in a twist. She wasn't wearing jeans and a tight tee shirt designed to reveal perky young breasts. Now her clothes were comfortable, expensive, and the latest style. But so many things about her had not change… her animation, attentiveness, and the way she used her eyes to convey more than words could say. She was definitely a looker. She was tall and slim, and she commanded the attention of other diners…especially men.

Cars began to pull into the parking lot. These would be the early diners arriving for the five-o'clock special. The watcher stepped back into the shadows. As the newcomers entered the restaurant, the women began to gather their things and slowly moved toward the door. Outside there were brief hugs and farewells and then each woman walked briskly to her car. She was walking in his direction. He waited until she reached her car and scrambled for her key to unlock the door.

He stepped out of the shadows, took her arm, and said, "Hey!"

She recoiled, forcibly wrenched her arm from his grasp, and squealed, "Ahhhh."

Then she was speechless. She'd heard of being so frightened that one could neither speak nor move. That was happening to her now. Although there were people just inside the restaurant, she couldn't cry out for help. She was frozen. Strong hands grasped her arms and whirled her around. Terrified, she gawped into the eyes of the intruder. The flicker of the neon lights in the restaurant window projected an eerie distortion of her assailant. Then slowly, slowly the figure coalesced into someone vaguely familiar. She suddenly realized she knew this man. From some time...some place. Who? Then recognition set in.

"Jeff?" she peeped.

He released his grip and smiled down at her. "So, you remember me, Sophie." he said.

She exhaled loudly. "Yes. I remember. But you just scared the daylights out of me." She went limp and leaned against her car.

"Sorry," he said, concern etched on his face. "I didn't mean to frighten you. I was watching through the restaurant window. I thought it was you."

She relaxed, took a deep breath, smiled slightly, and said, "I was meeting with some of our old classmates. We were firming up plans for a reunion tomorrow night. You should have come inside and joined us."

"Looked like a girl's-only party to me," he said.

"Not at all," she said. She was still trembling.

"Let's go somewhere and get a cup of coffee," he said. He took her arm and tried to steer her with him.

Sophie pulled away and said, "I'm sorry I can't, Jeff. It's getting late. Today's Friday...payday. I have to hurry home and give Gladys her check. She plans to grocery shop tonight. Maybe some other time."

He shrugged. "Shot down again," he said and started to turn.

"No, wait, Jeff," Sophie said. "I heard you were back. I don't know if you've gotten the word, but we're having a small high school reunion tomorrow night...not just for our class but for anyone left in Seaboard that went to high school with us. I hope you'll come. My place...eight o'clock."

"I'll see," he said. "...if I don't have to work." He turned and swaggered away.

"Good night, Jeff," Sophie called.

Jeff did not answer. He walked across the parking lot and leaned against his car. He watched as Sophie started her car and headed toward the exit. Then he opened his car door. On the door of the car were the words United States Marshal.

Jeff waited until her car merged into traffic. Then he drove slowly toward the exit. He waited for three cars to pass before he pulled out and headed in the same direction she'd taken. It wasn't hard to stay out of her sight in traffic, but it would be tricky when she turned onto a less traveled road. Jeff knew these back roads so well. He knew she'd have to take a road that went through a swamp and woods of Cyprus trees in order to get home...in order to reach Seaboard. Then he saw her car turn right. Two of the cars in front of him continued straight. The third one turned right. This was good. There was at least one car between them. He slowed more. Now it would be easy to keep her tail lights in sight on this flat straight road.

How many times he rode down this road with her. The drive brought back so many memories...tender yet passionate memories. Memories of her long white legs stretching out of a faded swimsuit; her bare feet pumping a bicycle down a hot dusty road; walks on steamy summer nights; and the kisses...innocent kisses that hinted there could be much more.

He could envision her now driving along thoughtlessly, radio blaring, singing along without a care in the world. Sophie was oblivious to danger. She'd always been like that...carefree, exhilarated, and foolish.

Jeff reached a sign that read 'Welcome to Seaboard'. The car between them continued straight, but he saw Sophie's turn signal flash. Careful to avoid being seen, he slowed and allowed her to complete the right turn before he followed. After all, he knew exactly where she was going. She drove across the railroad tracks and through town.

How Seaboard how declined over the years. It was an old town...a proud town. The small town was settled in 1751 by settlers that came from nearby Virginia. They had been attracted to the miles and miles of fertile farm land. They built a settlement and called it Concord. But in 1832 a railroad was built to connect Portsmouth, Virginia to Weldon, North Carolina and it ran straight through Concord. It was the Seaboard Railroad, known then as simply the Seaboard Road. Citizens of the small community were awestruck by the powerful engine that coughed black smoke and shook the earth. So hoping to capitalize on this new technology they changed the name of their town from Concord to Seaboard. Unfortunately the rewards for this name change were modest. The railroad did provide transportation to larger towns, and to the naval base in Norfolk. It allowed for daily shipments of fresh salt-water fish to the inland towns. But sadly the reign of the train ended and like other small towns, Seaboard declined with the railroad. Today the town consisted only of a mom and pop grocery, a bank, a post office, a John Deere farm implements dealership, a laundrymat, and several boarded-up wooden buildings.

Jeff watched the tail lights of Sophie's car disappear over the crest of the hill. He continued up Main Street pass several old Victorian homes hidden behind pecan and magnolia trees. There were two churches at the top of the hill...a Baptist Church and a Methodist Church. He reached the Baptist Church but stopped just short of the Methodist.

Sophie's house was across Main Street from the Methodist Church. It was a large yellow Victorian house complete with gingerbread and a wrap-around porch on which set two high-back rockers and a porch swing. The leaded windows sparkled with the reflection of a nearby streetlight. The house exuded an aura of comfort and serenity. Sophie parked in her driveway almost hidden by a row of giant English boxwoods. She bounded out of the car, and walked quickly toward the house. When the front door closed behind her, Jeff drove pass her house and headed toward Jackson, the county seat of Northampton County.

* * *

Sophie rushed through the front door, removed her coat, and tossed it on a waiting chair in the entrance hall. The entrance hall was a large, square 'shot-gun' hall meaning that the back hall door was directly behind the front hall door. In other words one had a straight shot from one door to the other. At one time the back hall door led to a porch, but Sophie had enclosed the porch and turned it into a sunroom. A large Oriental rug covered a portion of the highly-polished hall floor. A loveseat was positioned by the entrance to the den. There were several waiting chairs, an antique French commode, and a mahogany linen chest. Pocket doors on the left of the hall opened into a large den. On the right there was a pocket door that opened into a parlor and another into the dining room. Most impressive, however, was the staircase. There were three levels of steps, and at the top of each level was a small landing.

Sophie hurried to the kitchen looking for Gladys. Gladys came to work at the Singletary house when Sophie and her widowed mother moved in with Grandmother Singletary. Gladys cared for Sophie as a child and quickly became a strong mother figure for her. So when Sophie moved back home following a bitter divorce, Gladys assumed her previous station as if no time had passed at all. Gladys never seemed to age. Sophie thought Gladys looked the same today as she did when Sophie was a child. She had light almond skin, was pleasingly plump, and fashioned her hair in tightly-braided rows. Summer or winter, Gladys always wore cotton house dresses, black comfort shoes, and thick cotton stockings. And she smelled like freshly cooked pies or homemade bread.

When Sophie rushed into the kitchen she found Gladys seated at the kitchen table, wearing her coat and kerchief, and holding a large black pocket book on her lap. Gladys was not happy.

"Sorry to be late, Gladys," said Sophie. "I ran into someone I haven't seen for a long time and I lost track of the time."

Sophie reached into her purse, removed her checkbook, and began writing a check for Gladys.

"I ain't gonna say it's alright," said Gladys. "You know how I despise to stay in this house pass dark."

"I promise I'll try not to let it happen again," said Sophie as she tore off the check and handed it to Gladys.

"Well, **trying** mightn't be enough, Sophie. I tell you this place is preoccupied," Gladys said as she put the check in her pocketbook and clicked it shut.

"Preoccupied?" Sophie questioned. "I don't understand."

"You bet your sweet bottom, Sophie. You just think 'bout all them people what's died here. Them spirits are still 'round. Yeah. They ain't gone nowhere."

Gladys stood and walked toward the front hall. Sophie walked with her. She knew Gladys hated the gloomy hall after dark.

"By the way, I done the dips and appetizers you wanted. They're in the 'frigerator. You sure you don't need me tomorrow night...you know to do dishes and all that," said Gladys.

"No thanks," said Sophie. "Jan and Julie are coming early to help set up, and I'm just going to leave clean-up till Sunday."

They reached the door. "Well, I'll come by after church on Sunday to help clean up," said Gladys. "If'n I don't it'll be waiting for me Monday. Nothing worse than trying to wash dishes what's set for two days...caked with dried food and such."

"Thanks, Gladys," said Sophie. "What would I do without you?"

"I don't know," said Gladys as she reached for the door handle. "Half the people in Seaboard say this place be haunted. You'd be hard pressed to find someone to take my place."

Sophie rolled her eyes in disbelief. "Good night, Gladys," she said.

After her father's death, Sophie and her mother came to live in the house with her father's grandmother. To say that Sophie was spoiled would be an understatement. She was pampered, overprotected, and mollycoddled by the entire household. She was given free rein of the house and everything in it. Sophie investigated every nook and cranny. She and her little friends spent many afternoons exploring, playing hide and seek, and 'playing pretend'. Her favorite play place was the attic where old trunks and cupboards were filled with many childish treasures. She and her friends tried on the vintage clothes, old jewelry, hats, shoes, and moth eaten fur coats. They found old toys and baby clothes, cribs, and high chairs. The whole house was a little girl's dream.

It was on one of her summer explorations of the attic that Sophie found the trunk. It was a large, heavy old trunk. The kind one might have taken on a sea voyage. It was covered with stickers from different countries...Italy, Germany, England, and France. It was, of course, locked which served only to peak Sophie's curiosity. She felt no qualms about breaking the lock and found that a nearby rusty screwdriver served the purpose nicely. She was delighted to find that it was filled with personal memorabilia such as letters, journals, and pictures of people, some in period dress, smiling happily into the camera. Who were these people in the pictures? Who wrote the letters and made journal entries in such a lovely, flowing pen? Sophie felt compelled to search out the answers to these and other questions. And this fascination began Sophie's interest in family history which she enjoyed even now.

Sophie graduated from high school and enrolled in the university. Soon after graduation from the university she met and married the man of her dreams. However, as is often the case with over-protected young women, her dream soon turned out to be a nightmare. After years of hopelessness, Sophie returned to Seaboard, to her family, and to her home...that wonderful old house.

Returning to Seaboard provided her with opportunities to pursue her love for family research. She prowled old cemeteries in search of family members' final resting places and rummaged through aged dusty records in the nearby county library. She found the hours spent in these pursuits to be stimulating and restorative.

Sophie closed the door and stood with her back against it. The house was not a grand place. It was just a rambling old Victorian house filled with antiques and stuffy old furniture. It had been in her family for generations.

Sophie walked about downstairs clicking off lights as she went. Afterwards she climbed the stairs, stopped on the second landing, turned, and looked down into the dark hall below. How could she ever be afraid in this place? In this house she'd known love and security. So what if there were ghosts? They were her ghosts.

* * *

On Church Street, a street that ran beside Sophie's home, a rusty battered Chevelle was parked in the shadows. The car was positioned to stay clear of the light from the streetlight. Its windows were covered with condensation obscuring the people inside. Occasionally a hand went up to clear a spot big enough to give a view of the large yellow house. Tiny pinpoints of fire appeared and disappeared as the occupants pulled on cigarettes and filled the car with nocuous fumes. The smoke made it even more difficult for any passerby to identify the two people huddled inside the car and to determine their purpose for being there on such a bitterly cold winter night.

Chapter 2

Seaboard High School no longer existed. Now there was just a two-story brick shell of a building with broken windows, rotting stairways, and busted padlocks. It was a sad sight to behold. Sophie had attended school there for twelve years. This was before the state plucked such tiny schools out of their communities and bused the kids to a warehouse-like structure in another part of the county. The disappearance of community schools set in motion the demise of many small towns. The ball games, music performances, plays, Halloween carnivals, May Day celebrations, proms, talent competitions…were the glue that held small towns together. It was at these events that citizens gathered with common interests and for support. Parents knew teachers and teachers knew parents. No deed done by an errant student ever went unreported.

Sophie graduated from the tiny school twenty-five years ago, and there had only been sixteen students in her class. After graduation some of her classmates stayed in Seaboard, others moved away, and two died. A committee was formed to plan a class reunion. The big turnout the reunion committee hoped for seemed unlikely, so they decided to invite anyone who attended high school at the same time they were there. Word of the reunion spread like wild fire.

On the night of the reunion people showed up that Sophie hadn't thought of in years. Thankfully, some brought platters of appetizers to contribute to the fare. Others, however, simply brought a brown bag containing their choice of booze.

Because of the large crowd, Sophie found herself in the kitchen most of the time washing glasses and refurbishing platters. Now she wished she'd taken Gladys up on her offer to help out tonight.

"Boy-howdy! Things are really starting to take off!" The breathless excited voice belonged to Jan Ewing, one of Sophie's closest 'partners in time'.

Sophie lost her eastern North Carolina accent after a marriage that took her to live in so many places. Jan, however, retained hers along with an endearing sense of humor. She was short, and her full figure bore witness to her culinary skills. Short gray hair framed her smiling face that was virtually free of wrinkles. Jan was the motherly type, and now that Sophie was back in Seaboard, she felt a responsibility to care for her. Jan and Sophie went through twelve years of school together and knew enough *stuff* about each other to write a best-seller. When Sophie moved back to Seaboard, she and Jan picked up their friendship as if time and distance never separated them. Jan had married her high school sweetheart. Now she was a widow and lived alone on their family farm just outside Seaboard.

"You need to get yourself out there and enjoy your own party, girl," Jan said.

"In a minute," said Sophie. "I can't seem to keep up with the glasses."

"Told you to use paper cups or at least those disposal plastic kind otherwise you'd be stuck out here in the kitchen," Jan said. Jan never missed a chance to say 'I told you so' to Sophie. Unfortunately, she was usually right.

"*Paper* and *plastic?*" this indignant voice belonged to Julie Hinson, and Julie never missed a chance to point out what she thought was the *proper* way things should be done.

Julie always dressed to the nines and her bottle black hair was coifed in the latest style. She compulsively counted calories and was slim to the point of appearing anorexic. Julie was Sophie's oldest friend. They'd known each other all their lives. Julie left Seaboard soon after Sophie. She married a Yankee, divorced him, married a Texan, divorced him, married a chiropractor, divorced him, and then she moved back to Seaboard. Now she was Sophie's next door neighbor.

"You can't use *paper* and *plastic* at a momentous occasion like a class reunion," Julie said with contempt.

"Well wash glasses or enjoy your party...take your pick," Jan said with a shrug.

"I thought you'd like to know that Beak arrived," said Julie ignoring Jan's barb. "You really should be greeting your guests, Sophie."

Sophie abruptly stopped what she was doing, faced her friends, and said emphatically, "Just a minute. Please take care of things while I finish here."

Jan and Julie looked at each other, shook their heads, and walked out of the kitchen. Sophie knew she should have been out front to greet Beak. Beak. She smiled at the silly moniker.

Every student at Seaboard High School had a nickname. There was Beak because he had a hook nose like an eagle's beak. Spots had freckles on her face. Jigs was the guy girls like to dance with. Stilts had long legs. Squeaky talked in a high pitch voice. Einstein was smart. Sophie was Slim because she was slim. And Jeff was Stud...just because he looked like a Stud....and so on. Sophie shook her head and smiled.

Sophie reached for a cookie, bit into it, and frowned as crumbs toppled onto the front of her black dress. Suddenly, there was an explosion of noise from the front hall, and Julie rushed in with a big grin on her face.

"Guess who's here Sophie?" Julie spoke conspiratorially and grinned ear to ear.

"I have no idea, Julie," Sophie said testily as she rinsed a glass and placed it on a rack to dry.

Julie continued to smirk. "It's *Studdd*," she said. "And he's every bit the *Stud* he used to be...maybe even more so."

Sophie rinsed another glass, placed it on the rack, and gave herself a chance to recoup.

Then she said nonchalantly, "I'm so glad he could make it."

"Oh yes," said Julie, "I'm *sure* you are."

Jan appeared making it unnecessary for Sophie to comment further. "Hey girlfriend, the party's going on without you. You're missing all the fun. And guess who's here? Old Stud," Jan said as she answered her own question.

"I'm so glad he made it," Sophie repeated. Sophie grabbed two plates.

She shoved a plate of cookies at Julie and a plate of veggies at Jan and said, "Here take these. I'll be right out."

Julie took the plate and gave Sophie a knowing look. Jan simply grabbed the platter, walked out, and was back to join the party.

Sophie could hear the women's shrill giggles and the men's boisterous voices as they tried to impress the high school super star! Then someone put on oldies music and turned the volume up to an ear piercing level. There was a bumping noise, and Sophie envisioned Jigs and partner demonstrating his latest dance routine. Then she realized that the lights from the dining room and hall had been lowered. She grabbed a kitchen towel, dried her hands, and tossed it on the counter. Sophie knew she had to go out there. She couldn't avoid Jeff all night.

Suddenly she heard a familiar voice say, "Hey."

Sophie knew immediately who it was. She turned and smiled. "Hey, Jeff. So glad you could make it," she said for the third time that night.

Now Sophie was finally getting a **good** look at Jeff, and she understood why the women in the front hall were sniggering and tittering. To say that Jeff was handsome would be an understatement. He was gorgeous. His thick brown hair sported just enough gray to give him that sophisticated, mature appearance you see on television. He wore a leather jacket, tight fitting turtle neck tee shirt, and khaki pants. Sophie concluded that without a doubt he worked out every day. Yeah…Jeff was handsome, and Jeff was still a Stud.

Jeff leaned against the door with a drink in his hand and slowly studied the room. Finally he said, "Nice house you got here. You've done a lot to the old place."

"Yes, quite a bit really," said Sophie. "lots of painting, papering, a little bit of remodeling. But I think I'm just about through… at least for the time being. I've got one bathroom upstairs that I have to replace the tile. Not right now but maybe later in the spring." Sophie knew she was rambling, but she couldn't stop. She watched a grin slowly spread across Jeff's face. She felt like a fool.

"I could do that for you," he said slowly and took a sip of his drink.

"You, do what?" Sophie stammered.

"Do that for you. Replace the tile in your upstairs bathroom," he said, smiled, and lifted an eyebrow.

"Thanks for offering," said Sophie, "but I've already contracted with someone."

"I could do it cheaper," he said lifting his glass. "Where does that go?" He nodded toward the back stairs.

"It goes upstairs. It's a back stairs so if you're in the kitchen you don't have to go through the front hall to get to the stairs that go up…" Sophie stopped. Jeff grinned.

For some reason Sophie felt trapped…trapped in her own kitchen. Jeff was blocking the door. In order to leave the room, she'd have to squeeze past him. He might move, but then he might not. She remembered the encounter with him in the parking lot at the Tex-Mex Restaurant. To say he'd invaded her space was to minimize the situation.

Suddenly Jeff walked across the room and stared down at her intently. Then he slowly lifted his hand and brushed her cheek. Sophie froze. "A crumb," he said simply. Then he turned, and walked back to the door.

Sophie had been so startled that all she could do was squeak, "Thanks."

As if it were an afterthought, Jeff looked squarely at her. A dark expression crossed his face. Then he demanded, "Why did you dump me?"

"What?" Sophie said blankly.

"Why did you dump me?" Jeff repeated resentfully.

Sophie was stunned. Is this why he's acting so bizarre? Because he thinks I dumped him. Surely he can't be obsessing over a brief fling that took place while they were kids in high school. How old had they been? Fifteen…Sixteen? How dare he come here and harass her by bringing up a foolish thing like a teen age crush. Now Sophie was angry.

"**Dump** you?" said Sophie. "Jeff, I didn't dump you. *You* dumped me."

"That's not the way I remember it," Jeff said. He actually sounded angry.

"Well, that's the way I remember it," said Sophie standing her ground. Then she stomped to the door and pushed past Jeff. "Now if you will excuse me. I have to mingle."

"Wouldn't want to keep you from *mingling,*" Jeff said contemptuously.

Sophie worked her way through the crowd that had grown way beyond anything they'd expected. Who were all these people? Some were probably alumni she didn't recognize. Some might be guests of alumni. Others were most likely party crashers. Regardless, Sophie welcomed them all. Lights had been turned down even more, and now a few couples were slow dancing in the parlor where the only illumination was from the hall lights. Julie and Jan were really on top of things gathering dishes, passing platters and making friendly with all the guests. Sophie finally began to relax. She would just not think about Jeff.

She reached for a cracker topped with clam spread, took a bite, and watched as crumbs were strewn down the front of her dress again. "What a messer I am!" she mumbled to herself.

Sophie moved into the hall, leaned against the door jamb, and checked her memory by trying to put names with faces. Suddenly she felt a jab in her ribs. She turned sharply and found her face within inches of Jeff's. His face was expressionless. He reached up and brushed her chin. "More crumbs," he said simply.

"Will you please stop grooming me," Sophie said, and slapped his hand. She turned to walk away, but he caught her arm in a tight grip and wheeled her around. Sophie was startled. What's gotten into this man? His antagonistic attitude was beginning to scare her.

"Let's dance," Jeff said. And he steered her to the far corner of the dimly lighted parlor.

He placed his hand on the small of her back and pressed her close to him. They did not move for several seconds. He just held her and laid his face against her hair. She felt his warm breath on her ear. When they finally began to dance their movement was little more than a rocking motion. Ray Price sang his famous ballad *For the Good Times* in which he explicitly suggested passionate moves best for ending a fading love affair.

Jeff pulled Sophie even closer and whispered hoarsely, "Nice."

Sophie suddenly became tongue-tied but managed to stammer, "Yes, I think that's the best break-up song ever written and Ray…"

"That's not what I meant," Jeff snapped pressing her against him so tightly that she was sure he'd bruised her.

Sophie thought, "Why is he so angry?" Resentment flared. Every since the incident in the Tex-Mex Restaurant parking lot, Sophie had resented Jeff's arrogant, presumptuous behavior. Now she realized that this was a different side of Jeff…a side she never knew. As he held her close Sophie's thoughts wandered back to another time. Suddenly it felt right being with Jeff. She wondered where this was going. So many years had passed. So many miles had separated them. He had no idea what her life had been like after she left Seaboard. Those first years of marriage had been especially hard for Sophie who'd grown up in such protective surroundings, and Sophie had been terribly wounded. The experience left her guarded…even fearful. She remembered how she'd felt apprehensive at the Tex-Mex Restaurant parking lot when Jeff suggested they drive somewhere for coffee. At that time she certainly had no reason to fear Jeff.

But they had both changed. She wondered what his life had been like these past fifteen years. Jeff had surely had lovers… even a wife or two. Sophie wondered about this curious dark side of Jeff. He was so unlike the easy going, jovial guy she'd known years ago. Jeff had been the most popular guy in high school. Yet he was neither arrogant nor a bully. He was pleasant and friendly. She didn't understand this intimidating attitude she'd experienced. And yet, now that he was so close it was amazing…she felt inexplicably safe.

Ray Price ended his counsel on how to recover from the good times, and Jeff and Sophie stood motionless his lips were still against her ear. He whispered "Sophie, I want to…"

Suddenly, there was an explosion of racket from the hall…music off the Richter, yelling, and cat calling. Sophie and Jeff pushed their way into the hall. Then they stopped abruptly and gawked up at the scene on the first stairwell landing.

Rap music exploded from a boom box sending vibrations through the entire house. It jolted paintings that hung on the wall, and bounced knick-knacks about so precariously that Sophie felt the need to run around grabbing up precious heirlooms. The scene on the first stairwell landing was mind-boggling. Jigs and Spots were dressed urban style. Both had on faded wash jeans worn so low that they exposed more than anyone needed to see. Logos were splashed across the front of their wrinkled cut-off tee shirts. Jigs' shirt read 'Rap me Baby' and Spots' read 'Look Before Touching'. Both rappers were draped in gold-type chains, long earrings, and wore washed-out athletic shoes of some undeterminable color. Spots' hair was orange, and Jigs was white. Their gyrating movements were evocative as they lip synced the lyrics of the number one rap hit. Everyone laughed and whistled and clapped as the two rappers bumped and pulsated about on the stairwell landing. Sophie and Jeff leaned against the door and laughed and clapped.

Jeff moved in close behind Sophie. He let his arm fall gently around her shoulder. Sophie did not move. This seemed so right. She was here in Seaboard, in her home, and surrounded by old friends. And Jeff was here...Jeff with his arm around her shoulder. It was meant to be Sophie thought dreamily. Sophie let her head fall against him. Jeff responded by squeezing her shoulder gently.

Then Jeff leaned in close, put his mouth to Sophie's ear, and whispered, "The rappers--do they remind you of someone?"

"What?" Sophie asked.

Jeff repeated, "Do the rappers remind you of the low-life you took up with after you dumped me?"

Fury surged through her. How dare he jerk her around like that? Sophie wrestled his arm from her shoulder, spun around, and headed into the dining room. When she realized Jeff was following her, she turned and sputtered vehemently, "Low life? Did you say low life? Who are you to criticize? If I remember correctly you took up with that dim witted little bimbo with an IQ of a head of cabbage."

"You've given this a lot of thought haven't you? Well think about this...at that point in time, I wasn't thinking about IQ's," Jeff said with an infuriating grin on his face.

"Now that I can believe," Sophie replied bitterly. "**You** dumped **me** for some cutesy little bottle blonde tramp and then blamed it all on me." Sophie turned to walk away.

"Why you were jealous!" she heard Jeff exclaim.

Sophie wheeled around and snapped, "Jealous? Don't flatter yourself *Stud.*"

"Are you listening to yourself?" Jeff said. "Yes, Sophie, jealous."

"That's ludicrous. Now leave me alone, Jeff. Just leave me alone," Sophie barked. She could feel tears welling in her eyes. She thought, "For Pete's sake don't let me cry."

As Sophie stormed into the kitchen, Jeff cried out above the din, "...and you're still jealous."

In order to avoid another encounter with Jeff, Sophie busied herself in the kitchen stacking dishes and trays for Gladys to clean in the morning. The rap performance was to be the culminating event of the evening, and soon Sophie recognized noises that signaled guests were leaving. She rushed back into the hall. As she stood by the open door saying good night to old classmates, she heard the faint drum of sleet on the porch roof. She cautioned everyone to drive carefully. It was then that she realized Jeff must have already gone.

Sophie turned to see Jan and Julie picking up glasses and plates to carry into the kitchen. "No, stop," said Sophie, "It's late that can wait."

"Nonsense," said Julie who thought leaving a messy kitchen overnight was an abomination. "We'll have this cleaned up before you know it."

Sophie rushed across the room and took dishes out of Jan and Julie's hands. "No, you don't understand. Gladys is coming in after church in the morning. She won't like it if someone does her work for her."

Jan said, "Well, I don't hold with leaving dirty dishes over night, but since Gladys has her heart set on cleaning up that's fine with me. I've got to drive out to the farm, and I think that was fine sleet I heard out there." She was already moving to get her coat.

Julie was still not sure. "Well, I don't know, Sophie. Would she be offended if we just rinsed them off?"

Sophie steered Julie toward the coat closet. "Yes," said Sophie. "Gladys would be offended. Now Julie we've had a full day. You need to get on home." Now she was steering Julie to the door. "And be careful. Don't slip on ice."

Julie was out the door with Jan close behind. Jan turned and said, "She don't take no for an answer easily does she?" Sophie laughed.

Sophie closed the door. She could hear her friends continue to squabble. She smiled and turned to survey the chaos. "If this mess is any measure of how much fun we had, then it was one hell of a party. Knock yourself out, Gladys," Sophie said and began clicking off lights on her way upstairs.

* * *

On the side street, two men in heavy hooded parkas and thermal gloves sat shivering in a smoke-filled Chevelle.

"Looks like that's the last of the party," said the man behind the wheel.

"It's about time," said his partner unscrewing the top on a thermos. "I hate this kind of work in winter. All to do is drink coffee and pee. By the way, I gotta see Mr. Mason."

"Again?" asked the driver as he reached into the back and brought out a large canning jar with the lid screwed on tightly. Inside a brown liquid sloshed about. The label on the jar read, Mason.

Chapter 3

The whisper of the sleet on the bedroom window had a calming effect. In spite of the excitement of the party and the confrontation with Jeff, Sophie fell asleep immediately.

She was roused from a deep sleep by the ringing of the doorbell. At first she thought she was dreaming but reality slowly surfaced. She turned over and grabbed the digital clock. Five forty five. The doorbell rang again. She rolled out of bed and pulled on her robe. She felt around on the floor with her foot for her slippers but couldn't locate them. The bell rang again. She dropped on her knees and reached under her bed, but no slippers. The ring became persistent, impatient. Sophie tied her robe tightly about her and hurried barefoot to the stairs.

"Somebody better be dead," she growled.

As she reached downstairs the bell rang again. She stormed across the hall, threw open the door, and stood face to face with Jeff.

Sophie was furious. "What? What do you want?" she demanded.

Jeff's eyes roamed up and down Sophie's body from her disheveled hair to her bare feet. He grinned widely.

Sophie was embarrassed. She felt naked, but her embarrassment soon turned back to anger.

Sophie said, "Do you have any idea what time it is?"

"Sure, it's quarter to six," Jeff said showing her his wristwatch.

"What do you want Jeff?" Sophie said impatiently.

"I came to measure," said Jeff casually.

"Measure? What are you talking about? Measure what? Are you crazy?" Sophie said incredulously.

"Measure the bathroom floor," Jeff said simply holding up a metal tape measure. "I'm on my way to Roanoke Rapids and thought I'd go by Lowe's…take a look at their tile."

Cold wind blew in through the partially opened door and Sophie shivered. Jeff put his hand on the door and gave it a shove. "You're gonna catch pneumonia out here half naked. Let's go inside," Jeff said.

Sophie put her full weight against the door. "No Jeff. You can't come inside. Besides I already told you I've contracted with someone to do that job. Now go way."

"Sophie, I want to talk to you," Jeff said impatiently. "Now let me in."

He clasped his fingers around the edge of the door and began to push harder. Sophie pushed back as forcefully as she could. Jeff was caught by surprise and his hand became wedged between the door and the frame. He screamed and swore as he jerked his hand free.

"You almost broke my damned fingers, Sophie," Jeff said angrily.

"I'm sorry Jeff, but your hand had no business being in my door. Now goodbye," Sophie shouted back.

Jeff mumbled incoherently for a few seconds. Then he shouted, "At least lock your damn door," he roared. Then Sophie heard him stomping down the steps. She listened as Jeff revved his engine and the car tore away.

Sophie stood with her back against the door. She was breathless. Suddenly, she felt empowered. She had defied Jeff. Jeff…who gave her such a hard time at her own party in her own home. Then she smiled contemptuously and said, "Lock my doors? Ha…lock my doors in Seaboard? Now that's a joke." She looked down at her bare feet and wiggled her freezing toes to jump start circulation again. Then she sped back up the stairs, and dived into her bed.

* * *

Gladys was never happier than when she had a messy house to fuss over, so today she was as happy as a clam. As promised she showed up right after church. She threw off her Sunday hat and hung her big pocketbook on the hanger with her coat. Then she began immediately picking up glasses, plates, and platters that contained putrefied party scraps. She was humming a hymn she'd sung at church. Sophie sat in the dining room, nursing a cup of coffee, and trying to remember the words to the hymn Gladys hummed.

The doorbell rang again. A feeling of dread swept over Sophie. Suppose it were Jeff again. She wasn't sure she could go another round with him this morning. She heard the door open and footsteps in the hall. Now she wished she'd locked the door. Then Julie marched in. Sophie felt a rush of relief.

"What in the world is going on over here, Sophie?" Julie demanded.

"Going on? What do you mean?" said Sophie.

"You know what I mean," said Julie pulling up a chair and joining Sophie at the table. "I saw Stud's car over here this morning at five thirty. Have you two made up?"

Sophie was exasperated. "In the first place, Julie, it wasn't five thirty. It was a quarter to six. In the second place there's nothing to make up from…we were kids then. Look at me Julie. Now I'm a middle-aged woman," Sophie's voice was getting louder. Gladys cut her a quizzical look. "And in the third place, do you just sit over there all day watching my house?"

"Just about," Julie said undeterred. "So, what was Jeff doing here?"

Sophie sighed. She knew Julie would continue needling her until she got an answer. Sophie relented, "He was here to measure my upstairs bathroom because he wants to lay the tile there even though I told him already that I had contracted the job out and I threw him out and smashed him hand in the door," Sophie rattled breathlessly. She took a deep breath and added, "Satisfied?"

"Wow!" exclaimed Julie. "He still loves you."

"Stop saying that!" said Sophie. "We were kids, Julie. Just kids. I got over it, can't you?"

"Well," huffed Julie. "You know what they say about that first love…"

"No, Julie, I don't know. Why don't you…"

Gladys sensed tensions rising so she asked insistently, "Don't you want a cup of coffee, Julie?"

"No thank you, Gladys," said Julie. "Sophie, listen I'm just…"

"If'n you don't want coffee I gots some tea bags," Gladys persisted.

"No thank you," Julie snapped. "Now Sophie…"

At that moment the doorbell rang again. "Saved by the bell," Sophie muttered. Gladys shook her head, went back to work, and resumed humming.

The front door opened and closed and there were sharp footsteps in the hall. Jan burst into the room.

"Hey girlfriends," Jan said happily. "I don't know what cha' been talking about, but back up and fill me in. Hey Gladys. Could I bother you for a cuppa? I need one after that party last night. I'm plum tuckered out."

"I can understand that," said Gladys moving toward the kitchen. "Jest take a look at dis mess."

"Good old Gladys. She's in her element now," said Jan. "Now, what, what?"

Julie replied condescendingly, "I merely came over to ask Sophie why Stud was here at five forty five this morning. She took umbrage to what she implied was my meddling."

Jan's eyes grew as big as saucers and she exclaimed, "Stud? No kidding? Goooo…girl. You really work fast."

"Jeff wants to lay the tile in my bathroom, and he thought that five thirty in the morning was an appropriate time to measure the floor," Sophie said angrily.

"Ohhh," cooed Jan. "Already talking about laying stuff, huh?"

"Tile, Jan. Tile," Sophie said irritably.

"I know. I just said that for meaness. So Sophie, looks like you've hooked yourself a Stud. Yes ma'am, you're the gal," said Jan.

"Hardly," said Julie in an au fait manner. "This is not Sophie's first fling, so to speak, with Stud. There was another time. Right, Sophie?"

"What?" Jan screamed with delight and slapped her hands on the table. "How come I didn't know about this? How could you keep something this hot from me? Come on tell, tell."

"There's nothing to tell, Jan. We were just kids. It was very short lived…only a couple of months one summer."

"And then she dumped him," Julie said disgustedly.

"I did not dump him," Sophie yelled.

Gladys calmly entered the room again and set a cup of coffee in front of Jan. Then she gave Julie a cagey look, "You sure you don't want none?"

"No thank you," Julie said testily and continued. "Sophie dumped Stud and she knows it. He knows it too."

"Whoa, whoa, whoa," said Jan sloshing coffee onto her coat. She snatched up a napkin and began to dab at the stain. "What do you mean *HE* knows?"

Jan looked from Julie to Sophie expectantly. Finally Sophie said, "Why don't you tell her about it, Julie. You seem to remember much more than I."

Julie was delighted to be appointed narrator. She settled back, assumed a haughty expression, and began. "Well, not that there's that much to tell. It *was* very brief. One summer Sophie and Jeff had a *heated* love affair. They were together constantly, holding hands, kissing, whispering and such. The whole affair was...as they say...rather hot and heavy. Then toward the end of the summer, just like that (Julie snapped her fingers) Sophie dumped Jeff for no apparent reason. Just dumped him!"

Jan turned to Sophie wide-eyed and said, "Oh, that was cold. Is she telling the truth, Sophie? Did you dump Stud for no reason?"

"For the last time, I did not dump Jeff, and it was not a *heated love affair*. We were just kids for heaven's sake. That's the way kids are. They get together, fall head over heels in love, and then find someone else to get together with, fall head over heels in love, and then find someone else, and so on. It's a cycle. That's why they're called kids."

"Ah ha!" exclaimed Julie. "Then you admit you were in love."

Sophie stood up, and declared, "I'm not going to have this conversation any longer. Subject closed."

Jan said, "Well, even though I've been left out of the loop for years, I agree with Sophie. Let's change the subject before fur starts to fly over something that happened between kids. So, what about that party? Was it a smash or was it a smash?"

The next hour was spent reliving the events of the previous night and patting themselves on the back for a job well done. All three carefully avoided any further mention of Jeff or his early-morning visit.

Finally Jan said, "We oughta get out of here. I'm starting to feel restless."

"Where do you want to go?" asked Sophie.

Julie exclaimed, "Let's go shopping!" Julie was a firm believer that there wasn't any crisis that could not be solved by shopping.

* * *

Roanoke Rapids, North Carolina didn't have much to offer in the way of shopping. There was a Super Walmart, a Belk's Department Store, two Christian Bookstores, a couple of locally owned specialty shops, and a few chain restaurants clustered around the I-95 exit. But that didn't discourage Julie who charged through every little shop. She reasoned that it would be unfair to skip a single store.

Jan and Sophie spent their time carting clothes back and forth from the racks to the dressing room for Julie to try. Sometimes they fetched the same outfit more than once. However, they indulged Julie who boasted effusively about her shopping skills. She claimed that she knew the best brands, the best times to shop, the best ways to shop, and how to sleuth out bargains.

The morning passed quickly and soon conversation turned to lunch. The weather forecast warned that nighttime could bring frozen precipitation, possibly snow. So they decided to grab a bite at Ruby Tuesday Restaurant and then head straight back to Seaboard. The wind was biting, and they ran to the car. Crossing the parking lot was like picking their way through a mine field. The many potholes were filled with ice. Their balance was compromised further by bags filled with Julie's purchases. They slipped and slid and had several near mishaps, but no one hit the ground. They laughed and joked, and by the time they reached Jan's car, they were in high spirits.

Jan pulled onto the highway and said, "So Ruby Tuesday, right girls?"

Sophie and Julie shouted, "Right!"

Jan clipped along at a smart speed and soon reached the turn into Ruby Tuesday. She flipped on her left turn signal and pulled into the turn lane.

Suddenly Sophie shouted, "No, no don't turn. Keep going

straight…straight. Don't turn. It's him. Jeff is at Ruby Tuesday. Go straight."

Jan abruptly swung out of the turn lane without any regard to oncoming traffic. Suddenly there was the deafening sound of blaring horns and screeching brakes, as an eighteen wheeler swerved to miss Jan's car causing drivers behind him to take to the shoulder. Through the back window, Sophie and Julie saw the truck driver's mouth moving savagely, and spittle spewed against his windshield. He flipped Jan a finger and beat his fist against the steering wheel. Jan's car reverberated with shrieks and screams and cries from Julie and Sophie.

"What's the matter?" Jan asked nonchalantly as she continued down the road.

"Jan you almost killed us," Julie screamed.

"Not to worry," said Jan. "Everything's under control. Didn't you know I had everything under control?"

If the three women had been able to look back, they would have seen Jeff and most of the Ruby Tuesday Restaurant customers standing at the front window, mouths opened, and heads shaking.

They decided to drive back to Seaboard and grab lunch at the only fast food place in town. Julie and Sophie ordered salads and diet drinks. Jan ordered chicken salad, fries, cole slaw and a chocolate milkshake.

"You two don't eat enough to keep a bird alive," said Jan and she reached for another fry.

"I don't have much appetite after that near-death experience," said Sophie.

"Me either," said Julie. "I swear my whole life passed before me."

"Oh, come on, Julie," said Sophie. "We weren't in danger **long enough** for **your** life history to pass before your eyes." Sophie grinned slyly and took a sip of her drink. She felt her gibe was pay-back for the hard time Julie gave her about Stud. Julie, on the other hand, appeared impervious to her joke.

Jan said between chews, "I was only doing what Sophie told me to do. She kept screaming 'don't turn, don't turn…the big bad Stud is eating there'. So I didn't turn. I aim to please my passengers."

"Well, next time you may think twice before you take seriously anything that Sophie has to say about Stud. Where he is concerned, she's clueless. As nice a guy as I've ever known," Julie said.

"And you'd be the perfect judge of men *why*?" Jan said.

"Well I'm a pretty darn good judge about what happened between Sophie and Stud. After all, Jan, you just found out about it this morning. I've had years to analyze their situation."

"Hey you two," Sophie said angrily, "I'm here. Stop talking about me as if I weren't."

"Sorry," Julie and Jan said derisively.

Outside the wind began to blow forcefully. A large American flag in the parking area flapped so vigorously the pole began to shake. Dark puffy clouds blew in from the southwest and tiny specks of sleet peppered the concrete. A car pulled into the parking lot and a man opened the door. The wind caught the door and slammed it against the unsuspecting man and threw him back into the car.

"Oh, I hope he's not hurt," said Sophie. Then the man tried again. This time he was prepared for the gust of wind and successfully made his exit.

"I wish this weather would make up its mind," said Jan. "They've been predicting a big snow for two days. As for me I'd love to see a little of the white stuff."

"Me too," said Sophie. "A fire in the fireplace, a cup of hot chocolate, a warm throw, and a good book…who could ask for anything more."

"I could," said Julie. "I'd like someone to clean off the steps and shovel the walkway. I can do quite well without the 'white stuff'."

"Julie, you're just too darn persnickety," scolded Jan.

Sophie looked at her watch. "I've got to go. Gladys doesn't like to be in the house after dark. She thinks it's haunted. And Gladys is one person I can't do without."

Preparing to leave involved a lengthy conversation on the tips. Julie discussed the quality of the service and then used a calculator to figure her tip while Sophie and Jan haphazardly dropped coins on the table and started for the door.

Julie soon followed. "You shouldn't do that you know," protested Julie. "How will the help know if they've pleased the customer if you always tip them well?"

* * *

The watchers in the old Chevelle observed the three women as they left the restaurant, drove out of the parking lot, and headed for Main Street. Although they could not hear any conversation, the men watched as three heads bobbed about in silent animation.

"Don't those three ever shut up?" asked the driver.

"Nah," said the passenger. "Just be glad that all we have to do now is watch, not listen."

Chapter 4

Sophie sat on a tall stool in the kitchen. Her hands were wrapped around a huge mug of hot coffee and her eyes were glued to the television on the counter. She watched intently as a haggard weatherman stood beside a map of eastern United States. He was giving updated information on the approaching winter storm. The storm was moving slowly from the southwest leaving a heavy accumulation of snow in its wake. It was predicted that near blizzard conditions would soon reach the North Carolina state line, and Charlotte was already on a high winter storm alert. Schools were dismissed and commuters jammed the highways in an effort to reach home before the approaching storm hit. To Sophie the most troubling part of the report showed a projection in which a northeastern path of the storm would continue unabated through Raleigh and straight to Northampton County and Seaboard. A list of closings rolled across the screen accompanied by shots of children bursting jubilantly through school house doors.

"How many pieces of French toast you want?" asked Gladys who was busy cooking breakfast.

"Huh?" replied Sophie as she roused herself from her concentration on the weather report.

"I says…how many pieces of French toast you want?" Gladys repeated impatiently.

"Sorry. Only one," replied Sophie.

"Don't eat enough to keep a bird alive," huffed Gladys as she dropped a piece of toast in the frying pan. "There's preserves and sour cream on the table."

"Sugar-free and low fat?" asked Sophie mindlessly, her eyes never leaving the television screen.

"Don't start with that mess this morning," said Gladys impatiently. "It is what it is."

The telephone rang and Gladys reached for it one hand still attending the toast.

"Yes?" Gladys said loudly. Sophie had suggested several telephone greetings to Gladys, but Gladys rejected them all. Yes, was definitely her preference. "Here she is." With a scowl, she thrust the phone toward Sophie.

"Hello," said Sophie.

"Hey girl friend," said Jan much too cheerfully for Sophie who hadn't finished her first cup of coffee. "What the matter with Gladys? Who licked the sprinkles off her ice cream cone?"

"She's just worried bout the snow storm," said Sophie.

"Too bad," said Jan. "Can't change the weather. Might as well not waste time worrying 'bout it."

"Try telling her that," said Sophie. Gladys shot Sophie a blistering look.

"Whatcha up to this morning?" asked Jan.

"Just sitting here watching the weather report. Have you been keeping up with the winter storm?" Sophie asked.

"Couldn't help but," said Jan. "That's all they've been talking about for three days. Got any plans for today?"

"I'm going over to Jackson to the library. I want to do some more family research. Seems I have a missing ancestor. Can't find his grave," Sophie said.

Gladys removed the French toast from the pan, placed it on a plate, and shoved it toward Sophie. Sophie took the plate in one hand and the phone in the other and walked into the dining room.

"What are you doing today?" asked Sophie as she smeared low-fat sour cream on her toast and reached for the sugar-free blackberry spread.

"Well, I was hoping you'd be interested in going out to lunch, but guess I'll have to settle for a fun-filled day of shopping with Julie. Or should I say a fun-filled day of toting clothes back and forth to the dressing rooms for Julie to try on." Jan sighed, "Oh, well at least there's lunch to look forward to. If you change your mind, join us."

"Thanks," said Sophie, "but I'm really determined to find a certain grave."

"A grave? Sounds about as much fun as coming up on a wasp's nest, but 'to each his own'. See you later," said Jan.

"Right," said Sophie. She polished off the delicious French toast and wished she'd asked for two pieces. She looked up to see Gladys standing at the dining room door.

"You through?" Gladys asked.

"Yes," said Sophie. "That was delicious. Wish I'd asked for two pieces."

"Too late now," said Gladys. "Done washed the frying pan. You planning on driving out of town with that storm a-making its way here?"

"*Out of town* is only to Jackson. Seven miles away. It's not as if I'm driving to Raleigh or Greensboro," said Sophie.

"Well, you best keep your ear tuned to the weather reports," said Gladys. "And don't forget I don't like being here alone pass dark."

* * *

As Sophie walked into the library, she was struck by the smell of dusty books and furniture polish. Eilene Brown, the librarian, was busy polishing the large tables. She smiled brightly as Sophie entered. Since Sophie began her pursuit of family history, the two women had become close friends. Eilene didn't mind dusting. She was thrilled to have tasks other than checking out and shelving books, and she was invaluable to Sophie in locating documents, maps, and family histories relative to the Singletary family.

Sophie removed her coat, scarf, and gloves and hung them on the wooden coat rack by the entrance. She rubbed her hands together vigorously in an effort to return feeling to her numb fingers. Then she looked around the small library. Only a few hearty souls had braved the severe cold. They were the enthusiastic readers who were determined not to be without several good books when the winter storm hit. Eilene rushed to Sophie, her face flushed with excitement.

"Sophie," she whispered as she took Sophie's arm and began to lead her to the back of the library. "There's someone I want you to meet. You know that grave you are looking for. Well, if anyone can help you find it, this lady can. She knows more about Northampton County history than any breathing soul around here."

Sophie stopped. Eilene's excitement was contagious. "Tell me a little bit about her before you introduce us," Sophie said.

"Her name is Mrs. Carrie Kendricks. I understand she is eighty seven years old, and she's sharp as a tack. Her love is genealogical research, and she has researched practically every family in the county. She lives with her dead son's wife, and she brings Mrs. Kendricks to the library several times a week so she can read and do research. To be honest, I didn't expect her to come in today with the storm and all. But here she is and here you are. Can't wait to introduce you." She took Sophie's arm, and they headed toward the back of the room again.

Sophie had hit a dead end while trying to locate the grave site of her sixth generation uncle. Records indicated that he was a lively, colorful character, and such accounts peaked her interest in him. Although he was featured as a favorite family member in letters, diaries, and other documents, there was no mention of where he was buried. Sophie was immediately drawn to this ancestor who died so young in the Civil War. Not knowing where he was buried made his the only incomplete story from the sixth generation of the Singletary family. Now she was going to meet someone who might be able to answer her questions. She was eager to meet this woman who was an expert on Northampton County history and family genealogies.

They approached a table to find a little old woman surrounded by books and other materials. She was dressed all in pink. She huddled inside a large pink woolen coat, with a pink neck scarf tucked inside. White curls toppled onto her forehead from under a fuzzy pink angora cap. Blue veins showed through the white transparent skin on her hands, and well manicured nails were tipped with a delicate pink polish. She held an expensive pen and in front of her laid a yellow legal pad. The pad was covered with notes written in a beautifully flowing script. She looked up from her work and smiled as Eilene and Sophie approached.

"Excuse me, Mrs. Carrie," said Eilene. "There's someone who would like to meet you. Mrs. Carrie Kendricks this is Sophie Singletary. Sophie…Mrs. Carrie Kendricks."

"How very nice to meet you, my dear," Mrs. Carrie smiled with a twinkle in her blue eyes. "Do sit down."

Eilene excused herself, and Sophie sat. "Thank you Mrs. Kendricks," Sophie said as she chose a chair across the table from Mrs. Carrie Kendricks.

"Please call me Mrs. Carrie, dear. Now what can I do for you? I'm sure you must have a reason to share your library time with an old lady like me."

Sophie felt embarrassed. "I would have been honored to meet you without reason," Sophie said. "However, I have run into quite a conundrum while researching the sixth generation of my family, and would appreciate being pointed in the right direction."

"Of course. I'd be happy to help if I can. Your problem will become my purpose for being here today. We all need a purpose, you know. Now what is your family name again?"

"Singletary," said Sophie

"Ah, I know that family history well. It is so well-documented that I'm surprised you are having difficulty. What seems to be the problem?" Mrs. Carrie asked.

"It's my sixth generation uncle. Willis Singletary. I cannot seem to find where he is buried. When I returned to Seaboard, I began researching the Singletary family. There are, as you said, copious amounts of documentation…letters, diaries, wills and so forth. Everything was so completely documented. Then I went to the Seaboard Cemetery to do tombstone rubbings and was surprised to discover that Willis Singletary is not buried there with the rest of the family. I know his remains were sent home in April 1864 because there is a journal entry documenting the details of his wake, but nothing about the burial."

"Are you married, dear?" asked Mrs. Carrie.

"I was. I'm divorced, and I have taken back my maiden name, Singletary," said Sophie.

"I can understand that…a proud name, Singletary." said Mrs. Carrie. "Did you know that Willis Singletary was a twin?"

"Yes," said Sophie. "I am a direct line descendant of his twin,

Wilhimena, whose nick-name was Willa."

"Ah yes, Wilhelmina," said Mrs. Carrie. "It is said that there was a special bond between Willa and Willis…a bond that transcended this physical life. It is even recorded that before the family was notified of Willis' death that Willa already knew he was dead. The family did not question her intuition and began funeral preparation before they were officially notified."

Mrs. Carrie leaned forward in her chair and spoke in a whisper, "You know, Sophie, in research, we often discover information that does not always meet with our approval. For instance, did you know that your ancestor grandmother, Willa, had an illegitimate son?"

Sophie answered undauntedly, "Yes, I knew that. And my ancestor grandmother never married. She retained the name Singletary."

"Good," said Mrs. Carrie with great satisfaction as she leaned back. "You make a good genealogist, Sophie. There are those who would sanitize their family history so to speak. That is not good research."

Sophie's face took on an awkward expression. "What is it Sophie?" asked Mrs. Carrie.

Sophie said hesitantly, "In all the records I've examined there is no mention of the father of Willa's child. Have you any idea who he might have been?"

Mrs. Carrie said, "In genealogical research, I do not like to dwell on unfounded information. However, under the circumstances since you are a direct descendant, I shall pass on the old rumor that he was the son of a minister. The minister and his son left town very quickly after it became apparent that Willa was in a family way. But remember, that is conjecture, Sophie. As a genealogist, you must focus on fact. Have you any other questions about Willis?"

"There is so much I don't understand about Willis' death. According to my findings, Willis died in the Battle of Petersburg in October 1864, and his body was sent to Seaboard for a funeral and burial. In a time when there was no refrigeration and travel by wagon took days, how were bodies preserved for such long trips?"

"Arsenic," said Mrs. Carrie. "Arsenic is an excellent preservative. So during the Civil War arsenic was used as an embalming fluid. Massive amounts. Its use became widespread. Even today, care must be taken in exhuming remains from that time period. Although it was quite an effective preservative, it is deadly if one is exposed to it in large amounts and for long periods of time."

Sophie reached into her bag and retrieved a pen and pad. "Do you mind if I take notes," she asked.

"Not at all, dear. That **is** why you came here today isn't it?" Mrs. Carries replied.

"Please, tell me what you know about my Singletary family," said Sophie poised to record.

"My, my let me see. Where shall I begin," Mrs. Carrie mused. After some contemplation she continued. "Well, Dr. Singletary was a much beloved doctor in Northampton County and most especially in Seaboard. He never refused a call regardless of the time of day or night. He delivered babies in practically every family in town and took only what pay the family could afford. He was competent and compassionate. He knew more about Seaboard family secrets than anyone, and yet he held their most private business in strictest confidence. That is why when his daughter, Willa, gave birth to a little son out of wedlock the whole town embraced her as if she were their own. That was the least they could do for Doc Singletary and his beloved Willa."

"That explains why my ancestor grandmother wasn't tagged with a scarlet letter, so to speak," said Sophie as she frantically scribbled on her pad.

"Yes, it does," chuckled Mrs. Carrie. Then she sat quite still for a minute as she collected her thoughts. Outwardly Sophie waited patiently, but inwardly she ached for Mrs. Carrie to continue. Finally Mrs. Carrie said, "Did you know that Dr. Singletary was averse to the Civil War?"

"No," Sophie said with surprise. "How could he have been? Why he traveled ten miles by horse and buggy to help in Garysburg Confederacy Hospital."

"He began to serve there **after** his son Willis joined the Confederate Army. Willis was so young and joined on a lark never knowing how deadly a mission he'd chosen. Dr. Singletary chose to treat the young

Confederate soldiers at Garysburg Confederacy Hospital hoping that if Willis ever needed help a doctor some place else would treat him in kind. But, no, Dr. Singletary hated the war. And he hated slavery. He had several servants whom he declared free, but never owned a slave in his life," said Mrs. Carrie.

Sophie was writing furiously. "This is amazing. How fortunate to have come to the library while you are here."

Mrs. Carrie was delighted. She continued, "Did you know Dr. Singletary was a Freemason?"

"Yes," said Sophie. "I learned that from documents I found at the house. Also, the Masonic seal is on his tombstone and there's a big stone beside the back porch that bears the square and compasses."

"Really?" Now it was Mrs. Carrie's turn to show surprise. "I shouldn't be surprised. Did you know that many Masons were associated with the Underground Railroad?

"No!" exclaimed Sophie. "Do you suppose my ancestor grandfather was involved in the Underground Railroad?"

"I wouldn't be surprised," said Mrs. Carrie. "It was rumored that he was. Yet no one in Seaboard would have spoken against him. Assisting slaves to escape was a crime back then you know. However, he certainly made no secret of the fact that he abhorred slavery. And now that you speak of a Masonic seal on a stone by his back porch, it appears more and more likely that he might have been a participant."

"Why does the seal indicate that?" asked Sophie

"There were safe houses along the Underground Railroad. Those Masons who helped slaves on the trail to freedom would mark their homes in some way to indicate that theirs was a place where slaves could rest, get food, and help until they were able to continue on their flight," Mrs. Carrie explained. "Many houses had secret room in which the fleeing slave could hide. Such rooms can be found today under stairwells, in cellars, or in other well-hidden places. Would there perhaps be such a room in your house today?"

"Why yes there is," said Sophie. "Off the room that was used as my ancestor grandfather's office, there is a very small room. It's a most curious room. It's very dark and has no windows. As a child I never played there. Actually it's the only room in the house I avoided. My grandmother explained to me that my ancestor grandfather used the room to isolate extremely ill patients while he treated them for contagious diseases."

Mrs. Carrie chuckled, "How clever. That would be a perfect place to hide a runaway slave. People in those days steered clear of exposure to contagious diseases such as smallpox or consumption. Believing the room was used to confine such patients would certainly prevent the room from being entered. You might have hit upon something very interesting, my dear."

"So then you think my ancestor grandfather might have helped slaves run?" Sophie said.

"Most possibly," Mrs. Carrie said simply.

"Amazing," said Sophie. "Absolutely amazing! Mrs. Carrie, you've made my day!"

Mrs. Carrie simply smiled. Then Sophie looked somber. "You know this still doesn't help me find Willis' grave. Have you any ideas?" Sophie asked beseechingly.

"In 1864 soldiers were usually buried in one of two places," said Mrs. Carrie. "Some were buried in family plots, such as the one you searched in Seaboard. Other soldiers were buried with their comrades in cemeteries exclusively for Civil War dead. Since we know that Willis' body was transported from Petersburg then he must be buried nearby. Have you looked in the Civil War cemeteries in Seaboard and Northampton County?"

"There is no Civil War Cemetery in Seaboard. Eileen gave me a list and directions to some in the county. I've checked as best I can, but so far no Willis Singletary."

"Have you checked the grave houses?" Mrs. Carrie asked simply.

Sophie looked perplexed. "Grave houses? I don't know anything about grave houses."

"Grave houses are found throughout the South. They were quite popular prior to the Civil War and for a short time thereafter," Mrs. Carrie began.

"Are they sort of like a mausoleum?" asked Sophie.

"Oh no," said Mrs. Carrie. "Grave houses were little houses built over an "in earth" grave. They were constructed of stone, or brick, or wood. However, the remains of wooden ones are often difficult to find today due to years of exposure to the elements. Plus families no longer appear to be interested in maintaining grave houses. At any rate, some grave houses were quite elaborate. Different styles and decorations were used. There were windows (often with curtains), picket fences, and the name of the deceased was sometimes chiseled or burned on the door. Most houses were constructed so visitors could go right inside and sit beside the tombstone while visiting their loved one. From a distance a grave house can resemble a dog house. They can be quite difficult to find. Some can be found in graveyards, others in cemeteries."

"Graveyards *or* cemeteries? Is there a difference?" asked Sophie.

"Oh most definitely," said Mrs. Carrie. "Although the terms are used interchangeably, there is a difference. Graveyards are burial places that have a connection to a church. Cemeteries are burial places that have no such connection."

An impeccably dressed middle aged woman approached the table. Mrs. Carrie smiled and said, "Emily, I'd like you to meet Sophie Singletary from Seaboard. We were just discussing her family. It seems like she's missing an ancestor uncle…from about the sixth generation."

The woman smiled. "Then I'm sure you've had a good morning. I'm pleased to meet you Sophie." Then she turned to Mrs. Carrie, "Mother, we'd better go. The weather is taking a miserable turn. They say snow is barreling down on us." She began collecting Mrs. Carrie's things.

Sophie stood. "Mrs. Carrie I can never thank you enough for all your help."

"Please keep me posted regarding your research, Sophie," Mrs. Carrie said as she slowly stood, took her daughter-in-law's arm, and unhurriedly walked away.

Sophie gathered her things and hurried to the librarian's desk. "Eilene, what a generous lady and a valuable resource! She gave me enough information to keep me busy for weeks. Thank you so much for introducing us. She suggested that I search cemeteries and graveyards that contain grave houses for my ancestor Uncle Willis' grave. Do you know of any cemeteries that have grave houses?"

"Grave houses?" pondered Eileen. "Not right off hand, but I can do some research and get back to you."

"Thanks, Eileen." Sophie said excitedly. "What would I do without you?"

Eileen beamed. "So glad to help Sophie. By the way, you've picked up an admirer while you were here."

"What?" said Sophie. Immediately her mind raced to Jeff.

"Couldn't take his eyes off you the whole time you were talking with Mrs. Carrie. Yes, a real young fellow. Had dark black hair and wore it in a crew cut."

Sophie's mind drew a blank. She looked curiously about the room. "Where is he now?"

"Oh, he left in a hurry when he saw your meeting was breaking up. Must be real shy."

Chapter 5

As Sophie walked out of the library, she was hit with a blast of bitter, icy wind. The air smelled crisp, and her nose and chest stung when she breathed in the cold, damp air. Naked tree branches lashed frantically against the bleak gray sky as if seeking some refuge from the inevitable storm.

Sophie clutched her coat tightly around her and dashed to the car. When she grasped the door handle, she could feel the cold metal through her gloves. She wrestled the door open and quickly slid into the car. Although the car provided protection from the wind, it gave very little defense against the cold. As her warm breath hit the cold air, the windshields were immediately clouded with condensation. Sophie turned on the heater and defogger and waited until the windshield and back window were clear.

Sophie slowly backed out of the parking space, crossed the lot, and turned right toward Seaboard. In spite of the impending winter storm, Sophie felt elated. Her day had been exhilarating. She had not only met a gracious lady of the old school, but the lady was a genealogist who was knowledgeable about Northampton County and the Singletary family. And as a plus, Sophie felt that their meeting could turn into a genuine friendship.

Sophie was so deep in thought that she failed to notice the flashing blue and red lights in her rear-view mirror. When she glanced up, she swore to herself, "Damn…how long have I been getting lights?"

She slowly pulled onto the wide shoulder of the road at Ramsey's Fork, rolled down the window, and turned off the ignition. She immediately began rehearsing excuses for every infraction she might have committed. "Speeding? Tail light out? Brake light not working? I did give my turn signal back in town didn't I? I'm so sorry." Her mind was racing.

She looked in the rear-view mirror again and saw the door of the vehicle open. Then came the bombshell. Stepping out of the car and swaggering slowly toward her car was none other than Jeff. She banged her head against the steering wheel and beat her fist on her knees.

"Damn, damn, double damn," she swore.

Then he was at her window a smug expression of his face. "What do you want Jeff?" Sophie said.

"Get out of the car, Sophie," he said.

"I wasn't speeding," she said.

"Get out of the car, Sophie," he repeated.

"Why? Just tell me why. I won't get out until you tell me why," Sophie demanded.

Then Jeff reached down, grabbed the door handle, and swung the door open.

"Get out of the car," he said again.

Suddenly Sophie was afraid. As she stepped from the car the wind whipped her coat open, and the cold air seemed to tear through her clothes. She began to shake uncontrollably.

"Why Jeff?" Sophie spluttered through chattering teeth. "What? What do you want?"

Jeff stared hard into her eyes. Tears began to run down her cheeks. Were the tears caused by the cold wind or because she was afraid?

"Wh…wh…what do you want, Jeff?" she stammered, and this time she could only whisper.

Jeff pushed her against the car. Sophie again felt the cold metal against the small of her back. Then he leaned into her, put a finger under her chin, and lifted her face toward his. His eyes were dark and unsettling.

Sophie thought she heard a slight crack in his voice as he said, "I want to know why you are avoiding me, Sophie."

Sophie was dumbfounded. She brought her arms up and pushed him away. "Are you crazy?" she said almost hysterically. "Avoiding you? I'm not avoiding you, Jeff."

"I saw you, Sophie," he growled. "I saw you, and Julie, and Jan in Roanoke Rapids. Jan started to turn into Ruby Tuesday and when **you** saw my car you told her not to."

"Now I know you're crazy…" she began.

"No, Sophie, I saw you. And I saw you almost get killed. Jan pulled right back into the traffic without any warning to the cars behind her. Why if that truck driver had not been a professional you would have been squashed like a bug on a windshield."

Sophie was beginning to feel like a kid who had skipped school and was hauled into the principal's office. "Jan had everything under control," she said weakly.

"Under control? I saw the whole thing, Sophie, and so did half the people in Ruby Tuesday. There was no control there," he roared.

Then suddenly Jeff became very quiet and calm. Sophie found this more disturbing than when he was bawling her out. Finally Sophie said, "So, is that why you stopped me…to bawl me out? Is that what you wanted?"

"No, I stopped you because I want you to have dinner with me," he said simply as if the previous scene had never taken place.

"What?" stammered Sophie. "Dinner?"

"Yes, dinner," Jeff reiterated.

Sophie was not prepared for this. Every since she had reconnected with Jeff, their meetings had been confrontational. Now how could she simply have dinner with him as if nothing unpleasant had happened?

"Oh, I don't think so, Jeff," she said contemptuously.

"Why?" he insisted.

"Because I've been in a dusty library all afternoon, handling dusty books, and I don't want to get dressed and go out again," she rattled.

"Okay. I can see that," he said. "So how about my coming to your place for dinner?"

Sophie gave a weak laugh. "If I don't feel like going out to dinner, I certainly don't feel like cooking dinner for a guest."

"Okay, I can see that, too," he said. "How about my bringing dinner to your house?"

"Bringing dinner? Well, I don't know…"

"Pizza. Do you like pizza?" Jeff said hurriedly.

Sophie spoke hesitantly, "Well, I suppose I like pizza. I haven't had it in so long but yes, I sup…"

"Great," Jeff jumped in. "Pizza it is. And I'll bring wine. What kind?"

"Ah, ah, well let's see pizza…"

"Never mind, I'll surprise you," Jeff said.

"You've already done that," Sophie muttered.

"What?" Jeff asked.

"I said…I'll make a salad, and pizza would be nice," Sophie said weakly.

"What time?" he asked. Sophie was not quick enough. Jeff said, "eight o'clock okay?"

"I suppose. Yes, eight o'clock is fine," said Sophie still unable to absorb what was happening.

"Okay, eight it is," Jeff stepped back and opened the car door. "See you then."

Sophie slid into the car relieved to be out of the wind. "Okay, see you then."

Jeff slammed the door. "Lock your door, Sophie," he said. She did, and he walked quickly back to his car.

Sophie sat there for a few seconds. What just happened? What was she doing? Did she really want to get mixed up with someone whose mercurial moods bounce back and forth like a hand ball? She started the engine and looked in the rear view mirror. Jeff made a U turn and headed back towards Jackson. Then he stopped and sat there. What now? Then it occurred to Sophie that he was waiting for her to move. She put the car in gear and drove in the opposite direction.

Chapter 6

Sophie pulled into her driveway and stopped in front of the garage. She pointed the remote and clicked the door open. That was strange. The inside garage light didn't come on. Sophie seldom parked her car in the garage, but with the approaching storm, she felt it wise to house her vehicle. Fortunately it was not yet dark and she could find her way out of the garage by the remaining daylight outside. She got out of the car, rushed outside, and closed the garage door.

Sophie raced to the back door and into the kitchen. There she found Gladys stacking dishes in the cabinet while her 'matrimonial possibility', as she called him, sat patiently on a stool waiting for her to finish.

"Hello Melvin," said Sophie.

Melvin stood and said, "Good afternoon, Miss Sophie."

"Oh, please Melvin, don't call me **Miss** Sophie. Sophie is fine. 'Miss' makes me feel like an old woman," she said.

"Sorry. Good afternoon Sophie," he corrected himself. Gladys shot him a disapproving look. She did not think it proper for him to take such a liberty.

"By the way, Melvin, the light bulb in the garage is burned out. Could you please replace it?"

"Sure," said Melvin.

Gladys said, "Made you some of that chicken-vegetable soup you like…'nough to last two, three days. There's plenty of crackers in the tin. If'n that storm is as bad as they say, you might need it seeings you haven't been to the grocery and the pantry is near 'bout empty."

"I couldn't face the crowd at the grocery store. I know how people panic at the sight of a snowflake. I could only imagine what it would be like with a storm this size moving in. The stores would be swamped," said Sophie. "Besides, I knew you'd come through."

"Don't be depending too much on me," Gladys said. "One of these days you might get disappointed."

"I doubt it," said Sophie, and she gave Gladys a hug.

"Huh," grunted Gladys, and she headed for the front hall. "Come on Melvin. I want to be home before things get bad." Melvin trotted obediently after her.

"Don't forget…you're not to try to come in if the roads are bad," Sophie called after her.

"Don't even need to tell me that," Gladys replied, and Sophie heard the front door close.

* * *

Sophie showered and shampooed library dust out of her hair. She changed into a light green turtle neck sweater, dark green sweat pants, tan leather moccasins, and woolen socks. She pulled her hair back and fastened it in a pony tail at the nap of her neck with a clip. She didn't want Jeff to feel she'd done anything special for tonight. This was going to be casual…very casual. They would eat in the sunroom.

Sophie walked downstairs and into the sunroom and began to straighten pillows on the chairs and stack magazines and newspapers neatly. Then she eyed the fireplace with its gas log. A little fire might be nice especially if it begins to snow. She lighted the fire. She flipped on the overhead light. Too harsh. Candle light would be much more in harmony with the fire in the fireplace. She lighted several candles. She flipped on the floodlights outside the sunroom. No snow yet. She flipped them off. She turned and looked at the room. Suddenly she felt it was too much. It looked like she was trying too hard.

"Trying too hard for what?" Sophie wondered aloud then added, "Well, let **him** figure it out." And she walked back into the kitchen.

Sophie took the makings for a salad from the refrigerator, washed the vegetables, and began making the salad. She kept one eye glued to the television as scenes shot in Raleigh showed people standing in long lines at the grocery store and cars backed up on the interstate. One meteorologist called the event the 'mother of all snowstorms' for eastern North Carolina. Weather conditions had rendered the perfect storm, and it was being tagged the worse snowstorm to hit the area in twenty five years. Large accumulations resulted from the very slow movement of the storm, and graphics showed the storm moving toward Seaboard.

"Maybe he'll cancel," Sophie said to herself, but at that moment she heard the front door open and footsteps coming toward the kitchen.

It was Jeff. "You left the door unlocked again, Sophie," he said sternly. Then he smiled. He was carrying a large boxed pizza and two bottles of wine.

"You have a thing about unlocked doors, Jeff," she said. "Remember you're in Seaboard."

"Yeah, well I locked it anyway," he said as he set the pizza and wine on the counter. The spicy aroma wafted through the room. Jeff walked to the stove. "I'll turn the oven on warm and stick the pizza in so it won't get cold."

After placing the pizza in the oven he came to where Sophie was working. He stood close behind her and she could feel his breath on the back of her neck. Sophie quivered.   "Great salad!" he said. Then he turned and walked into the sunroom.

"Nice!" he said. "Fire and all. This is real nice."

Sophie cringed. She **had** done too much. She made an effort to play down her embellishments and said nonchalantly, "Oh, do you like it? I have supper out there a lot. The fire is so nice, and if it snows we can turn on the floodlights and watch the storm while we sit inside cozy and warm." She smiled at him impassively.

Jeff returned a knowing grin and said, "Well whatever, it's still nice."

Thankfully the doorbell sounded through the house. "It's the doorbell," Sophie said stating the obvious. "I'll get it."

"No, let me," said Jeff and he was already starting out of the room.

Sophie heard Julie's voice. "Oh Jeff! What a surprise! Sophie never locks the door. Where is she anyway?"

Jeff grinned, "I know she doesn't lock the door. And probably everyone in Seaboard knows it too. She's in the kitchen."

Julie practically skipped to the kitchen. "Oh Sophie, I didn't know you had company."

Sophie shook her head and smirked, "Oh, you didn't see Jeff's car out front?"

"Well, no…I guess I didn't," Julie stammered as she moved into the sunroom. "Oh, my, how lovely everything looks! And is that pizza I smell? That's nice although the cholesterol count for pizza is off the chart, you know. I didn't think you ate pizza, Sophie. And wine. White or red? There is a debate you know. Some say white with pizza and some say red. I would say that it depend upon whether the pizza has meat or is vegetarian. Does your pizza have meat?"

Jeff tried not to laugh. Sophie shook her head and looked impatient. "Was there something you wanted Julie?" she said.

"Oh, no. At least nothing that can't wait until tomorrow. I'm sorry I intruded on your date," she said as she moved toward the door. "I'll just run along. There's something I must do. And Jeff, I'll make sure I lock the door." And she was gone.

Sophie shook her head and laughed, "Yes, I'm sure she has something to do, and I bet I know what it is. She's rushing home to call Jan."

"Most likely," Jeff said. "Sophie, how is Julie going to lock the door? Does she have a key?"

"Yes, she does," Sophie said.

"Who **else** has a key?" Jeff asked. His manner turned grim.

"Well, let's see. Jan has a key, and Gladys has a key," Sophie said. "Jeff you are way too paranoid about this locking doors thing."

"Maybe. But things have changed, Sophie. Seaboard isn't like it was fifteen years ago," then his stern manner mellowed. He smiled, looked intensely into her eyes, and playfully tugged at her ponytail. His voice was soft, "I just worry about you, Sophie. You're too trusting."

Now that was way too serious and way too soon for Sophie. She lifted the salad bowl and walked to the sunroom. "Bring the wine and glasses?" she said over her shoulder.

Sophie sat on one end of the couch and Jeff on the other. "Glass of wine before we eat?" he asked.

"That would be nice," Sophie said. Sophie watched Jeff pour the wine. "Did you hear Julie? She said we were having a **date**. A **date.** Can you imagine that?"

Jeff cocked his eyebrow, handed her a glass of wine, and said, "Well, Sophie, I'd call it a date. What would you call it?" And he lifted his glass in a toast and took a sip.

Sophie hesitated, tilted her head to one side, and said, "I suppose I'd call it a date too."

By the time Jeff brought out the pizza, they had consumed almost a full bottle of wine. Sophie, who was not used to drinking so much wine so fast, felt giddy and uninhibited.

"Ummm...good pizza," Sophie said savoring the rich flavor. She didn't remember pizza tasting this good.

"Good salad," said Jeff. "More wine?" And he reached for the bottle.

Sophie covered her glass with her hand. "Not just yet," she said. Jeff leaned in close, lifted his hand, and wiped a bit of tomato sauce off her chin.

"You like doing that don't you?" Sophie said.

"I guess I do. It's just a way of taking care of you," Jeff said.

"Taking care of me, worrying about me...just where is this going?" thought Sophie. Suddenly she laughed loudly, unexpectedly. She put her hand over her mouth and giggled. Sophie knew immediately she sounded smashed. "I need to go easy on the wine. I'm not much of a drinker," she said.

"That's okay," said Jeff as he placed his glass on the coffee table. "Tell me Sophie Singletary, what have you been up to these last fifteen years."

"Well let me see," Sophie placed a finger on her cheek, gazed upward, and mused, "After graduating from Seaboard High School, I went away to college. Two years at St. Mary's, and then I transferred to Carolina for two years. I met my husband...or I should say my ex-husband...Andrew Temple one summer while I was vacationing on the Outer Banks. Actually Andy was the only man I really fell for after leaving home. Two months after we met, we ran off to Danville Virginia and got married."

"How did your mother and grandmother feel about that...the running away to get married?" asked Jeff.

"They were heart-broken. They wanted me to have a big wedding with all the trimmings right here in Seaboard. But Andy insisted on a small wedding with no *frills* as he put it," Sophie said.

"Why Danville, Virginia?"

"Simple," said Sophie, "no waiting period there."

Jeff reached for the bottle, poured some wine into his glass, and lifted the bottle to Sophie. She shook her head.

"Guess I'll just finish this off then," he said and poured the remaining wine into his glass. He raised the empty bottle and said, "Another dead horse."

Sophie stared into the fire. Talking about Andrew resurrected old feelings. Dreadful feelings she'd tried hard to suppress. Yet talking with Jeff about those terrible days seemed so natural, so appropriate.

"Hey," said Jeff. "You okay?'

Sophie wrested her thoughts from dark places she'd dared not go and looked beseechingly at Jeff.

Jeff reached across the couch and took her hand. "Sophie, if you don't want to talk about this, just tell me to butt out."

Sophie laughed. "No, Jeff. It's okay. Talking with you like this seems …well, seems okay."

"If you're sure," Jeff said. Then he asked cautiously, "Were you happy with him, Sophie?"

She said, "Yes, I was…for a short time. Andrew was extremely bright and very attentive. And he was quite handsome. He was a computer consultant. I don't know much about his work, and when I asked questions he just said I wouldn't understand. And we moved a lot. I mean a lot. There was never time to make friends before we had to move again. Actually we lived quite comfortably. In addition to his salary, Andy received money from a trust every month. We traveled abroad, stayed in five-star hotels, and ate at the finest restaurants. Even on our trips abroad he had business to take care of, and I spent many hours sighting-seeing alone. As far as material things were concerned, we had everything we wanted. He wouldn't allow me to work, yet he never denied me anything…anything except friends. And I missed having friends, and I missed my family."

"Your family?" Jeff asked.

"Yes. Andrew always found some reason why I couldn't visit them or mother couldn't visit me. I felt—alone, suffocated. Then his behavior became strange. He began checking on me," Sophie said.

"Checking on you?" Jeff asked looking troubled.

"Yes. When I went shopping or when he was out on consultation, either he called me or I had to call him at a certain time…a time determined by him. And if I missed a call, he was furious," said Sophie with a shudder. She went silent.

"Sophie, did he ever hurt you?" Jeff asked with trepidation.

"Only once," Sophie said. "Only once." And she stood up and walked into the kitchen. "More pizza?"

Jeff's face took on a dark, angry look, and his jaw pulsed furiously. His fists were clinched so tightly that his knuckles were white. But he said nothing.

Sophie returned with two slices of pizza on her plate. "Here," she said. "This is the last of the pizza." And she put a piece on Jeff's plate.

Sophie took her place at the other end of the couch and curled her feet underneath her. "I think I will have some more wine now if you plan to open that other bottle," Sophie said.

"If you're sure," said Jeff. He popped the cork and reached for her glass.

"Just a smidgen, please," she said. Jeff splashed a small amount of wine into her glass.

"It must have been a bitch having to handle the move back to Seaboard all alone," Jeff said.

"Not really there wasn't that much to take care of. We were living in Las Vegas, Nevada at the time. Andrew had gone on one of his long trip, and I took the opportunity to get a quickie Las Vegas divorce. Then I left in a hurry. I brought very little with me. I just threw my clothes in suitcases and cleared out," Sophie's face took on an ominous far-away look, and she sat silently for a few seconds. Jeff watched her closely not wanting to impose on a moment that must have been very private and painful for her.

Then she took a sip of wine and continued, "Now turn about is fair play. What have you been up to since **you** left Seaboard?"

"Not anything interesting enough to write home about," he said. He paused as if collecting his thoughts. She remembered that Jeff found it more difficult to discuss things than she, so she waited silently, patiently.

Finally he said, "I married her you know."

"Who?" asked Sophie knowing that he wouldn't continue without her urging him.

"The 'dim-witted bimbo with the IQ of a head of cabbage'.... the one you mentioned the other night," he said.

Sophie was horrified. "Oh Jeff, I'm so sorry. I had no idea. I thought she was a one- time thing. I didn't know she was your wife. No wonder you were so angry. I am so sorry."

"Forget it," he said. "You were right. She was brainless. But as I told you, when a guy is only eighteen he's not thinking about a girl's IQ. He's got other things on his mind."

"But still, I'm so sorry," Sophie reiterated. She sat quietly trying to decide if she should change the subject.

Jeff sensed her reluctance to go on with the conversation so he continued, "I joined the Navy right after graduation from high school. Then got married at Thanksgiving. Like that was something to be thankful for."

Sophie was shocked at the bitterness in his voice. "Any children?" Sophie thought Jeff would have made a terrific dad.

"Two. We had a boy nine months after the wedding. She was a disaster as a mother. She was just a kid herself...and so was I. But I was off at sea most of the time. Since she...we...screwed up so badly as parents the first time, she thought she deserved a second chance. So we had a second kid. Another boy. The second time around was no better. In fact, it was worse. When I got my next orders to go out, I talked her into taking the kids home to her mother. I thought Grandma might be a buffer for them. And she was. I breathed a sigh of relief when I came back and saw that my mother-in-law was definitely in charge. Can you imagine that—a man being glad that his mother-in-law was in charge?"

"What happened next?" Sophie asked.

"We divorced then, no hesitation—no regrets from either of us. It was just one of those things that should never have happened," Jeff said.

Sophie took a sip of wine. Then she asked, "Do you ever see them? Your sons?"

"Nope," Jeff said as he stared into the fire. Sophie thought she detected a note of sadness in his voice. "The older boy joined the Navy like me. Last I heard he was training to become a Seal. I think he took that track because he knew **I** always wanted to be a seal. I just didn't have what it takes."

"And your younger son?" Sophie asked.

"Grown up and still living with grandma out in Phoenix," Jeff said.

"Phoenix? How did a grandma from Northhampton County end up in Phoenix?" Sophie asked.

"This woman is no ordinary grandma. She snagged herself an air conditioning contractor, and she and her grandson moved out to Phoenix with him," Jeff said his palms splayed upward in a helpless gesture.

"And what happened to her—your wife or you ex-wife I should say," asked Sophie.

"Lord only knows," said Jeff. "I don't know, and I don't want to know. Lost track of her ten years ago."

"You sound so bitter," said Sophie. "So unlike the person I remember."

"I am bitter," said Jeff. "And I shouldn't be. We were both such kids. We never loved each other. It was just teenage hormones. We were damn stupid little kids. Intellectually I know that I shouldn't blame myself so much but it's just the boys. I hated it for them."

"I'm so sorry, Jeff," Sophie said and she reached out and took his hand.

"And after the divorce what did you do?" asked Sophie.

"I stayed in the Navy. Towards the end I did Shore Patrol. When I got out I decided I'd use some of what I'd learned on Shore Patrol, so I went and became a United States Marshal."

"The Shore Patrol experience qualified you to be a United States Marshal?"

"No…not exactly. There's a little more to it than that. There's some training involved. I had to go through a couple of programs, and the most fun of all is a seventeen and a half week basic training program down in Glynco, Ga. Ever heard of Glynco, Ga?"

"No. And then you're sent to work out of Washington?" she asked.

"No…Raleigh. Every state's divided into districts. North Carolina has three districts…Eastern District, Middle District, and Western District. I work in the Eastern District and Eastern Headquarters is located in Raleigh."

"But how did you end up back in Seaboard?" Sophie asked as she took another sip of wine.

"Northampton County is one of the counties in the Eastern District. So when *stuff* happens in Northampton County that requires the attention of a US Marshal, I come to the rescue," Jeff joshed.

"Like Superman," laughed Sophie.

"Yeah, like Superman," Jeff chuckled.

"So what kind of *stuff* throws you into action?" Sophie asked.

"Oh, stuff like protecting federal judges and courts, transporting prisoners, apprehending fugitives, protecting witnesses. Stuff like that," Jeff shrugged.

"Sounds pretty benign to me," said Sophie. "Which kind of stuff brought you to Northampton County this trip?" Sophie asked.

"Well, now that I can't say. Secrets you know. If I told you I'd have to shoot you," he joked. Sophie laughed at the old joke.

Jeff suddenly grew quiet. Sophie realized they had uncovered too many unpleasant memories. Then Jeff looked squarely into Sophie's eyes and said, "Sophie, during those years when things were really rough for you, did you ever wonder how it might have been if we hadn't broken up that summer?"

Sophie was taken aback. She pondered his question for awhile and then replied slowly, "I suppose there were times when I did, but it wasn't something I dwelled on. Occasionally when I was homesick for my family and old friends and Seaboard, I'd think about many foolish choices I'd made. And yes, I thought about you. Yes."

"Me, too," said Jeff. "I thought of you when the whole marriage began to unravel. But then I moved on…until I saw you the other night."

Sophie was beginning to feel uncomfortable. She was afraid of where this was headed. She'd begun to feel at ease about their getting together. They had been just two friends sharing memories, feelings, and pizza. Now she was afraid the evening would digress into another bitter war of words like the one they'd become embroiled in at the reunion.

"Jeff, please. I apologize for the other night. I said a lot of hurtful things, and I certainly wasn't a good hostess. Can we just forget it?" Sophie said. "We were just teenagers too. Can't we let it go at that?"

"I thought I had let it go until…"

Sophie blurted out, "Listen Jeff, toward the end of that summer you became cold, distant. I sensed you wanted to end our…our little summer fling, and I didn't want to be rejected at school in front of classmates. So I started flirting and acting silly. I knew you were proud and **you'd** end it then."

Jeff looked stunned. He took her by the shoulders and gently shook her. "Sophie, Sophie, do you mean to tell me that you dumped me because you thought I was going to dump you and you wanted to do it first? That's insane!"

"Jeff, I…,"stammered Sophie.

"Did you really think that **you** were the only thing I had on my mind that summer? It's not always about you, Sophie. Hell, my whole life was falling apart at home," Jeff shouted.

Suddenly Sophie felt mortified. Now it all came rushing back. She remembered that earlier in the summer Jeff's parents separated, but then they'd reconciled. Jeff only spoke of it once. But when school resumed in the fall, it was whispered that his mom and dad had divorced and Jeff's father moved to Richmond to work for the Richmond Fire Department. Of course, Jeff had had other things on his mind that summer. But as a selfish teenager Sophie felt being in love meant that she should have Jeff's full attention. So when his focus shifted away from her for some unknown, Sophie felt neglected. She sensed impending rejection, and made no effort to ferret out the reason for Jeff's preoccupation. If she had she could have supported him during what was surely one of the most difficult situations a teenager can go through. Instead she'd acted like a spoiled brat.

Tears welled up in Sophie's eyes, and she croaked, "Jeff…all I can say is I'm so very sorry that I wasn't there for you. What a stupid, selfish little monster I was. Please forgive me."

Slowly Jeff's demeanor softened, and he smiled. Sophie had not seen him actually smile. A grin, a raised eyebrow, a smirk. These were the kinds of expressions she'd seen since he walked back into her life at the Tex-Mex Restaurant.

Gently, firmly he drew her to him. "Sophie, Sophie, I didn't mean to make you feel guilty. I keep forgetting we were just kids. I wasn't forthcoming, and you were self-centered," he whispered without a hint of levity in his voice.

Sophie pulled away abruptly. "Self centered?" she squawked. And then they both burst into laughter. She settled comfortably into his arms, and he held her close. She felt a sense of resolve. They settled in front of the fireplace and watched the flames leap and crackle.

Then the wind set in with exceptional violence. Sophie and Jeff listened quietly to its howl. It rattled the windows of the sunroom like a beast trying to enter their safe chamber. The storm grew louder, and the wind sobbed, and cried like a child lost in the pine woods behind the house. Snow arrived with all the elemental forces of a true blizzard. The wind screamed, and snow and pellets of fine sleet beat against the windows. It was an event experienced in northeastern North Carolina only once in a generation.

Sophie slipped out of his arms, walked over to the window, and flicked on the outside floodlights. The snow was so thick they could hardly see the garage only a few hundred feet behind the house. "I've never seen it snow like this in Seaboard. It reminds me of the winter I lived in Denver. Snow can be daunting, but see how beautiful it is."

Jeff walked up behind her and wrapped his arms around her waist. "It is beautiful. Almost as beautiful as you," he said.

Sophia giggled, "Jeff, that doesn't sound like you. But thanks anyway."

"Can't blame me for trying," he said and kissed her lightly on the neck. Then he spoke more seriously, "It'll soon be unsafe to drive."

Sophie turned and put her arms around his neck. "I know where you can stay until it stops snowing," she murmured.

Jeff gave her a quizzical look. Sophie added softly, "Here."

"Are you sure?" Jeff said hoarsely.

"I'm sure," she said.

Jeff leaned down and kissed her softly, gently on the mouth reminiscent of the innocent kisses of summers past. Then his kiss became stronger, deeper, and less furtive. He snapped the clip from her ponytail and tousled her hair free.

Sophie pushed him away, took a deep breath and sighed loudly. Then she whispered, "I'll get the candles."

"And I'll get the fireplace and the outside light," Jeff said.

* * *

The hood and top of the rusty Chevelle were covered with snow, and wind rattled the beat-up car mercilessly. Inside two nearly frozen onlookers shivered without taking their eyes off the yellow house. Down parkers, woolen gloves, and woolen socks did little to protect them from the brutal cold. Then slowly light after light went out in the downstairs of the big house. Then a dim light in an upstairs bedroom snapped on.

"Okay, he's in," said the man in the driver seat.

"Good! Let's get out of here before it turns into a Popsicle."

It took several tries before the old car's engine fired. Slowly the car pulled onto the street and took a right. Its rear end swung from side to side on the snow-covered road. The car moved slowly, cautiously as it plowed its way toward Jackson.

Chapter 7

The woods outside the yellow Victorian house were transformed into a display of winter brilliance. Naked tree limbs were blanketed in white, and branches snapped under the weight of the ice. Accumulation had already exceeded predictions, and the wind blew tall drifts of snow against the house and outbuildings. Driveways and roads were completely obscured.

Jeff lay quietly and listened to Sophie's deep, steady breathing. They'd made love with all the eagerness of the teenagers they had been. Now she slept peacefully, contentedly. There was a pixie-like quality about her as she lay beside him. Her mouth was slightly open and a limp hand rested under her cheek. Her body was as white as the snow outside, and her auburn hair was spread in disarray on the pillow.

Jeff looked at the digital clock. Two-thirty. He carefully pulled back the quilt and swung out of bed. Not bothering to put on shoes or clothes, he picked up his cell phone and crept silently into the bathroom. He closed the door softly and without turning on the light tapped in a well-known number.

"It's me," he whispered. "Yeah...yeah...as long as it takes." Then he pressed end and snapped the phone shut.

He retraced his steps across the cold floor, gently pulled back the quilt, and settled back in the bed. Sophie stirred. "Jeff?" she said groggily.

"Yes," he said. "I just had to use the bathroom. Go back to sleep, Sophie." He gathered her in his arms and held her close.

Sophie moaned contently, settled in against him, and said softly, "I feel so safe in your arms."

* * *

They were awakened by the telephone ringing. Sophie rose up on her elbow and blinked like an owl. She reached for the phone, and Jeff reached for her.

"Jeff, no," she scolded. "If I don't answer, we might have some uninvited visitors. You know...Julie."

Jeff fell back onto the bed and in exasperation said, "Well grab the phone quick."

Sophie laughed and snatched up the receiver, "Hello."

"Hello yourself. Just checking up to see how you're making it."

"It's Gladys," mouthed Sophie to Jeff. Then she said, "Good morning, Gladys. I'm 'making it' just fine. How about you?"

"I'm snug as a bug in a rug," she said. "I'm one of those what's got enough sense not to try to go out in all this mess." The implication was that Sophie had no such sense.

"Well, believe me, I'm not going anywhere today," said Sophie and she ran her fingers lightly over Jeff's chest.

"Good," said Gladys. "Now don't you forget that chicken-vegetable soup I made for you, and there's saltine crackers in the tin."

"I know. You already told me," Sophie said and began softly tracing Jeff's mouth and ear with a finger.

"There's cake in the cake box and ice cream in the freezer chest, too," Gladys said.

"Goodness that's way more than enough for one person," Sophie said smiling at Jeff.

"Well, see that you eat then," said Gladys. "I'll be in as soon as this here weather breaks. I don't like the idea of you being there all alone for too long."

"Oh, don't worry Gladys," said Sophie as she smiled wickedly at Jeff, "I'm not alone."

"Now don't you go talking 'bout that ghost stuff. It's hard enough for me to put in time in that house without you always bringing up ghosts," Gladys said gruffly and hung up.

Jeff took the receiver from Sophie and placed it in its cradle. Sophie huddled close and swung her leg over his. "Now where were we?" Jeff said.

* * *

Snow continued throughout the day. The blizzard-like conditions of the night before had already left eight inches of ice-encrusted snow. The English boxwoods surrounding the yellow house and the tall pines trees in the back bowed under its weight. Limbs of less pliant trees broke under its weight and crashed to the ground making cracking noises that sounded like gunfire. No cars passed on Main Street, and the rusty old heap that had kept vigil on Sophie's house was gone.

Jeff made coffee and brought it upstairs. They sipped large mugs of coffee and watched coverage of the storm on the bedroom television. And they made love. Sophie felt as if they were the only two people in the world. By noon, they were starving. They showered, dressed, and hurried downstairs in search of Gladys's soup.

Sophie thought Gladys's soup never tasted so scrumptious. They filled bowls with the steaming potage, grabbed handfuls of crackers, and went into the sunroom. Sophie quickly polished off her cup and stood to get another.

"I'm getting some more soup," she said. "Gladys would be overjoyed if she knew I was eating this much. Want some more?"

"Sure," said Jeff. "That's some soup." And he handed her his bowl.

"We worked up humongous appetites this morning," Sophie said, and she grinned conspiratorially.

Jeff smiled as Sophie strutted out of the room, bowls in hand. He was beginning to see a glimpse of the Sophie of years ago. She'd begun to smile often and giggle in that childish way he found so appealing. She always looked directly into his eyes when he spoke. She hung on every word he said, and laughed at his jokes even when he botched the punch line. She was lively, uninhibited, and always approachable. While sitting on the couch with her feet curled underneath her she talked endlessly of faux pas she'd committed on trips abroad, the homesickness she'd felt after she married, and her sadness when her mother died. She told him about Julie's obsessions with shopping and how she and Jan were relegated to fetching clothes from the racks for her. She described at length Julie's compulsion for cleanliness and organization. Sophie told him about how sad she'd felt when she learned of the death of Jan's husband, Ed. Then she quickly described how Jan filled her emptiness by nurturing elderly relatives and supporting her friends. Sophie laughed about Jan's wit and her willingness to go along with any exciting adventure that her friends cooked up. Jeff cringed as he remembered how Jan had unwittingly pulled her car into the line of traffic in front of Ruby Tuesday's and ran an eighteen wheeler off the road.

They spent the rest of the day in front of the fire watching the snowfall. By late afternoon the snow receded and clouds moved out exposing dazzling sunshine. Then as the sun dropped below the tree line, a gorgeous sunset spread across the western sky. Orange and golden rays bounced and danced across the icy crust presenting a stunning display suggestive of stain-glass windows that adorn grand churches.

They finished the soup for supper and made a respectable dent in the ice cream and cake. Then with arms around each other, they walked slowly upstairs. They sailed into bed, wrapped their arms around each other, and made love as if this would be their last time together. Jeff was amazed at how natural it seemed to be here in Sophie's home in her bed. Years ago when, they were going out together, the house seemed gigantic. Now it appeared large but not extremely so. As kids he and Sophie explored every inch of the old Victorian house, but he'd never been in her bedroom and certainly not in her bed.

Sophie fell asleep her arm across Jeff's chest, but Jeff remained awake for hours. He lay there trying to identify house sounds. There was the click of the thermostat as the heat snapped on and off and a squeak in the front where the porch was attached to the house. There was a strange scratchy noise that sounded as if the house were breathing and a buzzing sound that floated up the steps from the kitchen. Old houses have eerie noises Jeff thought. Now he could understand Gladys's aversion to being alone in the house after dark.

Finally Jeff dropped into a deep heavy sleep unhampered by dreams or dreadful forebodings. It seemed like only a short time passed before Jeff was shaken forcefully.

"Jeff, Jeff, get up quick," Sophie cried, and she swung her legs off the bed and stood.

Jeff sprang up, and grabbed her arm. "Sophie, what's the matter? Are you okay?"

She yanked her arm away, ran across the room, and grabbed her clothes. "It's Gladys. Get up quick."

"Something's wrong with Gladys? What happened?" Jeff asked. He was already moving toward his clothes on the chair.

"Nothing's *wrong* with Gladys," Sophie said. She was already half dressed. "Gladys's down stairs. Hurry up, Jeff."

Jeff stopped holding his pants in mid air. He gawked at Sophie, and said, "Wait a minute. You've worked yourself into a frenzy and scared the hell out of me because Gladys is down in the kitchen?"

Sophie looked at Jeff incredulously. "Jeff, what'll she think? What'll we say?" Sophie was close to tears.

Jeff shook his head. He walked across the room, took her in his arms, and said, "We'll just say, *Good morning Gladys. What's for breakfast?*"

"Jeff, this is serious. What will Gladys think if she finds out you spent two nights here?"

"She'll probably be relieved that you weren't here alone with all the *GHOSTS,*" he said and fluttered his hands in a ghostly movement.

"Jeff...," she stammered.

Jeff looked grim. "Look Sophie, just because you moved back home doesn't mean you're still a kid. You're a woman. Believe me you're a woman! And Gladys knows that too. What do you suppose she and Melvin do when they're snowed in? You sell old Gladys short. Why I bet she could show us some moves."

"Jeff!" exclaimed Sophie. And slowly, slowly she began to smile.

"That's more like it. Now let's shower and dressed and go eat breakfast. I'm famished," he said, and he smacked her on her bottom.

During their shower Sophie muttered and shuddered, while Jeff just shook his head and scoffed in disbelief. Jeff dressed quickly, and Sophie rushed to keep up.

"Gotta go to work," he said as he hurried out the door.

Sophie was struggling to pull on a moccasin. "Wait Jeff," she pled. Then from the upstairs hall window, she saw Melvin's car parked behind Jeff's. "Oh, no!" she groaned.

Sophie followed Jeff hopping on one shoed foot. She was right behind him as he started down the stairs. Then when they reached the second landing, the front door suddenly burst open and there in all her glory was Jan. Jan came to a screeching hall, leered up the stairs, and beamed.

"Morning, Jay-eff," she crooned.

Jeff didn't miss a step. "Morning, Jan," he said with a smile much too bright, and he headed straight to the dining room.

Sophie moaned and crumbled onto the step. Jan ran up the steps and sat down beside her. "Tell me all about it. Don't leave out a thing," Jan said eagerly.

"Oh, Jan. What am I doing?" she said and covered her face with her hands.

"Well, I don't know less you tell me," Jan said urging her on.

Suddenly reality clicked in. Sophie looked at Jan questioningly. "Jan, what are you doing here? I thought you were snowed in at the farm."

"You don't think I'd stay out there with all this excitement going on do you?" Jan said.

"Julie!" Sophie said merely stating the obvious.

"Right. I've been over there two nights and a full day," Jan said shaking her head. "Believe me, you don't want to stay with her. You couldn't take it, Sophie. I tell you that girl can drive a person crazy with her obsession for cleanliness. Why I was afraid to potty for fear she'd start cleaning the toilet before I pulled my drawers up."

There were voices coming from the dining room. Sophie stood and said, "Good Lord! Jeff and Gladys are alone in the dining room."

"I really don't think you got anything to worry about, Sophie. Gladys's got her own boyfriend. Besides Gladys's old enough to be his grandma," Jan called. But Sophie was already bounding down the steps and heading for the dining room.

There seated at the head of the table was Jeff. Gladys was standing over him with a plate of scrambled eggs and bacon in one hand and a basket of hot biscuits in the other. Gladys was insisting that Jeff go in for seconds. She was delighted to cook for someone who ate as if he appreciated her cooking. Jeff took another biscuit and heaped more eggs onto his plate.

"Marry me, Gladys," he mumbled with his mouth full. "Marry me and make me a happy man."

Gladys laughed so hard that Sophie thought she'd drop the plate and basket. "Now, Melvin might have something to say about that." And she turned and sashayed back into the kitchen.

"He doesn't have to know," Jeff called after her. Gladys could be heard cackling from behind the kitchen door while Melvin mumbled something unintelligibly.

"What's become of old sourpuss Gladys?" Jan whispered to Sophie.

"A complete turnaround," Sophie whispered.

Jeff's biscuit was gone in two bites. He stood mouth still full and said, "Well, gals, see you later. I'm on the clock." Then he walked over to Sophie, brushed a kiss on her cheek, and sauntered into the hall.

Suddenly Sophie felt alone, defenseless. She scurried after him. He was pulling on his coat. "Jeff," she said cautiously, "Will I see you tonight?"

He paused and looked her straight in the eye. "Of course," was all he said.

"What time?" Now she was beginning to feel awkward. She was asking too many questions.

He walked over to her, "I can't say." Then he lifted her chin between his fingers, and kissed her hard. "Satisfied?" he asked.

"Only until *sometime tonight*," she said wickedly.

"Give it up, Sophie. I can't say *exactly* what time," he said and he walked across the hall and opened the door. "And don't forget to lock the damn door." Then he was gone.

Sophie watched him as he picked his way down the path and out of the gate. He started his car and turned on the heat and defroster. Then he got out and scraped ice from the windshield and back window. Sophie watched and when he finished he lifted his gloved hand in a slight wave. Just as he opened the car door, Julie appeared. Sophie saw them exchange a few words, and then Jeff climbed into his car. He made several attempts to drive off but the tires just spun stubbornly. Finally they caught traction and the car moved out.

Julie hurried up the path. She mounted the steps cautiously, and she and Sophie joined Jan in the dining room. Then they sat around the table as if waiting for some high level meeting to convene.

"Okay," said Julie as she struggled out of her coat. "Back up and tell me everything that's been said. Don't leave out a word."

"Not much been said," said Jan. "Sophie hasn't been very forthcoming."

"Not forthcoming? After two nights of unbridled passion with Stud and you tell me Sophie's not forthcoming?" Julie exclaimed. And she and Jan burst into laughter.

"Come on, Sophie," prompted Jan, "what's up?" And they laughed again hysterically.

Sophie feigned disgust. "I'm so glad you two are enjoying yourselves at my expense," said Sophie.

Jan stood up, rushed around the table, and gave Sophie a hug. "Oh come on, Sophie. You know I love you more than my electric blanket. We're just cuttin' up."

Julie retrieved a tissue and was wiping away her tears of laughter. "No kidding now. Tell us all about it. You know we'll eventually wrestle it out of you anyway."

"Well, for starters he was furious about our near-death experience in front of Ruby Tuesday," said Sophia.

"Has that guy got no confidence in me?" Jan said pretending to be hurt.

"It's because he loves her," said Julie. "One fears for the one they love."

"He's changed so much. He was nothing like the stubborn, arrogant, deceitful, misleading...," Suddenly Sophie stopped talking. Jan and Julie were staring at her as if antlers were growing out of her head. Sophie burst out laughing.

"I believe you said he'd changed," Jan said calmly.

Sophie looked embarrassed and then they burst out laughing. She smiled and continued, "Yes, changed. I told him about my unhappy marriage and he told me about his," Sophie said.

"That's good," said Jan. "Garbage out."

"By the way," said Sophie, "he married that floozy he started dating after we split up. But he divorced her, of course."

"Of course. I'd say good riddance there," said Julie.

"I don't know," reflected Sophie. "After he told me the circumstances I felt kinda sorry for the girl. She was like the rest of us...just a crazy, mixed-up kid."

They sat quietly remembering all the craziness of high school. "Then we talked through our brief romance and break-up back in high school," Sophie said.

Julie leaned forward with great anticipation. "So what was his take? Did you dump him or did he dump you?"

"It wasn't that simple," Sophie said rapidly. "Jeff explained the reason he became so distant and inhibited that summer. You see, his parents were going through a divorce and he was...was hurting. I misinterpreted his mood and thought he was going to reject me, so I rejected him first, and we moved on."

"Ah ha!!!" squealed Julie. "I knew it. I knew it. You dumped him!"

Jan looked shock. "Sophie! That was cruel. That's not like you at all...not being there when somebody needs you."

"I know. I know," Sophie cried wringing her hands. "I was so selfish and self centered. I could have died when Jeff told me. I remember finding out that his parents were divorced when school started but I didn't put two and two together."

"I knew it! I knew it!" Julie was still reveling in the confirmation that she was right.

"But that's not all," said Sophie. "Jeff shared the responsibility by admitting that he should have been more open and honest with me. After all we were kids."

Jan looked sage. "Yes Sophie, that's well and good, but just think how that false impression changed both your lives."

"I know," whispered Sophie. "I know. Oh, how I wish I could go back."

At that moment the kitchen door opened, and Gladys stood there with her hands on her hips. "What do y'all want for breakfast? This ain't no restaurant. Pretty soon I got to fix lunch and then start on supper. I can't get stuck in here on breakfast. Not with all I got to cook for today." Gladys was in heaven. She could now complain about having to cook too much.

"Oh, whatever is easiest for you, Gladys," Sophie said solicitously.

"Then it's bacon, eggs, and biscuits cause I got the biscuits already done," and she turned and walked back into the kitchen.

"And Gladys, I hope it wasn't too much trouble having Jeff here for breakfast," Sophie called.

"Trouble? Ha! Feels pretty good having somebody around here that eats," she said. "You don't eat as much as a goldfish."

Chapter 8

After serving BLT's for lunch, Gladys shooed Sophie and party out of the kitchen. "If I'm gonna be expected to do all this cooking then y'all gonna have to stay out from under my feet."

Sophie, Jan, and Julie moved to the den. The den was a large rectangular-shaped room. As was the custom in the nineteenth century, doctors' offices were usually in their homes. This room had been used by Dr. Singletary as a reception room, and his examining room was in a smaller room behind it. So what was now Sophie's den had a large front window and two smaller windows on the side. A large armoire that housed a flat-screen television, a CD player, a tape player, a DVD player, and even a turn table stood beside the stone fireplace. Two sofas were at right angles to the chimney corner while two armchairs directly faced the fireplace. Several small side tables were conveniently positioned about the room, and a large game table with four chairs was placed by the front window.

Melvin started a fire in the fireplace, and Sophie, Jan, and Julie spent the afternoon analyzing Sophie's rekindled romance with Jeff.

"You know, Sophie," Julie said, "not many people have a second chance at a botched relationship...especially if said person was the dumper."

"I didn't dump him. I told you it was a misunderstanding," Sophie protested tiredly.

"Oh, come on, Julie," said Jan. "Stop beating a dead horse. We've already put that debate to rest. Let's get back to the good stuff. Sophie, is Jeff going to spend the night tonight?"

"I don't know. I suppose..." Sophie began.

"Sophie, don't start supposing. You need to define this relationship right up front. That's what I always did," said Julie.

"And how did that work for you?" asked Jan grimly.

"Not very well," admitted Julie. "But believe me if you don't have expectations you'll be left alone with only a note that says *I don't need this any more*," Julie said reflectively.

"You sound like the voice of experience, Julie," said Jan, and she winked at Sophie.

"Yes Jan, I have been around the block a few times, and I've concluded that the success of an affair is determined by behavior early on in the relationship. Sophie, you'd be wise to do just that," Julie said emphatically.

"I don't know. We've just begun..." Sophie whispered.

Jan tossed in a question in an effort to change the subject. "Sophie, what's Jeff working on? I know he's a United States Marshal, but I'm surprised there's much of a need for high level police work in Northampton County, North Carolina."

"I don't know what he's working on. We haven't talked about his work very much," Sophie answered.

"See. There you go again. You don't know. Sophie, trust me. You've got to find out what you're dealing with," Julie insisted.

Jan looked annoyed. "Julie, you were about to wet your pants for Sophie to get back up with Jeff. Now, you're throwing up all these road blocks. What's the matter with you girl?"

"I'm just thinking of Sophie's well-being," said Julie sullenly.

"I don't think so," Jan said impatiently. "You're trying to muddy the waters just for the heck of it. Sophie's a big girl. She can figure it out for herself."

Julie began defensively, "I have never tried to 'muddy the waters'. If anything I'm making an effort to clarify the…….."

"Hey! Hey!" Sophie shouted. "I'm here. You're talking about me again as if I weren't here. We don't have a long-range plan. Jeff and I **just** reconnected. Right now we're enjoying each other's company and renewing our…our…ah… friendship."

"Well, if that's the way you want to play it," Julie said skeptically.

"She does," said Jan. "Now let's get out of here and give them some space." Jan was up and scrambling into her coat. Julies reluctantly followed suite.

As they reached the front door, Julie suddenly grabbed Sophie and hugged her hard. Then she said dramatically, "Remember, Sophie, I'm right next door."

"Oh, Julie, how can I forget," Sophie said.

* * *

Sophie had never seen Gladys so cheerful. Gladys spent the entire afternoon cooking. She cooked a corned beef brisket with cabbage, potatoes, onions, and carrots. Fresh rolls covered with cheese cloth set rising beside the stove. Having asked Jeff to name his favorite dessert, she'd baked a lemon pie with a mile-high meringue. She set the dining table with a lace cloth, candles, and Grandmother Singletary's fine Haviland china.

It was late afternoon now and dappled sunlight filtered through the stand of tall thin pines in the back. This was Gladys's cue to clear out of the *preoccupied house*. She was struggling to put on her coat when Sophie walked into the kitchen. Sophie helped her with her coat and then spontaneously hugged her.

"Thank you, Gladys," said Sophie.

Gladys was taken aback. "Like I told you...I like having someone around who actually eats."

"Everything looks so nice and the whole house smells delicious and cozy," Sophie said.

"Well to tell you the truth, I never thought of corn beef and cabbage as smelling cozy. But then that's just me," Gladys said with a shrug.

Sophie laughed. "Gladys, I have to say I was afraid you'd be upset because Jeff spent the night with me."

Gladys looked perplexed. "You ain't no child Sophie. You're a woman. Why should I have any say in it? Now I'm getting out of here. You gonna be okay here alone till he gets home?"

Sophie smiled as she thought of Jeff returning *home*. "I'll be fine. Now you be careful. Some of the snow has melted, and now it'll freeze again when the sun goes down."

Sophie walked with Gladys through the *dreaded* hall and then stepped onto the front porch with her. She watched as Gladys cautiously picked her way down the steps. Melvin, who had been waiting in the car, got out and opened the door for Gladys. Then he turned and waved to Sophie. Sophie returned his wave and went back inside. She started towards the kitchen. Then she abruptly stopped, returned to the front door, and locked it.

Chapter 9

Sophie showered quickly and went downstairs to wait for Jeff. She wandered through the dining room and kitchen. She peeped at the brisket and sniffed the vegetables. She opened the refrigerator and checked the lemon pie. She opened a bottle of red wine so it could breathe. Then she wandered back through the dining room. Gladys had done everything. There was nothing for Sophie to do but wait for Jeff to get home. 'Jeff to get home'. What a reassuring thought. Six o'clock came…then seven, then seven thirty, then eight. She went into the den, lighted a fire, and sat down to watch television. The aftermath of the storm dominated the news and Sophie became worried. Suppose Jeff were in an accident. The roads had frozen over again. No one would know to notify her. She walked across the room and clicked off the television. Nonsense, she decided. Jeff was an accomplished driver. He had to be in his line of work.

Sophie wandered back into the kitchen. She gently lifted the cheese cloth that covered the rolls. If they were not baked soon, they would begin to fall. She bent over, lifted the pot lid, and checked the brisket. It was covered tightly, so it shouldn't dry out.

Suddenly Sophie was grabbed from behind. Strong arms clutched her tightly around the waist and squeezed her hard. "Ahhh," Sophie screamed helplessly. She was whirled around and abruptly came face to face with Jeff.

"Jeff," she shouted. "You scared me half to death. Stop doing that!!!!!!"

Jeff pressed her close to him and kissed her hungrily. "Sorry. But when I saw you bending over that stove, I got carried away."

Then he began to cover her faces and neck with kisses making little smacking noises. "Ummm," he said, "smells so inviting."

Sophie laughed. "When I told Gladys dinner smelled delicious and *cozy*, she thought I'd lost my mind."

"I wasn't talking about dinner," Jeff said.

Awareness suddenly set in. Sophie pushed away from Jeff. "Jeff, how did you get in? I distinctly remember locking the door because you insisted."

Jeff grinned and held up a key. "Ah ha," he said.

Sophie looked concerned. "I didn't give you a key to copy. How did you get that?" Sophie insisted.

"I have ways," Jeff said slyly. Then he turned to the stove and lifted the pot lid, "Ummm...corn beef brisket." Next he checked the vegetables. "...and all the trimmings."

Then he lifted the cheese cloth. "Am I dreaming? Homemade rolls."

Sophie was momentarily distracted. "Check out the 'frig too," she urged.

Jeff opened the refrigerator door. "Lemon pie! If this is a dream don't wake me up. Looks like you've been slaving over a hot stove all day." And he grabbed her and hugged her again.

Sophie pushed him away and said, "Jeff, the key?"

Jeff looked serious. "Look if it bothers you I'll give it to you," he said and handed the key to Sophie.

Sophie shook her head. "What's to keep you from having another one made?"

"Nothing, but I won't if you don't want me to," he said. Jeff looked genuinely wounded. "Look Sophie, I just thought it would be more convenient if I had a key. You know like if you're in the shower, or if I am really late getting in and you're in bed. I didn't mean to act pushy."

Sophie was silent for a few seconds. Then she smiled and said, "Does that mean you'll be staying here at night?"

Jeff smiled and drew her to him. "As much as possible," he said. "So, let's get this show on the road," he said rubbing his hands together.

"I'll put the rolls in the oven," Sophie said.

"And I'll carve the brisket," Jeff said.

As they worked together in the kitchen, Sophie thought how

wonderful it was to have Jeff here. They'd have many nights like this. She wouldn't be alone in this *preoccupied* house as Gladys called it. And she'd be with someone she'd known so well for so many years.

They carried the food into the dining room and Jeff said, "Nice. Looks good, Sophie."

"Oh, I didn't do this. This is Gladys's handiwork," Sophie confessed.

"So, there's a romantic side to Gladys. I told you," he said.

They sat down, and Jeff ate ravenously. "Gladys says she likes cooking for you because you're a hearty eater. She thinks I just nibble," said Sophie.

"Shouldn't be like that, Sophie," said Jeff with his mouth full. "Got to keep your strength up." And he grinned and winked.

Sophie laughed and watched him. Jeff belonged here…here in her home, at her table, with her. No that wasn't right. It would be their home, their table, together.

"Jeff," Sophie said hesitantly, "I asked Gladys if she cared that you stayed all night with me."

Jeff stopped eating and gave her a curious look. "And what did she say?"

"She said it made no difference to her that I am a woman and should make my own decisions," said Sophie.

"I knew she'd think that. But if it makes you feel better to have Gladys's permission for me to spend the night then I'm glad you asked," Jeff said shaking his head.

Sophie looked ashamed, "Jeff, you make me feel so foolish. You have to understand that I haven't been allowed to make choices for many years. It's going to take me a while."

Jeff reached across the table and took her hands in his. "Sophie, I'm so sorry. I didn't mean to be patronizing. Of course, I understand."

Sophie felt it best to change the subject. "Jeff, will you be here tomorrow night?"

"Plan to," he said.

"Will you be as late as you were tonight?" Sophie asked carefully.

"Don't know," he said.

"Are you working in Jackson tomorrow?" she asked.

"Sophie, I can't talk about my work," he said emphatically.

"Oh, I understand that," she said. "It's just that I plan to go to the library tomorrow, and I thought we might have lunch together."

Jeff shook his head. "That wouldn't be a good idea," he said.

Sophie hid her disappointment, put on a smile, and said, "Well then, I'll just look forward to tomorrow night even more."

"Good," he said. "Now I'll clear away these plates and cut Gladys's scrumptious lemon pie."

* * *

That night they made love eagerly, desperately, and then Jeff fell asleep. But not so Sophie. She began to replay the conversation with Julie and Jan. Julie had raised some compelling questions about her relationship with Jeff. Sophie knew nothing about his work. She had known nothing about Andrew's work. She never knew what time Jeff would get in, and she'd never known what time Andy would be home. She wasn't sure when Jeff would spend the night, and there had been many nights that Andy had 'worked through the night'. She'd begun to think of this house as their home, but could it ever be *their* home.

Jeff stirred and sighed and reached for her hand. He stroked it gently and then quickly fell back into a sound sleep. Suddenly Sophie felt angry with Julie. Why had she fixed all these doubts in her mind? Yes, Sophie had botched her relationship with Jeff once…but she wasn't going to make that mistake again. She moved closer to Jeff. The warmth of his body was soothing…so reassuring. Sophie tried to replace troubling thoughts with happy ones, but it didn't work. She couldn't un-ring Julie's bell.

Chapter 10

Sophie awakened to excruciating pain as brilliant sunlight penetrated her eyelids. She squinted at the window that was the source of her pain. Long icicles hung from the eaves of the roof like icy daggers while avalanches of snow spilled from tree branches freeing them to spring back into an upright position.

Sophie rubbed her hand across the empty side of the bed. Jeff was gone. The bed was not even warm. A feeling of emptiness swept through her as she began to rerun earlier thoughts. She dragged herself out of bed, put on her slippers and robe, and headed for the bathroom. As she opened the door, she was struck by warm, moist air, and there was still condensation on the mirror. One step farther in and she banged her toe on something lying on the floor. She looked down and saw a large duffel bag. She looked inside. Jeff's clothes. On the sink was a black leather tote that held razor blades, deodorant, clippers and such, and Jeff's red toothbrush hung beside hers in the toothbrush holder.

"Eat your heart out, Julie," Sophie cried, and she tore out of the bathroom, down the stairs, and straight for the dining room.

Sophie rushed into the dining room anxious to see Jeff before he left for work. She stopped suddenly when she realized the dining table was cleared and there was no sign of Jeff. Sophie felt dejected again. How many times would her feelings soar only to plummet again? At first she'd had to deal with Jeff's mood swings. Now the uncertainties of their relationship were troubling. At first she'd blamed Julie for her suspicions, but now she was beginning to wonder.

Suddenly Sophie heard voices and laughter from the kitchen. She crossed the room and slapped the kitchen door open. There sat Jeff at the kitchen table with an empty breakfast plate in front of him. Gladys, Melvin, and Jeff were laughing genially. When the door burst open, Jeff looked startled and jostled the large mug he was holding. Coffee dribbled onto the kitchen table. His expression quickly changed. He smiled brightly, and said, "Well, good morning Sunshine."

Sophie looked at his empty plate. "Jeff, I thought you had gone to work, and when I realized you hadn't I thought we could have breakfast together."

Gladys moved wordlessly to the kitchen table and wiped up the spilled coffee. Then she turned and busied herself at the sink.

"Can't this morning," Jeff said and he stood and walked toward the door. "Thanks Gladys. If you keep serving up these farm-hand sized breakfasts, I won't be able to climb up the stairs." Then he bent down and whispered to Sophie, "And wouldn't that be a shame?"

Sophie followed Jeff into the hall and watched him pull on his parka. "Jeff, I wish you'd awakened me."

"Thought you needed your rest," he said with a wide smile.

He bent down and kissed her. At first it was a simple *goodbye-see you later* kind of kiss, but suddenly it soared into something far more arousing. Sophie slowly pulled away, gave Jeff an enticing look, and said impishly, "Want to go back upstairs?"

"I know that look. You're a bad influence, Sophie Singletary," he answered. Then he opened the door, stepped onto the porch, and started to walk away. Then as an after thought he turned, opened the door again, and said, "Don't forget to…"

"Yes, I know," said Sophie. "Don't forget to lock the door."

Sophie walked back into the kitchen where Gladys stood watching television. Gladys said, "They's saýng there might be another storm heading our way. I could have told them that much."

"What do you mean?" asked Sophie staring at the television where a large white blotch was traveling northeast through northern Georgia.

"My mama used to say if'n a snow lays 'round like this here one is doing, then that means it's just waiting for another snow," Gladys said as she turned to look at Sophie. "So what'll you want for breakfast now that Jeff is gone? I'll bet you won't eat nothing."

"I'll just have some yogurt and blueberries," Sophie said absentmindedly, her eyes glued the television.

"That man's got to start eating all his meals with you. It's the onliest way I can get you to eat anything," Gladys said impatiently.

Sophie sprinkled blueberries on yogurt and ate at the kitchen table. She tuned **out** Gladys who was scolding her for what she called 'silly eating habits'. To Gladys, a three course breakfast was the proper day starter. Sophie was, however, tuned **in** to the weather forecast. Seaboard had just experienced the largest snowstorm in a decade and now it looked like they were in for a repeat performance. Sophie poured herself a cup of coffee and headed upstairs.

She stretched out on the bed, reached for the phone, and dialed Jan's number.

"Morning, girlfriend," Jan greeted Sophie in her usual cheerful way. "How are things in the lives of my two favorite people today?"

"Good morning, Jan," Sophie replied. "You are awfully cheerful for so early in the morning."

"You would be too if you were waiting for two...not one now...but two handsome guys to show up early this morning," Jan quipped.

"Two guys?" Sophie repeated.

"You got me to thinking…if one guy is good, then two is better," Jan joked.

"Jan what are you talking about?" Sophie said.

Jan laughed. "Had a couple of mishaps down here on the farm. The outside water faucet froze and busted, and two limbs from that big old tree by the driveway broke and crashed on the garage. So I have a plumber and an arborist coming first thing this morning."

"It wasn't that big old pecan tree was it?" Sophie remembered as children she and Jan went to play with Ed at the farm. Even then Jan called him her boyfriend. They climbed the pecan tree and Ed's parents yelled at them to come down before they 'break their necks'. Back then, Jan never dreamed she'd marry Ed and live on that very farm.

"Yes, I'm sorry to say it was our old friend the pecan tree," said Jan. "I'm hoping the trunk isn't damaged and we can save the tree. But you never answered my question. How's your love life going...and don't leave out a thing."

Sophia sighed. "Not too well, I'd say," said Sophia.

Jan sounded concerned, "Come on, Sophie, what's happened? I can't leave you a day, and we've got a crisis."

"I think I'm having a panic attack," Sophie blurted out.

"What? Why?" Jan seemed genuinely concerned.

"It just seems like Jeff doesn't want to see me except in this house. I plan to go to the library today so I asked him about having lunch together. He turned me down flat just saying that it wouldn't be a good idea," said Sophie.

"Is that all? Good grief, Sophie, maybe the man had lunch plans with the folks he works with...you know like a business luncheon. If that's all you got then you're just looking for trouble where trouble ain't," Jan scolded.

"That's not **all** I'm worried about," Sophie said reluctantly.

"Go 'head," Jan said impatiently.

"I suppose I was upset because he got home late and then refused to have lunch with me. So I began to think about the issues Julie broached," Sophie began to explain.

"*Julie?* Well, there you go right there. That's your problem listening to Julie. How long you known Julie, Sophie?" Jan was practically screaming.

Sophie was embarrassed. "All my life, Jan. You know that."

"And have you learned nothing from that life-long association? Don't you know that, if anything, Julie is melodramatic? She thrives on drama. If things get too quiet, Julie will find some way to stir up the waters. We love the girl and all but, Sophie, you oughta know better than to listen to her high jinks."

"I know, Jan. I know. But listen some issues raised red flags. And I began to compare them to my life with Andrew," Sophie sounded distressed.

"Okay, tell me how Stud...Jeff...reminds you of Andrew," Jan sounded calmer.

"Well take work for instance. Jeff won't tell me anything about his work" said Sophie.

"He's a high level US Marshal, Sophie. I'm sure much of his work is confidential. You want him to blow a case or put his job in jeopardy?" Jan countered.

"No," Sophie said weakly. After a moment she added, "But there's this thing about his hours. I never know when he'll show up, and that's the way it was with Andrew. I never knew."

"Again the nature of his work, Sophie," said Jan. "Listen Sophie, you just lower those red flags Julie left you with and act like a woman. After all you got yourself quite a man…*Stud.*"

"I suppose so, but I can't help but make comparisons. Can't you understand that?" Sophie really wanted Jan to understand not just because she was her friend, but also because she valued her opinion.

"Sure, I understand. That doesn't mean your fears are justifiable though," Jan reassured her. "Now listen I think you're suffering from cabin fever. You got to get yourself out of that house. You want to come out here and help me supervise the guys' work?"

"No thanks," said Sophie. "I'm going to the library. The librarian has been researching some information for me."

"Good!" said Jan. "Oops, here come my guys and here I sit in my scruffy bedroom slippers with no makeup on." And she hung up.

Chapter 11

As Sophie drove to Jackson damage from the snowstorm was apparent. Pine trees bowed under a heavy icy burden. Snow had settled among the pine needles creating small mounds that looked like white cushions nestled among the branches. Limbs of larger trees lay splintered and crushed on the forest floor like defeated soldiers overpowered by some giant white beast. The marsh just beyond Ramsey's Fork was covered with a light layer of snow that concealed the treacherous swamp. Three deer stepped cautiously toward the quagmire in search of water. Instinctively they knew that one misstep would leave them trapped in the bog where they would freeze to death or worse be eaten alive by small scavengers.

Snow lay in small dirty piles on the shoulder of the road. Although it was obvious that road equipment had scraped the road, there was no traffic. Sophie had the road to herself. The drive was quiet, deserted, and somehow unsettling. Suppose she had an accident. Fumbling around in her purse she realized she'd left her cell phone. If Jeff found out she was traveling without a phone, he'd yell at her and then there would be another sparring match. Jeff…he was never out of her mind.

In spite of icy patches, the car made it to the top of a hill and rounded a curve. Finally, the first houses in Jackson came into view. Sophie breathed a sigh of relief. She drove pass driveways that showed no sign of tire tracks. Likewise, sidewalks were void of footprints. Sophie guessed that Jackson must be lying low and waiting for the next winter blast. She reached the traffic light and turned right toward the library. As she drove into the parking area, she saw only one lonely car parked directly in front of the entrance. Sophie recognized the car as belonging to Eilene Brown. She pulled up beside it, hurried out of the car, and scampered to the door.

Sophie was struck by the absolute silence in the library. Even as a child, Sophie found libraries to be comforting…their sheer size, their smells, and the books. But most soothing to Sophie, however, had been the silence. As she hung her coat, she scanned the room for Eilene.

"Eilene," Sophie called. When there was no answer, she tried again, "Eilene, where are you?"

Then from the back of the library Sophie heard a toilet flush. Soon a door opened and Eilene walked out.

"Sorry, Sophie. I was tied up in my private office," Eilene laughed.

Sophie smiled. "Not many customers this morning I see. I didn't pass a single car on my drive over."

"I'm not surprise," said Eilene. "I wouldn't be here myself if I didn't have to. Glad you made it though. I have some information I think you'll find helpful in your search for your missing ancestor uncle."

They walked back to Eilene's desk. Eilene reached behind the desk and pulled out a manila envelope with Sophie's name written on it in large black sprawl. Sophie took the envelope and anxiously tore into it. One page contained a list of the names of cemeteries. Some names were flagged with a red star. At the bottom of the page a key indicated that the starred cemeteries definitely contain grave houses. Two other pages included maps showing directions to the cemeteries. Another page gave the names and telephone numbers of the person who now owned the land where the cemeteries were located.

Eilene pointed to the page of names and telephone numbers. "See, some of these old grave places is stuck in the middle of cornfields and such. Others might include very recent burial sites of family members. I wouldn't go traipsing out into those old cemeteries without at least giving the land owners a heads up."

"Good advice," said Sophie. "Eilene, this looks promising. I can hardly wait to get started…that is if this weather will ever settle. Did you hear that we might have another winter blast heading our way?"

"Sure did," Eilene said disappointedly. "I wouldn't mind coming out in the cold and snow except that no one shows up." She waved her hands at the empty chairs and tables. "I get lonely here. That's why I'm so glad you made it today. Say, how about eating lunch with me? I'm sending out for a hot dog with all the trimmings."

"Oh, I don't know…" Sophie began. Then she remembered how Gladys chided her for not eating enough. Sophie changed her mind. "You know, that sounds fun. I'll have the same…a hot dog with everything."

"And how about a milkshake?" Eilene said as she reached for the phone.

"Oh, why not? What's a hot dog without a milkshake? Eilene you'll be my downfall yet," Sophie chuckled and shook her head.

Since the hot dog stand wasn't getting much business that day lunch arrived quickly. "Yours is the only delivery I've made this morning," said a breathless scrawny young man with a serious case of acne. A thin gold ring dangled from his pierced nose and the shirt that sported the restaurant's logo was covered by a heavy parka that could use a good washing. Sophie cringed but accepted the greasy brown bag and passed the kid a two dollar tip.

"Gee, thanks lady," he said, and Sophie didn't know if he were being sincere or sarcastic.

While they ate lunch Eilene talked to Sophie about the cemeteries with which she was familiar. Eilene was born and raised in Northampton County. And although she didn't claim to be an expert on cemeteries, she knew the back roads of the county well. Sophie listened carefully, took notes, and choked down the hot dog that was way too tough for her liking.

When they finished eating, Sophie said, "Thanks Eilene. I don't know what I'd do without you"

"Don't thank me yet," Eilene said. "You may not find a thing."

"I know," said Sophie as she held up the manila envelope. "But somehow I feel like this is a turning point. Things are going to really start happening."

* * *

As Sophie hurried to her car she sensed a change in the weather…and it wasn't a favorable change. It had turned bone-chilling cold again and when she breathed deeply, the cold air felt as if it were searing her lungs. She could smell approaching snow. It was only three thirty, but the sun was shrouded by ominous gray clouds making it seem to be much later. Her first inclination was to rush back to Seaboard.

Suddenly Sophie felt a strong urge to drive around Jackson and see if she could spot Jeff's car. Although it was the county seat, Jackson was a very small town. It shouldn't take long to drive through it. She pulled out of the library parking lot and headed to the downtown area. She still didn't pass a single car.

The Piggly-Wiggly had a large sign on the front door, OPEN. But obviously it had no takers for the small parking lot beside the store was empty. She passed two more store fronts with CLOSED signs on their door. Black paper was taped inside the store window of the next store preventing passersby from peering inside. There were no cars parked along the curbs in front of any of these stores.

Sophie drove pass the Northampton County Courthouse. There were no cars parked in front indicating that court was not in session today. Sophie had always marveled at the stately courthouse built in Classic Greek Revival that was popular in 1858. It was built of locally-made bricks. Sophie fell in love with this building when she visited it on a fifth grade school trip. She remembered being in awe of the massive Ionic columns seated on the second-level portico. Balustrades leading up to the portico were composed of handsome hand-turned spindles of North Carolina heart pine done in the shape of Grecian Urns. When she spotted a small Greek bonnet above the great wood paneled double doors she'd thought that surely these doors must lead into a magnificent place…perhaps the castle of the Wizard of Oz.

Jeff's car was not in front of the courthouse so Sophie took a quick left onto a street that ran beside the courthouse and ended in a back parking lot. Much to her disappointment the lot was vacant…**except** for one old beat-up blue Nissan pickup. Two grubby men in hooded parkas stood beside their vehicle smoking cigarettes and talking animatedly. As Sophie approached, the men looked startled as if smoking cigarettes were illegal. They gawked at her, dropped their cigarettes, and crushed them with their boots. Sophie felt uneasy at the way they stared at her. She focused straight ahead and drove to a rear exit of the parking lot. As she looked in the rear-view mirror, she saw the men still standing there staring after her with their mouths wide open.

"Hope you got a mouthful," Sophie said repeating a maxim often thrown at gawking young boys back in her teenage years.

Since the rear exit led Sophie into a different part of town, she decided to drive pass some old houses she loved in that area. Some of the houses dated back as far as the 1700's. Sophie's favorite one was the Pebbles House. She knew its history well. It was much grander than her Singletary home in Seaboard. The original Pebbles House was built circa 1775 and at that time consisted only of a broad main hall with two spacious rooms on either side. A stairway in the back led to two similar rooms on the second floor. The cookhouse was a separate building in the back. She wondered how Gladys would feel about that…her kitchen outside the main house. The house had been added to over the years until now it was one of the largest homes in Jackson and was still occupied by members of the Pebbles family. The white wood structure had a long porch that extended from one end of the house to the other. The tall windows had shudders, and in the "Gay Nineties" Dr. Pebbles added gingerbread to his home in preparation for his daughter's wedding. As a girl Sophie often fantasized that a glorious wedding celebration must have taken place there since the bride's father decorated the house in such a festive way.

Sophie took a back road that connected to the Seaboard highway. Since the two gawking guys appeared to be the only people in town, she wanted to make sure they didn't see which road she'd taken. As she turned right and headed toward Seaboard, the sun began to make its way toward the horizon dropping behind a large bank of gray clouds. Lights appeared in the windows and on the porches of the houses beside the road. Streetlights clicked on automatically, and smoke curled from chimneys. The reflection of the lights on the snow made the scene look like a Currier and Ives Christmas card.

As she passed the last house in Jackson, she suddenly felt anxious. Light from her headlights illuminated crusty ice on the road causing her to drive more slowly, more carefully. It would be dark when she got home, and

Gladys would be livid or perhaps even gone...Sophie hoped for the latter.

On the seven mile drive to Seaboard, Sophie didn't pass a single car. Suddenly her car felt stuffy, hot. She reached over and turned down the heat. The ice was mottled by the glow of the setting sun. Uncanny shapes danced across the snow as light moved behind one tall pine tree and then another. Movement of the shapes made Sophie feel dizzy and nauseated. She began to sweat and found it hard to breathe. There was a bitter taste in her mouth, and she knew she was going to throw up. But the shoulders were barricaded by heaps of ice and snow that had been pushed aside earlier by road scraping equipment. If she could make it to Ramsey's Fork there would be a place to pull over. She recalled that the shoulders at that intersection were clear that morning. She pushed ahead trying to focus on the front of the car and avoid looking at the shimmering shadows on the snow beside the road.

Sophie finally reached Ramsey's Fork. She pulled the car off the road, swung open the door, and threw up until there was nothing left to throw up except watery bile. Afterwards she felt weak and shaken. She hardly had strength to close the door. She sat inside the car with her head resting on the steering wheel. If only she could make it three more miles, she thought. Then suddenly lights appeared in her rear-view mirror...the first she'd seen all night. Maybe she could get help. The car slowed as it approached and she recognized the clunky old blue Nissan pickup. It did not stop beside her but drove several yards ahead, then stopped. The two men she'd seen behind the courthouse opened their car doors and stepped out. Sophie's heart raced. Her hands trembled as she fumbled for her car key. She turned the key, stepped on the accelerator, and the motor raced. Sophie realized the car was not in gear.

"Calm down, calm down," she said to herself. "Start all over."

So she turned the key, put the car in gear, and stepped on the accelerator. The car lurched forward. Sophie burned rubber as she pulled onto the road. "Please God, don't let me spin out." As she tore pass the old pickup, the two grubby men leered at her lecherously.

Sophie arrived home to find the house in total darkness. So Gladys had opted to go home. "Oh no," Sophie muttered.

Sophie was not sure she could make it to the porch and up the steps.

She opened the car door and the air felt cold, revitalizing. She stumbled out of the car, stood up shakily, and braced herself against the car. She breathed the cold air deeply and thought about how she was going to get to the front door. The house seemed miles away.

"Where is Julie when I need her?" Sophie said aloud.

Finally Sophie let go of the car, stood up straight, and took a step toward the porch. Not bad. She proceeded slowly, ever so slowly. She finally reached the front porch steps. This was just a small crumb, however. Now she was faced with climbing them. Holding onto the ice-crusted rail she gradually made her way up, walked across the porch, and to the front door. She grasped the door handle as if it were a lifeline and gave it a turn. Locked. She leaned against the door and fumbled through her purse for the key.

Sophie muttered, "Damn it Jeff. You and your stupid compulsions."

Chapter 12

Sophie was not sure how she got upstairs, but she found herself in the bathroom, sitting on the side of the tub, and vomiting violently again. She was still wearing her coat but somehow she'd lost one shoe. When the she could no longer vomit, she ached for the comfort and safety of her bed. She tried to stand but her knees buckled, and she crumbled to the floor.

"Well, I won't try that again," she thought.

Sophie dragged herself on hands and knees out of the bathroom, into her bedroom, and toward her bed. Her arms and knees stung from rug burn and she'd left small smudges of blood on the rug. She was cold and trembled convulsively, yet was wet with sweat. Climbing upon the bed would be a giant challenge. Her heart pounded, and she thought there was no way she could climb up there. She wasn't sure how long she lay on the floor beside the bed, but she tried to relax and focused on breathing deeply, regularly. Then somehow she found the strength to clutch the mattress, pull herself up, and drop onto the bed. She couldn't reach the comforter that lay at the bottom of the bed, so she clasped her coat tightly around her, folded herself in a fetal position, and let the darkness engulf her.

Sophie drifted in and out of consciousness and wasn't sure how long she lay there. Fragments of images played across her eyelids…grave houses, deer tromping through snow searching for water, courthouses, and rusty old pickups. There was no logic to the scenes just reruns of her day.

Then from a distance Sophie heard someone call. "Sophie. Sophie. Where are you?" It was Jeff.

"Jeff, is that you?" Sophie moaned. Her voice was barely a whisper.

"Sophie, Are you here?" His voice seemed to be moving to another part of the house. The kitchen?

Sophie no longer attempted to answer. She merely groaned and prayed to go back to sleep.

Jeff bounded up the steps two at a time, grabbing one of Sophie's shoes that lay on the stairs. He burst into the bedroom and was struck by the stench of vomit and sight of Sophie lying there so still that he feared he was too late. He rushed to the bed.

"Sophie, are you alright?" he cried as he gently shook her motionless body. "Answer me, Sophie. Tell me what's wrong."

Sophie forced her eyes open. They were unfocused, bloodshot, and tears rolled down the side of her face. "I'm sick, Jeff," she groaned. "So sick. I...I think I'm dying."

Jeff grabbed her and hugged her wet face to his. "No, Sophie. You're not dying. You're going to be okay now. And he lay her down gently. "Let's get this coat off and get you under a warm blanket." And he started to unbutton the coat.

"No!" screamed Sophie. "I'm cold, Jeff. So cold. Please don't."

"Okay," Jeff said holding his hands up in a surrender gesture. "I'll just put the blanket on top of the coat." And he spread the down comforter over her and snuggled it around her chin like he'd seen her do on very cold nights.

"Now you lay here. I'll be right back," he said as he kissed her on the cheek.

"As if I could go any where if I wanted to," Sophie mumbled.

Jeff smiled through tears. "See. You're already better," he said.

Jeff stepped into the hall, snapped open his cell phone, and clicked a number he knew only too well. "Yes, it's me...real bad...get a doctor here right away," he said. Then he yelled, "I don't care *how* just get one here and *now*. No, I want him *here*."

He ended the call and then tapped in another number. Ring. Ring. Ring. "Oh, come on," he mumbled. "Pick up the damned phone." After two more rings he said, "Gladys, Jeff here. We got a problem."

Gladys's slow voice said, "Well, I'm not surprised. What now?"

"It's Sophie," said Jeff. "She's real sick. Come as quick as you can."

"We're on our way. You tell her we're on the way," said Gladys, and she hung up.

Jeff rushed back into the bedroom. He knelt beside the bed and gently shook Sophie's shoulder. "Sophie, Gladys is on the way...and so is a doctor."

"Gladys? I want to see Gladys," Sophie moaned. Now the tears were flowing full force.

"Hang on. She'll be here soon. And so will Melvin," said Jeff.

* * *

Gladys stormed into the house and up the steps with Melvin right behind. She pointed to a waiting chair in the upstairs hall and ordered Melvin to sit there and wait for further instructions. Then she scampered into the bedroom. She stopped sharp at the door and gasped when she saw Sophie lying in a fetal position on the bed.

"What happened? How'd she get dis way?" cried Gladys as she tore across the room and began checking Sophie.

"I came home and found her like this," said Jeff.

Gladys felt Sophie's head and said, "Why she's burning up!"

"She says she's cold and won't take off her coat," Jeff said helplessly.

"Chills go with the fever," said Gladys, and she lifted her head and sniffed audibly. "She throw up?"

"All over the bathroom," said Jeff.

"Well, you get on out of here and let me clean her up and the bathroom too" said Gladys as she began to pull covers away.

"No, stop it, Gladys," screamed Sophie. "I can't stand it. I'm cold." Then she whimpered like a kitten.

"Now you hush, Sophie. Don't you worry none." crooned Gladys. "I'm gonna get you cleaned up and get you under some heating pads."

"Gladys?" moaned Sophie.

"Right here, honey," she said. "I'm not a going nowhere."

As he stepped toward the door, Jeff said, "There's a doctor on his way, Gladys."

"Then I best be getting things fixed up in here," said Gladys.

"Melvin..."

Melvin stepped closer to the door but positioned himself so he couldn't see inside the bedroom. "Yeah?" he answered.

"I needs my mop, some Clorox Clean-up, paper towels, plastic bags and lots of cleaning rags," she called.

"I'm on it," said Melvin, and he headed down the steps.

"Jeff," she called. "See if'n you can hunt down those two heating pads for me."

As Jeff followed Melvin down the steps he heard Sophie cry, "Don't Gladys. Leave me alone."

"You just be still, and I'll have you fixed up in a minute. Now be still!" was Gladys's firm yet caring response.

Jeff was relieved that there was something he could do to make him feel useful. After he found the heating pads and took them to Gladys, he put on his coat and went onto the porch to wait for the medics. It was snowing again although not yet with the fury that had been predicted. To Jeff it appeared that the halo around the streetlight created a sinister impression of gloom and hopelessness. He wished he could wait calmly like Melvin who felt confident just because Gladys was now in charge. He'd told Jeff that earlier in the hall when Jeff frantically threw down boxes from shelves and cursed because he couldn't find the heating pads. Jeff wished he had Gladys's know-how. He envied the composed, reassuring way she handled the situation. When Sophie was concerned the training that had required him to be cool, calm, and collected just went out the window.

Finally headlights materialized through a white curtain of snow. A car skidded to a halt in front of the house, doors opened, and three men stepped out. The man on the passenger side of the front seat rushed to the porch and up the steps.

"Show me," was all he said, and he followed Jeff inside and to Sophie's bedroom.

As he entered the room, he pulled off his coat and tossed it on a nearby chair. He immediately hurried to Sophie and began checking her.

Without interrupting his examination he asked, "How long has she been this way?"

"She was fine when she left the house this morning," Gladys said.

"No sickness…vomiting, diarrhea, dizziness?" he asked.

"None," said Gladys.

The doctor pulled down the comforter, removed the heating pads, and began pressing Sophie's stomach.

Sophie cried out, "That hurts. Gladys, the blanket."

Jeff cringed. The doctor said, "What time was it when she left here this morning?"

Gladys said, "About ten thirty."

"Gladys, my blanket," begged Sophie. The doctor nodded and Gladys covered Sophie again.

"This came on quite suddenly then," the doctor said. "When did she first get sick?"

"Around four or four fifteen," Jeff said. Gladys looked at Jeff questioningly. If Jeff hadn't been with Sophie then how did he know what time she got sick?

Suddenly there was a commotion from the hall. Two men clamored in with an IV pole and several boxes.

"Okay, y'all clear out," the doctor said looking at Jeff and Gladys.

"Ain't going nowhere, Doctor," said Gladys with determination. "I nursed this girl's mother and grandmother. There's not much I've not seen. So I'm staying right here with Sophie." And she planted herself firmly beside the bed.

The doctor looked at Jeff. Jeff nodded his head slightly, and the doctor said, "Okay, let's get some intravenous fluids going and then we'll put in a catheter."

Jeff slowly left the room, went into the hall, and sat beside Melvin. Jeff rested his elbows on his knees and covered his face. Melvin reached over and patted him on the back.

"Things gonna be okay. Just wait and see. My Gladys ain't gonna let nothing happen to Sophie," Melvin said with conviction.

They worked way into the night. They stabilized Sophie and started her on medication. Both her temperature and blood pressure went down slightly and she was finally experiencing a natural sleep.

The doctor was gathering his things to leave. "It would be best if someone could stay up with her tonight. I don't anticipate any set-back, but that's just my judgment."

"I..." began Gladys.

"No," said Jeff. "I'll sit up tonight, Gladys. You and Melvin sleep across the hall. She'll want you tomorrow, and besides it's snowing like blue blazes out there now."

"Good to know," said the doctor sarcastically as he pulled on his coat.

The other men were carrying equipment to the car and Jeff walked down with the doctor. They stood on the porch as the men loaded the car.

"Thanks Doc for helping us out again," said Jeff.

"Under other circumstances I'd admit her," said the doctor.

"Yeah, but we can't," said Jeff.

"I understand," said the doctor.

"So what do you think?" Jeff asked the doctor.

"I can't say yet," said the doctor.

Jeff was impatient, tired, and worried sick about Sophie. He was in no mood for a doctor-dance-around. "Look here, you've got to have **some** idea. Just give me your best guess. Food poison?"

"Well, I won't know for sure until after the results of the urinalysis," said the doctor. "But yes, I'd say probably poison...but not **food** poison."

Chapter 13

Somewhere in the deep, dark, recesses of his mind, Jeff heard his name being called. He tried to straighten, but his back and neck cramped causing excruciating pain. He recognized Sophie's voice. He'd listened for her all night, and now that she was calling for him he couldn't move.

He croaked, "Sophie, Sophie, I'm right here. I'm coming." And he pushed himself up cautiously from the chair he'd slept in all night and stumbled to her bed.

She was laying there her eyes opened, darting around the room as if she were seeing it for the first time. She looked frightened and confused.

"Jeff, are you here?" she asked. Her voice was rough and hoarse, barely a whisper.

"Yes, Sophie," he said. "I'm right here. How are you feeling?"

"Like hell," she said.

Jeff laughed. "That's my Sophie. Tell it like it is." And he leaned over and hugged her.

Sophie squealed, "Ouch, my arm." Then she looked up. She saw the IV bag, and then looked down at the needle in her arm. "Jeff, what's going on?"

"Sophie, you've been real sick," said Jeff. "The doctor came, and he gave you this IV because you were dehydrated. I think there's some medicine in there, too."

Sophie looked startled. "Jeff, please call Gladys," Sophie pled.

"Already done," Jeff reassured her. "She was up with you real late. Right now she and Melvin are sleeping across the hall."

Sophie thought for a moment. Then she smiled a weak smile. "Then you stayed with me **all** night?" she asked.

Jeff grinned. "Yeah, and I behaved like a preacher," he said

"That's not saying much," Sophie teased.

Sophie turned her head toward the window and realized that a white curtain of snow obscured the view beyond. "Jeff, is it snowing again?" she asked.

"It's a whiteout," he answered.

"Guess you can't go to work today then," she joked in her new husky voice.

"Not even if the sun comes out and we have a spring thaw," he said and buried his face in her shoulder.

Chapter 14

Gladys was up and going at the first sound of voices. The first thing she did was check on Sophie. She shooed Jeff out of her room and simply told him to go downstairs with Melvin. The kitchen smelled like baking biscuits and a pot of coffee gurgled on the counter. Melvin stood at the stove frying turkey bacon.

"Don't have much taste for this here turkey bacon," he said. "Turkey's for Thanksgiving. Some things just need to be cooked the way they're suppose to be cooked."

"I see Gladys has you cooking," Jeff said wearily. The adrenalin that took him through the night was spent. He was exhausted, and he found it impossible to concentrate on anything but Sophie. He poured a cup of coffee, sat down at the table, and rested his chin in his hand.

"Believe it or not," said Melvin, "I does most of the cooking at the house. Gladys claims she's cooked out by the time she gets home. I don't really understand that 'cause in the next breath she's going on about how Sophie don't eat nothing. 'Course, I'm sure her cooking has picked up since you moved in." Then Melvin felt embarrassed. "I apologize. I didn't mean to speak out of turn."

Jeff smiled a weary smile. "Don't worry about it."

Melvin seemed relieved. "How you want your eggs?" And he lifted a pan of biscuits from the oven.

Gladys came in all business. "Well, she's fixed up for the morning. She seems to feel stronger today." Then she gave Jeff a probing eye. "You sure don't. Melvin, give this man some breakfast."

"It's on the way, woman," Melvin said as he cracked an egg into the frying pan. "Fried okay?"

* * *

Jeff looked in on Sophie. She was sleeping peacefully. She was wearing a fresh gown, and her hair spread on the pillow. Gladys still thought of Sophie as her little girl. Sophie's face was scrubbed until it shined and the harsh reddishness that accompanied the fever was gone. Her breathing sounded normal, and Jeff thought she looked beatific with the fluffy white comforter pulled up round her shoulders.

Jeff turned on the television and muted the sound. He clicked to the weather channel and watched the crawler and weather map. Snow was predicted to end by mid-day and move out to sea followed by freezing temperatures and low winds. Jeff glanced out the window but saw no indication that the snow was abating.

Jeff walked quietly into the hall, took out his phone, and dialed. After a single ring there was a pick-up. "Hello."

"Doc...Jeff. What you got?" Jeff asked.

"I was just getting ready to call you, Jeff," the doctor said. "We got some very interesting test results."

"Shoot," said Jeff pen and pad ready to take notes

"Remember you asked about the possibility of food poison last night?"

"Yes," said Jeff.

"And if I remember correctly I said I thought it was poison but not food poison. Well I was right on the money," the doctor seemed pleased with himself.

Jeff was impatient. "Just give me the results, Doc," he said.

"Okay. What we've got here is arsenic...arsenic poisoning," the doctor said.

"Arsenic? Are you sure? Where did Sophie come in contact with arsenic?" Jeff wondered aloud.

"Now Jeff, this isn't a case of accidental exposure to arsenic. This poisoning was intentional. Sophie Singletary was **intentionally** poisoned," the doctor said. There was silence at the other end. "Jeff, Jeff are you there?"

"Yes," Jeff was stunned. "I'm here. How do you know it was intentional?"

"We did a urine test. Urine test is the most reliable for acute poisoning if it's done in 24-48 hours. Now a fatal dose of arsenic is around 70-180 milligrams. I can't pin point the exact amount Sophie had except to say it would have been lethal, and it's a miracle you got to her when you did. Oh, we also did blood work which verified what the urine test showed."

"What about hair and fingernail tests?" Jeff asked.

"Hair and nail tests are used to measure exposure to arsenic in small amounts over a period of months. In Sophie's case the arsenic was administered in one shot...large amount," said the doctor.

Jeff's head was spinning. "So what'll we do now?" asked Jeff.

"Well, arsenic disrupts the entire digestive system. That's why she had vomiting, diarrhea, and stomach pain. She was having some trouble with urination which is also symptomatic but then too she was dehydrated. We've got to really watch her blood pressure and temperature, too."

"So how is this treated?" asked Jeff who was on the verge of panic.

"Well, we have some isotonic intravenous fluids going. (Thank goodness Gladys has some nursing experience.) And we're already using a drug called dimercaprol. There's an interesting thing about this drug, Jeff. It was developed by the Brits during World War II as an antidote to arsenic-based warfare agents. Now we use it to treat all kinds of metal poisonings like mercury, lead, arsenic, and such. That's so often the case, you know drugs that are developed for war purposes end up being used for everyday medical purposes. Don't you think that's interesting?"

Jeff could not have cared less about the history of the drug. "Yeah, yeah, that's real interesting, but will it work?"

"We've had pretty darned good success with it. Like I said, the fact that you caught this so quickly works strongly in Sophie's favor. Cautiously I'd say, she'll be okay. Oh a couple of more things, she may have a little tingling in her fingers or toes and might sound hoarse. Have you noticed either?"

"She hasn't complained of tingling, but hoarseness, yes," Jeff said.

"That should improve as the drug takes effect. So knowing all this do you still plan to keep her at home?" the doctor asked.

"Yes," said Jeff. "I think she's safer here."

"Right. Let me speak to Gladys. I need to give her some instructions, and tell her she'll be in charge of the patient," said the doctor.

"I'll get Gladys, but you don't have to tell her she's in charge. She's already taken charge," Jeff said, and he found great comfort in that. "And by the way, let me tell Gladys it was arsenic poison."

"Got 'cha," said the doctor. "I can instruct her without revealing that."

While Gladys spoke with the doctor, Jeff checked on Sophie. She was awake and lay peacefully watching the snow.

"Hi," said Jeff as he moved across the room and sat on the side of her bed. "Can I get you anything?"

She smiled and said, "Just you."

"Well, you got me," he said, and he leaned in for a kiss. He looked out of the window where she'd gazed. "It's suppose to stop snowing this afternoon."

"It's beautiful. We so seldom have this much snow here. Now two snows only a few days apart."

Jeff noticed that she was still hoarse. He was anxious to begin searching for the source of the arsenic that almost killed Sophie. Although he had several theories, he had no idea where to begin.

"Sophie, do you remember going to Jackson yesterday?"

Sophie smiled, "Of course, I do. I am sick to my stomach not my head."

Jeff beamed. He was relieved that a little of the sassy Sophie was back. He continued, "What did you eat while you were there?"

Sophie thought for a few seconds and said, "Well, since I couldn't have lunch with you, Eileen and I ordered hotdogs and milkshakes. It was a carry out, and this weird looking boy delivered them. He was young and very thin. He had red hair cut in a crew cut, and a terrible case of acne. And...and his nose was pierced. He had a gold ring in his nose."

Jeff suppressed his eagerness and continued calmly. "Did you and Eileen order the same thing?"

"Yes, I just told you we had hotdogs and milkshakes. Jeff do you think the hotdog was spoiled? Mine wasn't cooked very well and tasted awfully funny."

"That's possible," said Jeff concealing growing concern. "Where did you order the hot dogs from?" he asked.

"I don't know," said Sophie. "Eileen placed the order." Suddenly Sophie looked alarmed. "Jeff, do you suppose Eileen is sick too?"

"I don't know," he answered. "But we need to find out right away. If she is sick, she needs to get to a doctor immediately."

At that moment Gladys walked into the room. "Get off the patient's bed, Jeff. The doctor says I'm in charge of her and I don't want nobody sitting on her bed."

Jeff jumped up and Gladys smoothed the place he'd sat. She handed him his cell phone and said to Sophie. "How about a little chicken broth and some jello?"

Sophie made a face. "No thank you."

"Well you gonna try it any ways," Gladys said and left the room.

"That doctor didn't know what he was doing when he put me in her charge," said Sophie.

Jeff sat in a chair beside the fireplace cell phone in hand. Melvin had built a fire in the fireplace and the logs snapped and popped sending sparks up the chimney like a fireworks display on the Fourth of July. Sophie alternated watching the silent snow, then the crackling fire. She found the contrast fascinating.

Jeff dialed a number. "Me," he said. "Get me the number for Eileen…" He looked questioningly at Sophie.

"Brown," said Sophie. "Eileen Brown."

"Eileen Brown. I'll wait." Only a few seconds passed before Jeff said, "Got it." Then he dialed a number.

He smiled at Sophie encouragingly. "It'll be okay." Then his attention went back to the phone call. "Yes, this is Jeff Sands. I'm trying to reach Eileen Brown. Do I have the right number?"

"Oh yes, you have the right number, but Eileen isn't here." Jeff sensed concern in the woman's voice.

"Do you know how I can reach her? This is very important," said Jeff.

"I can tell you where she is, but I doubt you can talk to her. Eileen is in Halifax Medical Center in Roanoke Rapids. She's in intensive care and she's real sick. I thought you were the doctor calling to give me an update. I can't get to the hospital in all this snow, you know."

Jeff thought she was going to cry so he hurriedly said, "I'm so sorry to hear about Eileen. Just a couple of questions. Can you tell me her doctor's name?" She did.

"And this may sound foolish, but can you tell me where Eileen might place an order for a carry-out hotdog and milkshake?"

"Why yes, a little fast food place right outside of town. They sell barbecue, burgers and such, but their specialty is hotdogs. It's called The Winner Dog. Why do you think..."

Jeff interrupted, "I'll get off the phone now in case the doctor's trying to reach you. Thanks and best to Eileen."

Sophie looked at Jeff eyes wide with alarm. "Is Eileen..."

"She's in the hospital," Jeff said. "I got to make a call."

At that moment Gladys came in with broth. "Well, make your call out in the hall. Sophie don't need no more excitement," she ordered. Then her tone abruptly changed and she said sweetly, "Now here you go, honey." And she lifted a spoon to Sophie's clamped lips.

In the hall, Jeff dialed up the doctor again. "Me again. Just found out the likely source of the arsenic...hotdogs and milkshakes. There's another person in critical condition. Eileen Brown, Halifax Medical Center..." and he gave him the name of the doctor.

"I'm on it," said the voice at the other end. "Let's hope we're not too late."

Chapter 15

After Sophie took a few swallows of broth she fell asleep. Jeff called a conference in the kitchen. Melvin and Gladys sat with full attention at the table and looked at Jeff expectantly. Jeff hardly knew how to begin. It was imperative that they realize the extent of the danger Sophie was in, but he didn't want to frighten them away. He recalled how Gladys avoided staying in the house alone after dark. Would learning that someone poisoned Sophie cause her to take off? He had to take the chance. He needed them now, but it wasn't fair for them to be unaware of what they were up against.

"I've talked with the doctor," said Jeff. "At first we thought she had food poisoning…"

"Not from my food, she didn't," Gladys interrupted defensively.

Jeff immediately mollified Gladys. "Oh no, we never thought for a minute it was anything you cooked."

"Well, I should hope not," Gladys seemed satisfied.

Jeff continued, "But for a while, we thought it may have something to do with a hotdog she ate yesterday."

"Hot dog?" scoffed Gladys. "Why she don't ever eat junk food."

"Well she did yesterday and so did Eileen Brown, the librarian. Eileen is in the hospital," Jeff paused to give them a minute to absorb what he'd told them.

"Well all's I can say is that place ought to be shut down," said Gladys.

"That would certainly be the answer," said Jeff, "If Sophie and Eileen were suffering from food poisoning, but that's not the case."

"I'm confused," said Melvin.

"I can understand why," said Jeff. "We were too. You see Sophie and Eileen were poisoned with arsenic and most likely it was either in the hotdogs or milkshakes."

Gladys threw up her hands and screamed, "Arsenic!!! Why that's what you use to kill rats. Oh my dear Lord please help her." Then she covered her face and began to cry.

Jeff tried to comfort her. "Gladys, please. The doctor has her on a medication that is real effective in treating arsenic poisoning. It's in the IV. And this morning you said yourself that she's already stronger. You've just got to keep on doing what you're doing."

Gladys looked up at him with fear in her eyes. She was scared yet determined. "Well you can count on one thing," she said, "If'n anybody can bring her through this, it's me. I've nursed that girl most of her life. I know what makes her tick."

"How'd the arsenic get in the food?" Melvin asked. Melvin was a man of few words, but he was always on point.

"That's just it," Jeff said reluctantly. "I'm afraid it was put there intentionally."

Gladys and Melvin gasped. "Who'd do that to that sweet Eileen Brown? Why I've known her and her family all my life. Why would someone want to poison her and my Sophie too?"

Jeff suddenly felt enraged. "Well that's another thing," he said angrily. "I don't think Eileen was the intended victim. I think Sophie was."

"What?" they both screamed.

"I'm sorry," said Jeff, "I don't mean to scare you but I need your help. I need you to stay here and take care of Sophie."

"You don't even have to ask me," said Gladys. "Ain't nobody gonna get anywhere near that girl. Not while we're around...and we intend to be around. Right, Melvin?"

"Right," said Melvin.

"Thanks," said Jeff. "I felt sure you'd feel that way but it's only fair that you know what really happened."

"The other thing I need to talk with you about is I'm going to have to leave for just a few hours. I need to go to Jackson to...ah...file a report. Earlier I promised Sophie I wouldn't leave her, and now..." Jeff looked distressed. "Now I'm going back on my word at a time when she needs..."

Gladys interrupted, "Now listen here, Jeff. You don't give Sophie enough credit. If you are just straight with her, she'll understand. Stop treating her like she's pathetic. Sophie's a strong woman."

"You mean tell her that I think someone tried to kill her?" Jeff said. "I doubt she's that strong especially right now."

"What? You gonna slink off to Jackson and tell her you just remembered you have to go to work? Now how do you think that will make her feel *especially right now*?"

Jeff was silent. He thought carefully about what Gladys said. After all no one knew Sophie better than she. "Okay," he said, "I'll tell her that someone tried to poison either her or Eileen...most likely her. But that's as much as I'll tell her."

"You mean there's more?" asked Gladys. "Lord have mercy!!! I wondered why you moved in here all of a sudden. I knew it wasn't for my cooking, so I thought it was a courting thing. Now you say there's more."

"It is a 'courting thing', Gladys," said Jeff. "But there's more. Lots more."

Melvin suddenly spoke with great authority. "Well, just bring 'em on....whoever it is. I'm ready." And he patted his coat pocket.

Jeff was stunned. "Melvin," he barked. "Are you carrying a gun?"

With that Melvin stood, reached under his coat, and waved a hand gun. "Yes sir," he said in his creaky old voice, "We'll take care of them...me and my Iver Johnson 32 caliber revolver."

"Whoa, whoa, there Melvin," said Jeff. "Take it easy. I...I'm not sure...I mean be careful with that..."

Gladys interceded, "Melvin, you fool, give me that gun before you shoot somebody."

Melvin obediently handed her the gun. "Ain't got no bullets anyhow. I gots 'em my pocket," Melvin mumbled.

Jeff slowly recovered from seeing his life pass before his eyes. He took several deep breaths and waited for his heart to stop racing. Then he said as calmly as possible, "Well I guess I'll go talk to Sophie."

* * *

Jeff found Sophie wide awake. "I wondered where you were," she said. "Look, it's stopped snowing."

Jeff bent down and kissed her. Her cheek was still warm but not as hot as it had been that morning. "I think your temperature's going down."

"I feel better," she said, but she was still hoarse.

"Sophie, I have to talk to you," Jeff said.

"Oh, this sounds serious," she said.

Jeff spoke quickly knowing what he had to say would upset Sophie. "Remember I promised you I wouldn't go anywhere until you were well. Well, I have to break that promise."

Sophie was silent. She looked hurt, mistrustful, and then a tear rolled down her cheek. "Are we experiencing a spring thaw already?"

"What?" Jeff asked.

"Oh, nothing. Just something you promised," said Sophie, and she turned to look out the window. Snow-covered tree limbs glistened as the sun eked its way through a gray mist.

"Sophie don't turn away. I have to talk to you. Please," Jeff pleaded. He took her shoulders and gently turned her to face him. "Listen."

She looked up at him, and now he saw anger. He thought of what Gladys said about Sophie being strong and he actually felt relieved to see anger not hurt. Jeff spoke quickly, "Sophie, when I talked with the doctor this morning, I didn't tell you everything he said. When they ran tests on you to determine why you'd gotten so sick so fast, they made a shocking discovery."

Sophie's expression turned from anger to fear. "Jeff," she said, "What's wrong? What's wrong with Eileen and me?"

"The tests showed conclusively that you were poisoned. Poisoned with arsenic. And that's probably the cause of Eileen's hospitalization. Her doctor is being notified of what we found from your tests, and I'll check to see what they found from hers later."

"But how did we get arsenic....Oh no," Sophie said. "The hotdogs and milkshakes. We ordered the same thing. But how did arsenic get in the food?"

"That's the most troubling part. Right now, we have to assume that it was put there intentionally," Jeff said.

"Why? Why would anyone want to poison us?" Sophie asked. Now she didn't sound so brave. Her voice quivered with fear.

"Why? I don't know. One thing that makes us feel it was intentional is the large quantity that you ingested. Sophie, there's so much we don't know. That's why I have to go to Jackson and track this down. Do you understand?" Jeff asked.

"Of course you must go, Jeff," said Sophie. Jeff was relieved. "Do you think Gladys will stay..."

"Of course, Gladys's gonna stay right here." Gladys had been ease dropping in the hall and she marched into the room. "...and so is Melvin. You ready to try a little broth now?"

"Uh, yes, thanks," said Sophie. "Right away." And Gladys was gone.

"Jeff, before you go will you do one thing for me?" begged Sophie.

"Anything," said Jeff.

"Make Gladys stop treating me like a five-year-old."

Jeff threw his head back and laughed. "You want **me** to make **Gladys** do something. You're kidding, of course."

* * *

While Gladys was warming broth the telephone rang. Caller ID identified the number. Jan. "Oh goodness, what am I gonna say to her?" Gladys said as she reached for the receiver.

"Hello," Gladys yelled. Gladys always spoke loudly on the phone especially if it were an out-of-town call, and she knew Jan was out at the farm.

"Hey, Gladys," said Jan. "How'd y'all make out during this last one?"

"Pretty good, Jan. Just warming up some broth here," said Gladys.

"Sounds good. Nothing better on a snowy winter day than Gladys broth. Hey, let me speak to my buddy."

"Ah, can't do it Jan. She's sick. Real sick," said Gladys.

"What's the matter with her?" Jan asked anxiously.

"She ate something that made her sick," said Gladys.

"What?"

"A hotdog," said Gladys. "Now I gots to get this broth up to her."

"Well tell her we called....Julie got snowed in out here with me. This time I got an entire tree blocking my path. Tell Sophie we'll call back later."

Jan hung up the phone, turned to Julie, and said, "Sophie's sick. She ate a bad hotdog. Food poisoning I guess."

"That's strange," said Julie. "Sophie didn't used to eat junk food. First pizza, now hotdogs. I tell you, Jan, Stud is wreaking havoc on Sophie's good eating habits."

Chapter 16

After lunch Jeff drove to Jackson. His feelings were a mixture of fury and frustration. Jeff looked out into the woods. It was a winter wonderland. A glaze of snow on the tree branches sparkled like diamonds. How could something so evil happen in such a beautiful setting?

In contrast to the splendor of the wintry scene in the woods, piles of dirty snow lay beside the road indicating that the snow plow began scraping the roads as soon as the snow stopped. A couple of miles outside Jackson, Jeff pulled up behind the plow, and it was moving at a snail's pace. Mounds of snow on the side of the road made it impossible for him to pass. The driver of the machine turned when he realized there was a vehicle behind him. He gave a friendly wave and flashed a pleasant smile. There was nothing for Jeff to do but smile disingenuously, return his wave, and seethe. When they reached the intersection in the middle of town the plow turned right toward the library, and Jeff turned left. There was no other traffic on the roads from either direction.

Jeff reached the building where a black covering hung in the storefront window completely concealing the interior of the store and a huge sign on the door read *Closed.* He pulled into an alley that ran beside the store and ended in a rear parking area. He parked between an old rusty Chevelle and a blue Nissan pickup, slapped the hoods of the vehicles, and noted they were cold. He dashed across the lot, up the back steps, and used a key card to unlock the door.

On the first floor there were three old surplus desks, a couple of filings cabinets, a computer station, and two work tables where scattered papers and open file folders lay. The room smelled like coffee, cigarette smoke, and sweat. The room reflected organized chaos except for one spot. Behind the desk in the least conspicuous part of the room sat a handsome young man, dressed nicely in heavy khaki pants, and a long-sleeve LL Bean flannel shirt. His thick black hair was fashioned in a crew-cut. He was tilted back in his chair, feet on the desk, and working a find-a word puzzle.

Jeff approached him. "What's happening?" he asked.

The young man looked up and grinned, "Nothing much. Nothing happening at all." And he went back to his find-a-word.

Jeff raised a fist and banged it loudly on the desk. The young man cringed, bolted upright, and almost landed on the floor.

"Well, *make* something happen," yelled Jeff. He reached into his pocket, brought out a small notebook, tore off a page, and threw it on the desk. "Here…see if you can find out where the hell this place is." Scribbled on the page was *Winner Dog*.

Jeff whipped around, stormed across the room, and took steps to the second floor two at a time.

The second floor was basically a balcony overlooking the lower floor. When the store had been in operation, the first floor was used for retail and the second floor was used by the manager and the managerial staff. Furnishings were sparse. It held two desks, two filing cabinets, a computer station, and a large work table with several chairs shoved underneath. Jeff walked to one of the desks, took off his coat, and tossed it angrily upon the work table.

"Little hard on the kid weren't you?" said Jesse, a gray haired man of about fifty who was working at the computer.

"Yes, Jesse, I suppose I was, but that *kid* has to learn to take things seriously. You don't stop working a case because nothing's happening," Jeff snarled.

"Well, just to top off your day," Jesse said, "we're having company."

"Damn! Who?"

"Big guys. Raleigh," Jesse said. "They view these two murder attempts as taking us to a *whole new level*. Guess they want to be in on the action."

"Or be underfoot," Jeff said. "You brief our guys here on the latest?"

"Yep…as well as Raleigh. Everybody's up- to-date."

At that moment a door in the back of the room opened and two burly, scruffy men dressed in jeans, long-sleeve flannel shirts, work boots, and showing a two-day stubble walked into the room carrying large mugs of coffee.

One man yawned and said, "Hey Jeff. Just catching a few winks. You want us here or back in Seaboard?"

"Tonight, you'd better go over to Seaboard. I don't know how late I'll be here…especially since I have to get ready for company," Jeff said contemptuously.

"We're on it," said the second man.

"And you need to be aware of a new development. It seems that our friend Melvin is packing heat. So don't go get yourselves shot," Jeff warned.

"Good God! What's he got a shotgun?"

"Nope. He's got himself an Iver Johnston 32 caliber revolver."

"Whoa grandpa! He *do* mean business."

At that moment the young man Jeff chewed out bounded up the stairs. "I found the Winner Dog location, Jeff," Buddy said breathlessly. Then he paused as if waiting for an ovation. When he didn't received one he handed Jeff a sheet of paper with directions and a phone number written on it.

"Did you try calling this number?" asked Jeff.

"Yes, sir," Buddy said proudly.

"And???" coaxed Jeff.

"No answer," Buddy said. This response was a little less enthusiastic.

"Okay," said Jeff. "Get your coat. Let's check out the Winner Dog."

Jeff was up and reaching for his coat. "Uh, one other thing," Buddy said. "I have copies of the information Eileen Brown gave Sophie Singletary." He handed Jeff a folder. Jeff opened it. Several sheets contained rough drawings of maps. Another sheet listed names and telephones number of cemeteries.

Jeff asked, "How did you get this?"

"Eileen Brown printed copies for Sophie Singletary. I found some copies she discarded because they weren't dark enough. I kept them, brought them back here, and enhanced them."

"Now that's the kind of thinking I'm looking for," said Jeff. "Let's go."

The young man beamed and rushed to get his coat.

Buddy drove. Jackson city streets had been scraped. Then they drove pass the sign that read, *You Are Leaving the City of Jackson, Come See Us Again.*

"Why do you suppose they call every little town a 'city' on those welcome and leaving boards?" the young man said trying to make conversation.

Jeff said, "I don't know. Why don't you see if you can find the answer to that one," said Jeff. He wasn't going to let the kid off the hook so fast.

The farther they drove, the rougher the road became. Only a few brave drivers with serous cabin fever dared to venture out on the ice-coated road.

"Thought you said the place was just outside the city limits," Jeff complained as they reached a shady spot and the rear tires spun helplessly in an effort to get traction.

"It is. It is," said Buddy, and he pointed. "See right back behind that hedge."

They reached what they supposed was the entrance to a parking area.

Jeff said, "Stop. Right here. Don't pull into the parking area."

"Right here on the road?"

"Right here on the road. I don't think we have to worry about being hit by speeding traffic," said Jeff.

They walked to the culvert that cars crossed in order to access the parking lot. "Stop," said Jeff. "What do you see?"

The young deputy looked around the parking lot. "Well, there's two cars parked there. One is up beside the door and the other is parked back and to the side."

"Notice anything unusual about them?"

"Well...."

Jeff was impatient. "They're both covered with new snow. The top, the hood, and the wind shield. What does that tell you?"

The young man's face brightened. "That those cars weren't driven today. They've been here all night."

"There you go," said Jeff. "Anything else?"

Buddy was beginning to catch on. "No footprints," he said.

"Right," said Jeff. "Now we don't want to leave any more prints in the snow than we have to, but we gotta find out who drove those cars in here and when."

The young man nodded and looked deep in thought. Jeff wasn't going to wait for ideas so he continued, "You check the front door and the car on the right. I'll check the other car and the back door. And remember no more footprints than necessary."

Jeff nodded and the young man moved out first. He walked straight to the front door. There was a sign that read *Open* but when he tried the door it was locked. He turned, looked at Jeff, and shook his head. Jeff motioned him toward the car on the right. When Buddy reached the car he tried all four doors, looked at Jeff, and shook his head.

"Okay," Jeff called, "I'm going to check this car and move on to the back. You walk back over your old path there and follow me."

Jeff found the second car also locked and started toward the building. Buddy fell in behind him. When they reached the back of the building, the door was partly open. Fresh snow covered the stoop and the door threshold. Jeff unzipped his coat, unsnapped the holster attached to his belt, and took out a 9 mm Beretta. His young companion followed suite. Jeff stepped on the stoop and banged loudly on the half-opened door.

"US Marshals," he yelled. "We want to talk to the owner." When there was no answer, Jeff tried to push it open. It wouldn't open. Jeff hit it with his shoulder. It still didn't budge. Jeff turned to Buddy and said, "Give me a hand here."

The deputy hurried to the door and together they pushed steadily against the tremendous weight that prevented the door from opening. Slowly, slowly the door opened. Jeff squeezed through and found himself in a vile-smelling, cluttered kitchen. Jeff looked on the floor and saw the source of the stench.

"What you got in there?" Buddy asked.

"Come on in and see for yourself," said Jeff moving aside to let Buddy inside.

On the floor lay a fat white man. He must have weighed three hundred pounds if he weighed an ounce. He wore black sweatpants and a black sweatshirt that was sprinkled with a white powder…probably flour. Over the front of the sweats was a long dirty white apron coated with unidentifiable stains. He wore black athletic shoes and black socks. He was lying on his back with his face turned upward. His eyes were set and dull and looked like black marbles staring at the ceiling. His hair was long and greasy, and a badly stained Boston Red Sox baseball cap lay nearby. It looked like his head was lying on a dark reddish-black cushion, and in the middle of his forehead was a small round hole.

Buddy accepted Jeff's invitation to come on in. He pushed his way through the door, looked down at the fat man on the floor, turned, and dashed back outside. Jeff couldn't resist yelling, "Remember now…don't mess up the scene."

When Buddy came back inside, Jeff was kneeling beside the body scrutinizing it closely. He looked up at Buddy and said, "Don't worry. It happens to all of us. Check out the rest of the building, and be careful."

Buddy gladly moved passed the body with his gun raised and walked into the seating area. He called, "All clear here, Jeff." Then he moved to an area closed off by folding doors. He slid open the doors slowly. Then he yelled, "Oh Jesus. Jeff, here's another one."

Jeff rushed to the room. On the floor lay a strange-looking young man. He had spiked red hair, a serious case of acne, and a gold ring hooked through his nose. The filthy jacket he wore lay open, and they could see a money pouch buckled around his waist. There was money inside. In the middle of his forehead was a round red dot. The kid looked like he was sleeping on the same kind of pillow as his fat friend.

This time Buddy stayed put. Jeff knelt beside the body and studied it carefully. "Looks like a twenty-two. This might be the work of our guy," Jeff said. He pointed to the pouch around the victim's waist that still contained money. "Wasn't robbery."

"Want me to check the cash register?" asked Buddy.

"No," said Jeff. "Let the scene guys do it." He reached for his cell phone and clicked a number. After one ring there was a pick-up. "Hey Jesse, we got us two bodies here. Send the guys…and call up the locals."

Jeff reported exactly what they had, gave directions to the Winner

Dog, and said they had the scene secured. "Any word from our *guests?*"

"Not yet," was the response. "Let you know as soon as we hear."

"Right," said Jeff. He clicked off, dialed up another number, waited, and then said, "Gladys...Jeff. I'm gonna be a while."

Chapter 17

"Just what in tarnation do you think you're doing up?" demanded Gladys. "And how did you get that IV pole over there?"

Sophie was sitting in a chair by the fire with the IV pole beside her. "I just felt like getting up, Gladys, and I rolled the IV with me. I got stiff lying in bed so long."

Gladys grabbed the thermometer and inserted it in Sophie's ear. When it beeped, she looked at it intently. "Well, it don't look like you got any temperature," she said. "So I suppose it's alright. What about something to eat?"

"You know...I think I'd like some cream of wheat with honey," Sophie said. When Sophie was a child Gladys always gave her cream of wheat while she was sick.

"Cream of wheat," beamed Gladys, and she turned to go.

"Gladys," Sophie said. "Have Jan or Julie called?"

"Not today," Gladys said.

"I was thinking that it may not be a good idea not to tell them about the arsenic poisoning. Just let them think food poisoning."

"Okay with me except I don't want them thinking it was my food," Gladys said.

"And Jeff...has he called?" Sophie asked.

"He has. As a matter of fact that's why I came up here. Says he'll be longer than he'd expected. Something musta come up," Gladys said. Gladys switched on the telephone ringer as she walked to the door. "Since you're up, might as well answer the phone yourself."

Gladys was no sooner out the door than the phone rang. Sophie reached for the receiver. "Hello."

"Hi girlfriend," said Jan. "You sound pretty chipper this morning."

"I'm feeling so much better," said Sophie. "So you and Julie are stuck out in the country…just the two of you."

"Yes Lord. I've spent more time with Julie this winter than I ever intended to," said Jan.

In the background Sophie heard Julie shout, "It cuts both ways you know."

"So how's Jay-eff?" Jan teased.

"Jeff's fine. We're fine. Jeff's working," said Sophie.

"See I told you…all you had to do was stop listening to Julie," said Jan.

Again Sophie heard Julie shout, "Remember, I speak from experience. Lots of experience."

"So Jeff's back at work," Jan said. "No doubts…no fears?"

"None," said Sophie. "When do you think you two will be able to drive back to town?"

"The tree guys haven't even made it out here to check things. When they do, they'll fix us a path so we can drive out. Probably a day at the most before we can get to town. In the meantime, take care. You sound just great," Jan said and signed off.

Sophie looked out the window. The sun sank low in the western horizon creating a purplish hue that was reflected on the newly fallen snow. Boxwoods that lined the walkway to the house looked like giant balls of grape-flavored cotton candy. Trees were completely still as if they feared movement would shake off their winter blanket. The trees were still. The boxwoods were still. The house was still. Suddenly the stillness was disquieting. Sophie didn't want to be alone. She stood up slowly, rolled the IV pole beside her, and walked into the hall. This was the most activity Sophie had experienced since becoming ill, and she felt extremely weak. She struggled to the balcony railing that overlooked the downstairs hall, looked down, and called for Gladys. Suddenly she was struck by a wave of dizziness and teetered at the edge of the overlook. The next thing she knew there was a scream and strong hands grabbed her arms. Sophie collapsed.

"Lordy, Lordy! Melvin come a-running and help me get this girl back to bed," yelled Gladys. "I can't leave her one second less she goes and almost kills herself. Melvin, where are you?"

Soon Sophie found herself back in bed. "Why did you go out in the hall like that, Sophie?" asked Gladys.

"I suddenly felt frightened," Sophie admitted. "I've never felt that way before, but suddenly I was afraid to be in my house alone."

They were silent for a few minutes. Then as Gladys straightened the pillows and covers on Sophie's bed she scoffed, "Well it's about time you was afraid! How many times I got to tell you this house has spirits. Now most of them is good spirits, but some are evil. It's the evil ones that you've got to look out for."

Sophie murmured, "It's not spirits I'm afraid of, Gladys."

* * *

Jeff and Buddy waited as the scene investigators did their job. They worked the parking lot first as they raced against nightfall. They concluded that body evidence inside would be protected by cold air entering the building through the opened back door. As the sun set the temperature plunged. Jeff and Buddy took refuge in the car with the heater running full blast and watched the outside activity.

"Does it always take this long?" asked Buddy. "Pretty soon there won't be any light at all."

"They're taking it slow and easy now because anything they miss might be lost for good when people start traipsing through the parking lot," said Jeff. "Forty eight hours and additional snowfall is bad enough. No point in making it worse."

"Do you smoke?" asked Buddy.

"No," said Jeff.

"Me neither," said Buddy, "but I think if I did this would be a time when I'd go through a whole pack."

At that moment a guy with a jacket that had *Crime Scene Investigator* stamped on the back walked into the middle of the parking lot and gave the all's clear signal. Jeff and Buddy rolled out of the car and headed to the back of the building. As they walked Jeff's phone vibrated.

Jeff clicked on the phone. "Yeah?"

"They're here," said Jesse. "Their car just pulled up in the parking lot."

"Well they'll have to wait. The scene guys just finished in the parking lot, and we're going back in." Then Jeff added sarcastically, "Give them my apology and tell them we won't be too much longer."

"Will do," said Jesse.

"Oh, Jesse," Jeff said, "what about Seaboard?"

"Got it covered," said Jesse. "They left here when you did."

"Good," said Jeff and he clicked off.

When Jeff and Buddy reached the back door, it was apparent the inside scene men were already collecting evidence. Fingerprint guys were dusting. A photographer was snapping pictures of anything unusual and usual. Jeff noticed that the cash register door was open and there was money inside. A medical examiner was examining the young man in the far room. He turned the victim's head slightly and studied the exit wound.

"Twenty two?" asked Jeff.

"Be my guess," said the examiner. "We'll see when we dig the slug out."

Two gurneys arrived. Black body bags were opened, the bodies zipped inside, and they were wheeled away to waiting vehicles. Jeff talked with several of the scene investigators and the consensus was that this was definitely a professional hit. Jeff noticed that Buddy seemed to move around the scene with more confidence and ease. He was interacting well with the other investigators and asking relevant questions. He was definitely on a roll and Jeff didn't want to stifle his initiative.

Jeff approached Buddy, "I got a call from Jesse. The guys from Raleigh are here. I need to get on back. Think you can get a ride in later."

Buddy was raring to go. "Sure. I'll keep an eye on things here and report back to you."

"Good. Just stay alert and let everybody do their job," Jeff said, and he turned and walked away leaving a keyed up Buddy behind.

* * *

When Jeff pulled into the parking lot he spotted a familiar black Crown

Victoria. The plates showed it was a government issue. He took a deep breath, swung open his car door, and hurried across the lot. As he entered the first floor room he was struck by the quiet activity taking place. No loud joke sharing. No raucous laughter. No dirty coffee mugs or fast food wrappers on the desks. One man stared intently at the computer screen while another watched over his shoulder. A third man with knitted brow studied the contents of a file folder. Jeff smiled, shook his head, and sprinted up the steps to the second floor.

Two men in suits and ties sat at the work table. Jeff saw his chair was occupied. The high-back desk chair was facing the wall and all Jeff could see was the top of a shiny balding head with a bad case of dry scalp. Jeff stopped short and began to unbutton his coat.

"Mr. Bryant," Jeff greeted the chair snatcher.

The chair turned slowly and a humongous round face set atop a fat neck grinned and said, "Jeff. Good to see you." Then he waved his hand over the scene below and added, "You run a tight ship here." And he grinned even wider.

Jeff grinned back. "We try."

As Bryant stood six feet two of blubbery mass unfolded. His cheeks were bright pink and tiny red veins showed through the thin flesh on his nose. He had bulging lackluster brown eyes and his red-tipped ears lay so flat against his head that he appeared to have no ears at all. He wore a dark gray suit and a white shirt with the top button open. He looked like an enormous walrus as he waddled to the table.

"Let's sit here," he said assuming a managerial role. "I only sat at your desk because your chair is more comfortable...and bigger." He sat down at the head of the table.

Jeff, Jesse, and the two other men took side chairs. Bryant cleared his throat and spoke in a commanding voice, "These two men are Powell and Talbot...Jeff Sands." They all nodded in acknowledgement.

"Now, what can you tell us about the two murders at the Winner Dog?" Bryant demanded.

Jeff took a deep breath, leaned forward with his elbows on the table, and reported rapidly, "Not a lot right now. The murders took place before the last snowfall...that would be before forty eight hours. Two locked cars in the parking lot. No footprints in the parking lot. Front door locked. Back door unlocked. Owner was face up on the kitchen floor. The second victim was in another part of the building…maybe tried to run. No robbery—money in the delivery boy's change pouch and in the cash register. They were both shot once in the forehead with a small caliber gun. Locals notified and assisting. I left one of our men on site…Buddy Turner. We'll have to wait for test results etc. Now this part is supposition. I believe that somehow the shooter was able to put arsenic in the hotdogs that were delivered to Sophie Singletary and Eileen Brown. Maybe he landed a job there as cook, who knows…anyway while the delivery was being made the owner was killed to prevent him from identifying the poisoner. The delivery boy returns, sees his boss dead, tries to run, and he's shot. As I said this last part is supposition, but it's the best I can come up with at this point in the game."

Bryant eyes were riveted on Jeff while he rattled off his condensed version of the murders. When Jeff finished Bryant drummed his fingers loudly on the table and continued to stare intently at Jeff. His frown boded no good news. Finally he said "Jeff we made this trip down here because of the attempts on the lives of Sophie Singletary and her friend Eileen Brown. Now we have the additional complication of two murders. As you know, your mission is to protect Sophie Singletary in the event her ex-husband should try to make contact with her. And in such an event, we would all move to apprehend him."

"I'm aware of the objectives of the mission," said Jeff. "We all are."

Bryant leaned forward in his chair as far as his waistline would allow, put his fingertips together, and said, "Now Jeff, we chose you for this job because we know you are familiar with the territory."

Jeff nodded. "I grew up here."

"I know," Bryant said. "And you know Sophie Singletary very well."

"We have a history going back to grade school," said Jeff.

"Yes, and that's all right. History is good," Bryant said. "But there's one thing we didn't count on, Jeff." Then his mood changed abruptly. He banged his fist on the table and shouted, "You went and jumped the fence."

Jeff didn't flinch. He sat quietly fingering a ball point pen. He hoped that after venting Bryant would cool down. But there was more. Bryant said, "So let's take a look at what we got here. First we had two innocent women almost killed with arsenic poisoning, and one is a possible witness to our case against Andrew Temple. Now we have two murdered men…both of them probably innocent citizens. So I got to ask myself, Jeff, are you the best person for this job?"

The whole place was as quiet as a tomb. No papers rattled. No computers clicked. No soft voices. Just quiet. Jeff let the pen he was holding drop on the table. It sounded like bomb.

"I don't know if I'm the best one for the job or not, Bryant, but I didn't ask for this assignment. In fact when I learned that Temple was a suspected assassin and that he was the ex-husband of Sophie Singletary I tried to bow out. It was you who said my history would make the job easier. I didn't count on getting involved with Sophie again but it happened and there it is. Now if you want to pull me off the case…go ahead. But that's not going to make me leave it alone, and it's not going to make me move out of Sophie's house. So the decision is up to you."

It was Bryant who went quiet this time. Then he looked at Jeff steadily and slowly asked, "Do you mean you'd jeopardize your career over this?"

"If that's what it takes," Jeff said obstinately.

Silence again. Finally Bryant shook his head slowly. "You're a stubborn man, Jeff. Sometimes stubborn makes a good Marshal but other times it can get him killed. Okay Jeff, we'll leave things the way they are…just don't screw it up."

Silence again. Bryant looked frustrated. Talbot jiggled his leg so hard that the second floor balcony shuck. Powell decided that this would be a good time to stare at a water stain on the ceiling.

Finally Bryant said, "Who's covering the girl now?"

Jeff look miffed. "I've got two guys on her right now although I'm not sure they're needed all that much."

"What do you mean?" Bryant looked skeptical.

"Sophie's old housekeeper, Gladys, and her boyfriend are staying in the house with Sophie. They're both devoted to Sophie, and I wouldn't want to cross either one of them…especially Melvin. He's armed."

Bryant threw his head back and banged his forehead with his fist.

"Holy Jesus, Jeff. What are you doing here?"

"The best we can, Bryant. The best we can," Jeff said.

Bryant settled for the third time and asked halfheartedly, "So what do you plan to do next?"

Jeff sighed. "Hit the streets. Ask store clerks, restaurant workers, man on the street if they've seen anyone resembling Andrew Temple. Doubt we'll get much since people around here have been snowed in, but we have to try. He'll surface sooner or later. We didn't do this sooner because we didn't want to scare him off. Now it seems like Temple doesn't scare easily."

"Then what?" asked Bryant.

Jeff looked tired. He put his elbows on the table and rubbed his eyes with the heels of his hands. "Then I talk to Sophie. I'm not going to leave out anything, Bryant. I haven't told her that Temple is an assassin and he's why I'm here. I wanted her to behave normally, and I didn't want to frighten her. Now things have turned nasty. Her neck is on the line, and she has a right to know everything."

Bryant nodded.

Jeff continued, "Then she and I are going to search every piece of clothing or anything that she brought with her when she left him."

"Thought you'd already done that," said Bryant.

"I have but not as thoroughly as I plan to now," said Jeff. "We may just rip up everything she has."

"Then you don't think he's just after revenge because she left him?" Bryant asked.

"I don't think he'd take these kinds of risks just to exact revenge on a wife who left him. He's too much of a pro," Jeff said. "I think he's after something. Something he thinks Sophie knows or has…and I think she's totally oblivious."

Bryant scooted his chair back, pushed himself up, and hiked his pants that had slipped below his belly line. "You're a smart guy, Jeff. Just use your head…and you know which head I mean."

Jeff let that one slide. He was too damned tired to take a swing at him.

When Bryant was out of the building, Jeff yelled, "Somebody print up some pictures of the son-of-a-bitch…Temple that is."

Chapter 18

The next day Jesse manned the office while Jeff and the other men went from business to business, picture of Andrew Temple in hand, and asked if anyone had seen a person resembling the suspect. Since Jackson was such a small town it was easy to divvy up the business district among the small force and the job went quickly.

Jesse and Buddy took the library. They found a young assistant librarian at the check-out desk. When they identified themselves, she immediately asked about Sophie. "She and Eileen have had a time of it," she said. "Makes me never want to eat another hotdog."

"Yeah, me too," said Jeff.

She looked at the picture carefully and said 'no' to ever having seen Andrew Temple. Jeff thanked her, and he and Buddy turned to leave.

Just as they reached the door, the young woman said, "Wait a minute. Could I see that picture again?"

Jeff turned, walked quickly to the desk, and handed her the photo. She studied it again carefully. "You know," she said, "he does look vaguely familiar...like I might have passed him briefly or that he may have been wearing different clothes or something."

"A disguise?" prompted Buddy. Jeff shook his head. He did not want Buddy to lead the witness.

"The hair. It looks so...so neat. You see, if the hair were down on his forehead then his eyes would look smaller and...and it would change his appearance," she said.

Jeff was excited. He took a deep breath, waited, and said calmly, "If an artist made these changes, the ones you mentioned, do you think that would help you remember?"

"I'll be glad to give it a try," she said.

Jeff walked toward the back of the room, took out his cell, and clicked up a number. "Hey Jesse, get Mal over here...the library...tell him to bring his sketch pad."

Jeff asked to see a record of books that Sophie had checked out. The librarian pulled up Sophie's sheet on the computer and then went off to work with Mal. Jeff and Buddy scrolled down the check-out sheet and studied Sophie's page. Mostly she checked out materials on genealogy, but there were a few mystery reads.

"Nothing here," said Jeff.

"What were you expecting to find...*life with an assassin*?" Buddy kidded.

Jeff didn't smile but he let the bad joke go. He saw no point in letting personalities take him off point. Soon the assistant librarian walked toward him with a bright smile on her face.

"He's remarkable," she said. "Just a couple of minor changes and it all came back. He's absolutely remarkable!"

"She's remarkable too," Mal said, and Jeff could tell he was smitten. Mal handed Jeff the sketch.

Then Jeff looked into the eyes of a scowling unkempt Andrew Temple. Jeff's mouth went dry and he cleared his throat before saying, "Do you remember exactly when you saw this man?"

"Absolutely," she said. "It was the day Eileen went into the hospital. I know because I was asked to fill in for her."

"Was there anything about him that was unusual?" Buddy asked.

"Good question," thought Jeff.

"Yes there was something unusual...and rude," she said. "He asked me to get him a book from the stacks. The stacks are upstairs and to the rear of the building. I'm not supposed to leave the desk if there isn't another person on duty, but there were no other people in that morning...it was snowing, you know. I searched and searched for the book he wanted but didn't find it. When I came back down, he was gone."

Jeff smiled and said, "Thank you. You've been a great help." And they turned to go.

As they reached the front door, the librarian called, "Oh Mr. Sands. You know what else was so peculiar?"

Jeff turned. "What?" he asked.

"The next day I found the book he'd requested in the children's section."

Jeff said, "By the way what was the title of the book?"

"Methods of Applied Calculus in the Nineteenth Century," she said.

As they walked to the car Buddy said, "He just wanted her out of that room didn't he?"

"That's right," said Jeff.

"What do you suppose he was after?" asked Buddy.

"The same as we," said Jeff. "He wanted to see her check-out sheet."

Jeff and Buddy returned to the office. Jesse could tell by the look on their faces that they found something.

"So you got a hit, huh?" Jess asked.

Jeff said, "You bet."

Jeff didn't bother to take off his coat. He sat down at his desk, pulled out his cell, and clicked off a number. Three rings and a pickup.

"Hey Bryant. We got a positive ID on Temple."

"Who, where, when?" Bryant asked excitedly.

"The assistant librarian. At the local library. He was there the day after the poisoning," Jeff said.

"Hot damn we're on the bastard now," Bryant was jubilant. Then he asked soberly, "Okay, what next Jeff?"

"Next I talk to Sophie," Jeff said.

Chapter 19

It was snowing again. This time the flakes were small and fluffy and looked like blossoms falling from an apple tree. Gladys said small flakes meant it would snow for a long time but Jeff doubted there was any actual science to bear out her prediction.

Sophie stood at her bedroom window and watched the new snow. She was no longer attached to an IV, and she'd gotten rid of her gown and robe. Now she wore a yellow sweat suit and fuzzy brown house slippers. Jeff sat in a chair beside the fireplace. He was leaning forward with his elbows on his knees watching her carefully.

Without turning Sophie spoke in a raspy voice. "So what you're telling me is that for ten years I was married to a murderer?"

"Yes," said Jeff.

"An assassin?" she said.

"Yes," said Jeff.

"And the reason we moved so often is because he was afraid he'd be caught if he stayed in one place too long," she said.

"Yes," said Jeff.

Sophie raised her hand and covered her mouth as if to suppress a scream. Then she whispered, "And those times when we were traveling abroad and I was sightseeing alone, he was…let's see how did you put it…carrying out a contract."

"I'm sorry, Sophie," Jeff said, "so sorry."

She turned to look at Jeff. "But why take me along? Why involve me in his unspeakable *work*?"

"Cover," said Jeff. "He thought no one would expect an assassin to travel with a wife…especially one who looks as harmless as you." He smiled. "And it worked. It worked for a long time."

"There was no trust?" Sophie asked.

"No trust," said Jeff. "just money for his *work*. That's how we tracked him…the money."

"And you think he is here?" she asked. Jeff caught the frightened tone in her voice.

"We know he's here. He's been IDed," Jeff said.

"By whom?"

"By the assistant librarian in Jackson," Jeff said. "He was there at the library."

"Andrew was in the library?" she whispered, and this time she really sounded scared.

"Yes," said Jeff. "The day after you and Eileen were poisoned."

"And he did that…he poisoned Eileen and me?" Sophie asked.

"Looks that way," Jeff said.

"And killed two men at the Winner Dog?" Sophie asked.

"Yes," said Jeff.

Sophie suddenly felt cold. She crossed the room and sat facing Jeff. The flames from the fire felt comforting and warm. She looked intently into Jeff's eyes.

"I don't know what to say," she said helplessly.

Jeff reached out and took her hand. "Sophie, I wish you'd never had to learn about this. But I knew eventually you'd have to know."

Sophie sat quietly for a long time collecting her thoughts. Jeff waited. Finally she said, "Now that I know about Andrew, I need to know about you…your involvement." She didn't withdraw her hand. "So tell me how you were chosen for this job."

Jeff moved forward in his chair and took her other hand. "Okay. Here it is…about the time it was determined that Andrew Temple was our man, he went missing. About that same time, you left him and came back to Seaboard. Now it was felt that Temple might follow you or try to get in touch with you. It was also known that I grew up in Northampton County and that I knew you. So I was chosen for the assignment."

"Exactly what was your assignment?" Sophie asked.

"My assignment was to protect you in case Temple might be a threat to you...which he was. Also I am to assist in the apprehension of Temple," Jeff tried to be as concise as possible.

"He's dangerous, Jeff," she said.

"I know," said Jeff.

"No, what I meant is he is mean. Real mean. And he'd gotten worse," said Sophie.

"I know," said Jeff.

Sophie was silent for a long time. Jeff knew she had a lot to process and he waited patiently. He had decided to answer her questions as fully as he could yet not give more information than necessary.

"How did you intend to protect me?" she asked.

"I've tried to be with you as much as possible, and I had some men watching you, too," he said.

"Men watching me?" she was shocked.

"Yep. Two," Jeff said. "They're not much to look at, but they're two of the best. When I'm not here, they're parked around the corner watching your house. Sometimes they're in an old Chevelle and sometimes in a blue Nissan pickup."

"Blue pickup?" repeated Sophie. Sophie began to experience flashbacks...blue pickup behind the courthouse...blue pickup when she stopped at Ramsey's Fork...two men walking toward her when she was ill.

She said, "Jeff on the day I got sick there were two men behind the courthouse in Jackson and they were in a blue pickup. They followed me home. Were those two men my...my bodyguards?"

"Behind the courthouse?" Jeff said with a wide grin. "What were you doing behind the courthouse? Sophie, were you checking up on me?"

Sophie snapped, "Don't change the subject. Were they?"

"Yes," said Jeff. "That's how I learned you were ill."

Sophie became quiet again. She withdrew her hands, stood, and gazed into the fire. Jeff waited.

Finally she eyed him directly and said, "Jeff, I have to know—why are you here? Is it just because I'm part of your assignment?"

"No," said Jeff.

"Then why? I don't know what to believe any more. For years what I thought was reality was in fact just illusionary. I lived ten years with deceit, lies. Hell, I don't know if I'll ever trust anyone again," Sophie declared angrily.

Strangely Jeff was relieved that Sophie was angry instead of frightened or hurt. He knew those emotions may come later, but for now it was reassuring to see that spark that had made her so uniquely Sophie.

Jeff stood, moved close to Sophie, and clutched her shoulders. He looked directly into her eyes and said, "Alright Sophie, here it is straight. I was chosen for this case for two reasons. One, I am from Northampton County, and two, because I knew you." Sophie looked disappointed and shrugged away his hands.

Jeff continued. "I also want you to know that I tried every way I could to get out of the assignment but I couldn't. So I reasoned...I'll just go down there, do the job, and avoid any camaraderie. But it didn't happen that way, Sophie. I think I knew that night at the Tex-Mex Restaurant that there was still a connection between us...at least on my part. And I fought it...Lord knows I tried...to put space between us. I suppose that's one reason I was such an ass at the reunion. I didn't want to get caught up in something that would complicate my job. Well, you see how that worked out."

Sophie was silent. She knew how difficult it was for Jeff to open up, so this time she listened.

Jeff continued, "You know I'm not very romantic, Sophie, and I don't always handle things well. I can be...ah...abrasive. Comes from working around hard-nosed men and women so long I guess. Anyway, when we danced at the reunion I knew I wanted you back in my life, but I was afraid it might compromise my work. I fought it real hard, Sophie, but it didn't work."

Then Jeff saw tears welling up in Sophie's eyes. He smiled widely, laughed, and said, "Then when I saw you almost get killed in front of Ruby Tuesday, I thought that woman needs a keeper. So here I am."

Sophie laughed. Jeff wrapped her in his arms and held her close. Her hair smelled like lemons, and she felt so frail. How did she become so thin so fast?

Finally Jeff said, "So, Sophie Singletary, I'm here to stay. If you kick me out, I'll just camp out on the front porch."

"Snow and all?" she said.

"Neither, rain, nor sleet, nor snow, now gloom of night will keep me from my watch," he said with a smile.

Then Sophie slowly pushed away. "Jeff, I'm so tired," she said. "Can we lie down for awhile?"

Jeff looked concerned. "Sure. You've had a trying morning, Sophie Girl." So they lay together on the bed watching the fire and the snow and holding each other close.

Finally Jeff said, "Sophie, promise me something."

Sophie said softly, "Sure...if I can."

"Promise me you won't leave the house without me or one of my guys until we apprehend Andrew," he said.

Sophie was silent for a while, and then she said, "I can't promise you that Jeff. Andrew controlled my life for ten years. When I left him and came back to Seaboard I promised myself nothing would ever control me like that again. Not leaving the house alone because Andrew is out there is giving him power again. I hope you understand, Jeff, but I can't make that promise."

Jeff said wearily, "I understand, Sophie. I don't like it, but I understand."

Sophie lay on her side, her shoulder under Jeff's arm, and her head resting on his shoulder. He held her close and fingered the strand of hair that had twisted itself free from the ponytail. Soon they were both asleep.

Chapter 20

Gladys was right. The snowflakes remained small and fluffy, and the snow stayed around for awhile. Although it was extremely cold, the sun peeped out intermittently. Its dazzling shine concealed the unsightliness of broken limbs and damaged shrubs that had been shattered by earlier ice buildup. For four weeks the winter weather monopolized the news. The amount of snow, ice, and biting cold were being labeled a winter phenomenon for northeastern North Carolina. In spite of the harshness of the wintry weather, the county and town road maintenance crews did a remarkable job of keeping the roads and main streets passable.

The arborists finally removed the fallen tree from Jan's drive and Jan and Julie traveled back to town. Of course, their first stop was Sophie's house.

"Hey girlfriend," said Jan as she hugged Sophie. Then she pushed Sophie back, took a good look, and added, "You still look a little bit peaked."

"I know," Sophie said, "but I am feeling much better."

"Well if you ask me," said Julie, "hot dogs should be taken off the market. Why, there's no telling what goes in those things…skin, ground-up uneatable body parts, gristle. Why one time my second husband bit into a hot dog with lots of gristle and broke a crown. Can you believe that…a $750 crown? That's the kind of ingredients that goes into a hot dog. So if you ask me…"

Jan interrupted, "Well, regardless, you're looking great. Food poisoning ain't no picnic."

"I'll say," said Sophie.

"It won't **my** food. I just want that to be known. Nobody ever got poisoned eating my food," said Gladys who was dusting at the other end of the room and ease-dropping on the conversation. She felt it imperative to defend her cooking.

Sophie supported her, "I can certainly vouch for Gladys's cooking. Had it not been for Gladys, I don't know what would have happened to me. So now I'm feeling stronger, but I am getting restless. I need to find something to do."

"I know what we should do," exclaimed Julie.

"NO!" cried Jan and Sophie at the same time.

"I don't feel strong enough to go shopping with you, Julie," Sophie laughed.

* * *

The next morning Jeff sat in the kitchen eating a hearty breakfast and laughing and talking with Gladys and Melvin. Sophie walked in. She wore woolen slacks, a heavy woolen sweater, woolen socks, and snow boots. Gladys and Jeff glanced at each other.

"What are you all dolled up for?" demanded Gladys.

"I think I'll go to the library today," said Sophie.

"Are you sure?" asked Jeff.

"Yes, I'm sure. I feel fidgety and besides I need to face my demons," Sophie said.

Gladys looked alarmed. "What sorta demons you talking about?"

"My demons...my *fears*," said Sophie and she looked at Jeff. "Andy was in that library and if I don't go back there soon, I never will."

Jeff felt a hard, dry lump in his throat. "As I said, Sophie, I don't like it but I understand. I'll see to things."

"Thanks, Jeff," she said, turned, and walked out of the kitchen.

"See...I told you she was strong," Gladys said proudly.

Jeff reached for his cell phone, "Yes she's strong, and stubborn," he said.

* * *

144

Sophie walked into the library, removed her coat, and looked around the room. There were only a few regulars who had grown weary of the winter weather and needed a change of scenery. In an effort to combat boredom they braved the snow and cold and trekked to the library. There was no one at the desk. In the back of the room Sophie spotted a group of very young children sitting on the floor in front of Josie Clark, the assistant librarian. Josie was reading a story, and their eyes were glued to the picture book she held. Three women stood close by. Sophie recognized one attractive red-haired woman, named Ms. Ann, as the owner and operator of a day care center in Seaboard. She guessed the other two women were mothers who volunteered to help out on a field trip to the library. Josie spotted Sophie and smiled.

When she finished the story Josie said to the children, "Now choose your book and bring it to the checkout desk. Then you can take it home with you." Mayhem broke lose as fifteen children squealed, jumped up, and raced to the bookshelves.

Josie walked to Sophie, hugged her, and said, "Sophie, it's good to see you again. How are you feeling?"

"Actually pretty well," said Sophie. "How is Eileen?"

"Eileen is still weak, but she's getting stronger every day," Josie said. "Can I help you today?"

Sophie took a quick look at the wiggling, squirming, squealing children and laughed. "I think you have your hands full right now. Talk to you later." And Sophie walked to the genealogy section and pulled a book about tombstone icons from the shelf.

Suddenly a woman's voice shrieked, "**Andy**.......what are you doing? **Andy???**" Sophie sprang from her seat and gawked in the direction of the scream her heart racing a mile a minute. No, no!!! Andy couldn't be here. He was too shrewd, too conniving, too much imagination to return here.

Then Sophie spotted the source of the commotion. A small, blonde haired boy of about three was hanging from the fourth shelf of a bookshelf. Ms. Ann was wrestling him down as he screamed, "It's not fair! Let me go! I want that one!" And he pointed to a book on the top shelf.

Ms. Ann snatched the book, handed it to the kid, and said, "Here!"

The little boy shouted, "Oh boy!" and raced toward the checkout desk squealing, "I'm next. I'm next."

Sophie sunk back down in her chair and waited for her heart to stop pounding. She tried to turn the pages of the book and realized her hands were trembling fiercely. She was sweating, and she felt weak. Maybe she wasn't strong enough to face down her fears after all.

The children lined up to leave and Ms. Ann thanked Josie for being so patient. After the group of children was herded out the door Josie looked at Sophie and breathed an audible sigh of relief. She walked to Sophie's table and sat down.

"So can I help you now?" Josie asked breathlessly.

Sophie laughed. "The question should be, 'can I help you'."

"I'll admit they're a handful," said Josie. "My hat is off to Ms. Ann. So what about you?"

Sophie pulled out the list of graveyards and cemeteries containing grave houses. "Eileen gave me this list. Can you tell me which place is closest?"

Josie read the list carefully. Then she said, "Sure. That's easy. This one right here." She pointed to a name and phone number. "I know this place well. It's only about a mile or two down the Garysburg road."

"Good," said Sophie. "I don't want to drive too far just yet. Eileen suggested I call before going out. That's the reason for the phone numbers."

Josie said, "Would you like me to call? As I said I know these people real well and sometimes old folks don't trust strangers."

"Would you?" said Sophie.

"Sure," said Josie and she was up and walking to her desk.

Josie looked at the phone number, dialed, and waited patiently. "Sometimes it takes him a long time to get to the phone." She said to Sophie. Finally a pickup.

"Hello Mr. Howard," Josie spoke very loudly. She mouthed to Sophie that he didn't hear well. "This is Josie Clark…Josie Clark at the library….No sir…you don't have an over-due book. Mr. Howard, there's a young woman here who wants to come out and see the grave houses on your property….Yes sir, the grave houses. Would that be okay….She's looking for the grave of an ancestor uncle….Civil

146

War....I'll tell her how to get there. How's Mrs. Howard....Say 'hey' to her for me…. Okay....Goodbye Mr. Howard."

Josie hung up the phone. "That was Mr. Howard," she said and handed the list back to Sophie. Sophie smiled. "He said it would be fine to come out today. He said Mrs. Howard just baked sticky buns and they want you to stay for coffee."

"Thanks, Josie," Sophie said excitedly. "Now how do I get there?"

Josie said, "Go out of the parking lot, turn left, go about two miles. It's a big, two story bird's-egg blue farm house on the left, and there's a bright yellow mail box shaped like a school bus beside the driveway. Can't miss it."

Sophie stopped before pulling out of the library parking lot. She looked around for a blue pickup or an old Chevelle. She saw neither. She thought that was strange, but presumed they'd probably gone for coffee while she was safe in the library. She considered whether she should wait for them but decided she'd be safe with the Howards. So Sophie shrugged, turned left, and exited the parking lot.

* * *

Josie was right—you couldn't miss the Howard's house. The bright blue paint was in stark contrast to the glistening white snow on the lawn. And, of course, the vibrant yellow mailbox couldn't be missed. Mail was placed in the box by opening the door of the school bus.

Sophie cautiously pulled into the driveway careful to steer her car into furrows already left by other cars. An old man dressed for an artic expedition stood on the porch. He leaned on a big walking stick, and this wasn't just a short cane but a tall stick often used by hikers. Peering out of a front window was a smiling gray haired woman. She gave Sophie a little finger wave and Sophie returned the greeting.

The elderly man walked cautiously out to meet Sophie. "So you want to see my grave houses, huh?"

"Yes sir," said Sophie "Thank you for letting me come out. I'm Sophie Singletary. Just call me Sophie." And she extended her hand.

He took her hand, gave it a firm shake, and said, "You can call me Mr.

Howard."

"Yes sir," said Sophie. He was already walking toward the back of his house so Sophie fell into step.

"Can't see too much today," he said back to her. "The snow and all, you know."

In the back of Mr. Howard's house was a clearing, and as they approached it Sophie was surprised to see large rock-solid headstones reaching stalwartly out of the snow. There must have been at least twenty such stones in this family cemetery. Sophie was astonished to see such a large cemetery in a backyard. Then she spotted a building that seemed out of place. In the middle of the cemetery stood a small white house with a gable roof, two windows, and bright green shutters. It had gingerbread trim along the roof line and was enclosed by a white picket fence.

"What a strange place to put a child's playhouse," thought Sophie.

"Well, there she is," said Mr. Howard pointing to the playhouse.

"What? I don't understand," Sophie said.

"There's a grave house," said Mr. Howard.

"I thought it was a child's playhouse," said Sophie.

Mr. Howard laughed. "No, it's a fancy one ain't it? But it's a grave house. It's such an oddity around here that the wife keeps her spruced up. Come on. I'll show you," he said and began picking his way through the snow toward the grave house.

He reached down and unlatched the gate of the little picket fence that was only knee-high. "Back when this was built, the fence was supposed to protect the grave from being desecrated by animals. Didn't help much in that respect if you ask me...but it's an eye-catcher."

Sophie followed him to the little house. When they reached the door Mr. Howard said, "Now watch your head. This ain't really tall enough for folks now days, but it **was** intended to accommodate visitors."

Sophie bent forward and stepped into the house. The house had been built over an "in earth" grave. The burial spot was covered with a gravestone and a headstone stood at the top of the tomb. The identity of the deceased along with other information was chiseled into the headstone. Sophie leaned forward, took out a notepad and pen, and copied down the information.

"What was the purpose of grave houses," said Sophie.

"Well, as I already said, they were supposed to protect the dead from being dug up by animals. Also they protected the grave from the elements...rain, snow, and all. And most importantly, they were supposed to keep away the grave robbers. You know sometimes corpses were buried wearing jewelry and such. Personally, I don't know how much protection from anything the little houses provided...but it made the living feel better knowing they'd tried to look after their dead."

They turned to go and Sophie said, "Thank you, Mr. Howard. This is amazing... truly amazing. One other question. There are quite a few graves in your cemetery and only one grave house. How did they decide who deserved a grave house?"

Mr. Howard opened the door and Sophie stepped outside where she was hit by a rush of cold air. He said, "Well actually I've got more than one. I'll show you the others. But to answer your question, grave houses were usually built for very special people like a child, a beloved mother or grandmother, or a soldier. This here one is the grave of my great grandmother. Why she's raved on about to this day. I could go on all day telling you stories about Katie Howard. She was a much beloved person...a real matriarch of the Howard family."

Sophie said, "You say that grave houses were often built for soldiers. The ancestor uncle I'm trying to find died at Petersburg during the Civil War. Mrs. Carrie Kendricks is the person who suggested that I search grave houses. So then you agree that Civil War soldiers might have been buried in grave houses?"

"Yes indeed," said Mr. Howard. "I agree...but it's not like anybody's gonna disagree with Mrs. Carrie on genealogy." And he chuckled. "Now walk over here and I'll show you some other grave houses."

Sophie followed Mr. Howard to another part of the cemetery. "There they be," he said and pointed to other structures that looked a lot like dog houses. Two buildings were made of rude logs set on large rocks. There was a door but no windows. The gravestones were outside propped beside the door. A third grave house was set behind and to the left of the two. It was built of rough cut field stones and the roof was built directly on top of the stones. There was a door and the gravestone for this grave was inside. A fourth house was in the back of the cemetery and to the right. It too was built of stone with a cedar shingle roof, and it had neither door nor windows. There was also no gravestone outside.

"How strange," Sophie said. "Why isn't there an entrance to that grave house?"

Mr. Howard replied, "Haven't the foggiest. Always wondered if not having a door was to keep people out…or to keep the corpse in. Hee, Hee," he laughed.

Sophie smiled. "Thank you, Mr. Howard. Your grave houses are incredible, and you've maintained them so well."

"Well, they're family you know," he said. "Don't make no matter if it were hundred or so years ago that they died, they're still family. Besides it means the world and all to Mrs. Howard having folks drop by like this."

As they plodded back across the cemetery Mrs. Howard stepped onto the back porch and waved. "You-who," she called. "Your sticky buns are ready."

Sophie smiled and thought about what Jan could do with that line.

* * *

Sophie stopped before pulling out of Mr. Howard's driveway. She looked for any sign of Jeff's men on the highway, the side road, and the surrounding fields. No old rusty Chevelle. No blue pickup. No Jeff. In fact, there was no traffic from any direction. Sophie had finally accepted having bodyguards and found it somewhat disquieting to find herself on her own. She turned right and headed back towards Jackson.

"Why not do another drive-through when I get to town?" Sophie said to herself. She remembered Jeff was annoyed when she "checked up on him" earlier, but Sophie rationalized it was easier to ask forgiveness than permission. So she carried on…she did a drive-through in Jackson. She drove pass the Pebbles House, the Courthouse, the Piggly Wiggly, and the line of storefronts on Main Street. There were only a couple of cars parked along the curb in front of the stores, and none of them looked familiar. Parking spaces in front of the courthouse were empty. Apparently court was not in session again today, but she thought she may as well circle the courthouse via the back parking area. Empty.

Sophie had experienced a full day, and she was beginning to feel bushed so she headed back toward Seaboard. The road had been scraped and asphalt was visible through the thin crust of icy slush. Dusk was settling in as she approached Ramsey's Fork. This is where she was forced to pull over when she got sick. Unexpectedly she felt a tightening in her chest and she could hear her own heart beating. She swallowed hard, gripped the steering wheel, and stepped on the accelerator. The tires spun in response to the engine's sudden acceleration.

"Whoa," Sophie cautioned herself. Then she looked in the rear-view mirror. Headlights. "Oh no. Not again," she said.

Ignoring how her car had reacted, Sophie stomped on the gas pedal and this time the tires gripped and the car barreled forward. She took hurried glances at the lights behind her. It appeared that the trailing vehicle sped up too. Just a few more miles to Seaboard. Where was the blue pickup when she needed it? Then she reached the city limits sign that read 'Welcome to Seaboard...A Good Place to Live".

Sophia breathed a sigh of relief and slowed the car as she approached her house. It appeared that every light in the house was on. Gladys! Gladys had discovered how to 'stay pass dark'. She just turned on all the lights in the house and pretended it was daylight.

Sophie breathed a sigh of relief, turned into her driveway, and drove to the garage. She pointed the remote and activated the garage door opener. The door yawned open, and Sophie stared into a black cavernous hole that was the entrance to her garage. Sophie was not feeling very brave at the moment. She inched the car into the garage, threw open her door, and rushed to the safety of the fading daylight.

When Sophie entered the kitchen she found Gladys kneading a bowl of biscuit dough and Melvin peeling potatoes and complaining that the knife wasn't sharp enough to cut hot butter. Sophie took a deep breath and relaxed in the familiar setting. How comforting it was to get back into her own kitchen...or more accurately Gladys's kitchen.

Gladys looked up from the mixing bowl and said, "So how did you make it today?"

"Oh, I feel okay," Sophie said. "Hear anything from Jeff today?"

"Not a word," Gladys said and she dumped the dough onto a floured board, reached for her rolling pin, and began to roll out the biscuits.

"Guess what?" Sophie said, and without waiting for a reply announced, "I visited a grave house today."

Gladys dropped her rolling pin and slapped her hands to her breasts. "Good Lord, Sophie!!! What are you thinking? Don't you have enough spirits here in this house without going out looking for more? You don't know what kind of lost souls are trapped in those old grave houses. Sometimes you act like you ain't got sense God gave a billy goat!"

When Gladys dropped her hands there was a flour handprint on each breast. Melvin gawked. Sophie laughed.

Sophie darted across the room and hugged Gladys. "Gladys, I love you, but you drive me crazy with your mumbo-jumbo."

Gladys pushed her away. "Mumbo-jumbo, my sweet tea!" she scoffed. "Just you wait missy, one of these days you're gonna wish you'd listened to me."

Sophie started to walk out of the room. Then she stopped, turned to Melvin, and said, "Melvin, would you please replace the light bulb in the garage. It's *spooooky* having to pull into a dark garage." Then she looked at Gladys, laughed, and sashayed out.

Melvin looked at Gladys with a puzzled look on his face. "I done replaced that bulb once. We musta got a bad batch of light bulbs."

Chapter 21

Sophie slept sporadically. She listened to the house sounds, the wind, and the occasional crash of a limb that could no longer bear the weight of snow and ice. She kept reaching across to Jeff's side of the bed, and each time she found it empty, she was seized by a hollow, lonely feeling. She heard Melvin snoring across the hall although both his door and hers were closed. Once she told him he snored loud enough to wake the dead, and Gladys reacted with alarm. "Sophie Singletary, stop thinking up ideas like that. This house comes up with enough mischief of its own. Don't need no help from you," she'd admonished.

Sophie heard the digital clock roll over but was too exhausted to look at the time. Then the phone rang. Sophie sprang up, reached across the bed, and the phone clamored to the floor. Instantly she was up and on her knees scrambling for the phone.

"Damn," she swore. Then she finally found the receiver, clicked on 'talk', and said, "Hello...hello."

"Sophie...Sophie, are you there?" It was Jeff.

"Jeff, yes. Where are you? I've been worried sick," Sophie said.

"Sophie, are you okay?" he said.

"Yes, Jeff. I'm fine. But where are you? What's going on?" she said.

"We almost caught him, Sophie. We almost caught Andrew Temple," he said excitedly.

"Jeff are **you** okay? Jeff, Andy is mean. I mean real mean and he's...cunning," Sophie said.

Jeff heard the fear in her voice. "Well we got to see cunning today. He's as slippery as an eel. We had a report he was spotted out on Garysburg Road heading west. We pursued, but by the time we got out there, was no sign of him. We searched all the way to Roanoke Rapids, but we lost him."

"Jeff, he's dangerous isn't he?" she asked.

"That's putting it mildly. He's treacherous, Sophie. I already told you that," he said. "By the way, your guys helped pursue Temple. They'd come in to the office for a break leaving you in what we **supposed** was a safe place…the library. While they were there we got the report of the sighting and they joined in. Later when we got back to Jackson you weren't at the library. Where were you?" Jeff asked.

Sophie was suddenly aware that Andy might have followed her to the Howard's farm. She was horrified. "Jeff, I left the library to visit some grave houses."

"Where?" Jeff asked.

"At the Howard farm…on Garysburg Road," Sophie said softly.

"What?' Jeff exploded. Then there was a long pause. "Sophie, you must have been at the Howard's farm while we were searching for Temple down Garysburg Road."

"Yes," Sophie whispered.

"And that means …that means that Temple probably followed you out there and ran when we showed up."

"Yes," Sophie said, and this time he could barely hear her.

Jeff shouted, "We had no idea where you were. The guys went back over the route you drove when you were checking up on me. Then they went back to the library. They were frantic. Finally they spotted you just before you reached Ramsey's Fork."

"Jeff, I'm so sorry," Sophie said. "I looked for a blue pickup or a Chevelle when I left the library and again when I left the Howard's place. When I saw headlights in my rear view mirror at Ramsey's Fork, I thought…I thought…"

"You didn't think, Sophie. Don't ever do that again. Don't change your plans without letting us know. This isn't a game. This guy is a real wacko." Jeff had never chewed her out like this before, and Sophie was stunned.

"Okay, okay," she said. "I won't."

Silence again. Then Jeff said, "Sorry. I just don't think I could stand to lose you again."

"Me too," said Sophie. "When will you be home?"

"Not sure," he said. "I'll keep you posted...and Sophie, don't go tramping around in any more cemeteries until we bag this guy...please."

"Okay, okay," she said. "Since you said *please*."

* * *

"Was that Jeff that called last night," asked Gladys. She was whipping eggs, cheese, and chives for an omelet.

Sophie sat at the kitchen table staring into space. The Daily Herald and the Virginian Pilot newspapers lay on the table open to the story of two murders at the Winner Dog in Jackson, North Carolina. There were dark circles under her eyes and her face looked pinched and thin. Sophie didn't hear Gladys.

"Sophie Singletary, did you hear me? Was that Jeff that called last night?" she asked this time much louder.

Sophie flinched. "Yes, that was Jeff."

Melvin walked to the stove, poured a large mug of coffee, and set it in front of Sophie while casting an anxious look towards Gladys. He could tell that Gladys was concerned too.

"When's he coming home?" Gladys asked.

Sophie was still lost in thought and didn't hear her. "I said...when's he coming home?" This time Gladys spoke slowly and even louder.

This roused Sophie from her distraction. "Oh, he's not really sure. He told me they almost caught Andy yesterday," she said. "*Caught Andy.* That sounds so bizarre." Then she added, "Jeff was angry with me too for going to see the grave houses... but not for the same reason you were."

"Well you see, he's a man with his head on straight," said Gladys. Melvin nodded in agreement. "What you want with your omelet?" Gladys asked.

"Noth...," Sophie began. Gladys shot her an impatient look, and

155

Sophie said, "Whole wheat toast. No butter."

When Sophie bit into Gladys's delicious omelet she realized she was hungrier than she'd thought, and she didn't refuse a second piece of toast Gladys put on her plate.

The day was overcast and hinted of impending snow. Sophie remembered that her grandmother told her about big snowstorms in Seaboard when she was a child. She'd walked to school undeterred. She claimed the snow was so deep that it came above the top of her boots so when she got to class her boots were packed with snow. She'd dumped the snow from her boots, placed them beside the stove, and then had to sit in school all day in wet socks. Sophie thought her grandmother had embellished her snowstorm stories. Now she thought they were probably true.

The weatherman projected only a thirty percent chance of snow that day, but Northampton County folks had grown dubious of his predictions. Anything given thirty percent chance or greater was seen as a real threat and grocery lines lengthened.

Sophie was agitated. The possibility of being confined again was frustrating. She poured herself another mug of coffee, walked into the den, and settled in front of the fire. Immediately the phone rang. It was Julie. Sophie grabbed the phone and clicked on talk.

"Hello," was all Sophie had a chance to say.

"Sophie, have you heard that weather forecast? What's this about global warming when northeastern North Carolina is in the deep freeze? If you ask me global warming is a doggone conspiracy. Why I don't ever remember weather like this when I was a child. As a matter of fact, it seems like we hardly had a winter at all...."

At that time Gladys walked into the room to clean. She mouthed the word, "Jeff?"

Sophie held the receiver out at arms length and mouthed back, "Julie." Gladys shook her head and continued what she was doing.

When Sophie put the receiver to her ear again, Julie was still babbling on. Sophie interrupted loudly, "Julie, sounds like you've been listening to talk radio again this morning. What are your plans for today?" hoping to change the subject. Sophie knew better than to attempt a logical debate with Julie.

Julie paused. Sophie could almost hear Julie's brains changing gears. Then Julie whined miserably, "Well since no one wants to go shopping and out to lunch…even if it's on me…then I suppose I have no plans."

"Tell you what," said Sophie, "why don't I call Jan and the two of you come here for lunch. I'll have to check with Gladys first…" She looked at Gladys, and Gladys nodded 'yes'. "Gladys just said yes".

"That sounds good," said Julie. "Are you sure Gladys doesn't mind? It's most thoughtless of us to come for lunch on such short notice."

Sophie smiled, "Gladys can manage. Shall we say twelve thirty?" Again she looked at Gladys, and again Gladys nodded.

"Want me to call Jan?" Julie asked eagerly.

Sophie knew that Julie was anxious to be the bearer of good news so she said, "Sure. See the two of you then," Sophie said.

Sophie sat for a long time lost in thought. Gladys watched her carefully and said, "I just got pot-luck for lunch. That okay?"

Sophie did not respond. Gladys repeated loudly, "Pot luck okay for lunch?"

Sophie was shaken from her trance. "Yes," she said. "That will be fine. Gladys, I think I'll tell Jan and Julie about Andrew."

Gladys frowned. "You sure?"

"Yes, I think I should," said Sophie. "Suppose something happened…" Gladys started to object but Sophie raised her hand in a stop jester. "I'm not saying it will, but if it should, they would be devastated not to have known what was really going on."

Gladys walked to the sofa, sat down beside Sophie, and asked, "How much you gonna tell them?"

"That's what I was thinking about. I think I'll just tell them that Andrew has come here and he is stalking me. I think I'll also say that Jeff thinks he could do me real harm."

"What do you think Jeff will think about you telling them that? His job and all you know," Gladys asked.

"Oh, I'm not going to tell them he's an assassin. I'll just be vague and say that I'm afraid and Jeff is afraid for me," Sophie said.

"You might want to tell them that Andrew is the reason Melvin and

I are staying here," added Gladys.

"Right—good," said Sophie. "I'm sure Julie has realized you're staying overnight."

Gladys stood and said, "Well I guess I better go find something to fix for your lunch. I guess I agree that you might as well tell Jan and Julie else what they guess may end up being worse than what's really happening."

Sophie nodded. Gladys walked to the door, turned, and added, "Sophie, you just be careful exactly what you tell them. You don't want to put them in danger too."

Sophie looked Gladys squarely in the eye. "Gladys, is that what I have done to you and Melvin...put you in danger too?"

Gladys shrugged. "I don't know. Wouldn't make no difference no how," she said. "Melvin and me can take care of ourselves." And she walked out of the room.

* * *

As usual Gladys's 'pot luck' was exceptional. She served tomato basil soup, mixed green salad with her special dressing, hot roast beef sandwiches, and for the grand finale—spicy peach cobbler with a golden crust to die for. She was praised lavishly for the cobbler.

"Glad you liked it," she said as she poured steaming aromatic coffee into Grand mother Singletary's Haviland china cups, "but them was canned peaches you know."

"Let's take our coffee into the den," suggested Sophie as she picked up her cup and stood. Julie and Jan followed suite.

Melvin had built a fire in the fireplace and the smell of the burning wood combined with the smell of the coffee created a tranquil mood. Jan and Julie sat in chairs on either side of the fireplace and Sophie burrowed into the plush sofa pillows. They sat silently for a few moments and let Gladys's delightful lunch work its magic. So content were they that Jan fought to keep her eyes open.

Sophie interrupted the tranquility. "Ah-huh," she said. "I'm so glad you two could come over today. I have something very important to tell you..."

And that was as far as she got. Julie shot forward in her chair and burst out, "You and Jeff are getting married!!! I knew it! I knew it! What did I tell you, Jan? Their kind of passion never dies...never! Now we haven't a moment to lose. I've been thinking about this every since that first date...you know the pizza date—not that I ever thought that was a good choice of menu to rekindle a romance—but that's neither here nor there. I have the perfect menu in mind for the engagement announcement party and for the wedding reception. Now we also have to think about the church. You'll have it at the Methodist..."

Gladys had entered the room to collect the cups and saucers. She looked at Sophie, shook her head, and said, "Don't nobody make up menus around here but me."

"Of course, Gladys," said Julie condescendingly, "but a wedding...that requires a special touch. A refined touch."

Gladys lifted Sophie's cup and mumbled, "I'd like to *touch* her."

Sophie cried, "Whoa, whoa, Julie. That's not what I wanted to talk to you about. Jeff and I have no plans at this time to get married."

"Yeah, Julie," said Jan "cool your jets. Let Sophie say what she wants to tell us."

Julie looked deflated. "Not getting married?" she muttered, and she shrank back into her chair.

"Go 'head, Sophie," coaxed Jan.

Sophie positioned herself on the couch with her legs tucked underneath her. She took a deep breath and began. "As you know, I divorced Andrew before I returned to Seaboard. I don't know if I ever fully explained just how controlling and threatening he is..."

Julie was up again, "Threatening? I wish I'd known he was threatening you. Why I could show him threatening..."

"Julie, if you don't hush up Sophie will never get through her story. This isn't about you, you know," Jan said impatiently. Julie settled down again.

Sophie continued, "Anyway, after coming home I didn't hear anything from Andy. Now suddenly he's turned up, and his actions are pretty scary. He is stalking me and harassing me and in general just frightening the hell out of me."

"Is that why Jeff is staying here?" asked Jan.

"Not the **entire** reason," Sophie said coyly. "He wants to protect me, yes, but Andrew's threats aside, Jeff would be here anyway." She smiled.

Julie was recharged. "Now Sophie," she said patronizingly, "are you sure Andrew is a menace. Perhaps he's just experiencing separation anxiety…separation from his wife of ten years. Maybe he loves you and realizes he's made unwise decisions and wants you back. You have to agree Jeff would seem like formidable competition to any man," and she rolled her eyes. "But you know, love hath no fury like a man scorned, don't you think?"

"No Julie, I don't think that," said Sophie angrily. "Some of the things he's done go way beyond jealous competition. Jeff has even assigned two men to shadow me. Jeff doesn't think this is simply the actions of a jealous husband."

"Is that why you've got Gladys and Melvin staying here all the time?" asked Jan.

"Yes," said Sophie.

"Now let me be clear about this," said Jan as she leaned forward in her chair and said meticulously. "You got two bodyguards, Gladys, Melvin, and Jeff staying here at the house right?"

"Yes," said Sophie.

There was a long silence. Then Jan said, "Sophie, I think you better tell us just what Andrew's done." She turned to Julie, shook a finger at her, and said, "And Julie, don't you say a word."

The three were so engrossed in Sophie's story that they didn't notice Gladys reenter the room. "I…I'm not sure how much I should divulge," Sophie said glancing at Gladys. "Gladys?"

Gladys nodded her head. "Go 'head, Sophie."

"Well," said Sophie, "for starters he tried to poison me." Jan and Julie gasped. Sophie paused letting the gravity of her statement sink in. Then she continued, "And he also tried to poison Eileen Brown, the librarian. Eileen is still not able to go back to work."

Jan and Julie stared wide-eyed with their mouths open. Gladys moved closer to Sophie and eased down on the sofa. She patted Sophie's hand encouragingly. The fire crackled and sparks popped and bounced against the fireplace screen. A log fell and hot ashes dropped through the grate.

"Go 'head," Gladys encouraged. "Tell them what happened yesterday."

Sophie looked down, covered her face with her hands, and shook her head. Gladys patted her reassuringly on the shoulder.

When Sophie lifted her head tears welled up in her eyes. Sophie said hesitantly, "Yesterday I went out to the Howard's farm outside Jackson on the Garysburg Road. I went to see the grave houses in Mr. Howard's cemetery. You know—part of my genealogical research. What I didn't know was that Andrew followed me. At the same time Jeff received a report that Andrew was sighted on the Garysburg Road so he and the other Marshals pursued. Andrew, of course, spotted them, ran, and got away. If it hadn't been for Jeff and his men I'm not sure what Andrew would have done. I wasn't aware of Andy's presence or the pursuit until I came home. Jeff told me."

"And he bawled her out for going to them grave houses," Gladys interjected.

"Jeff wasn't upset about the grave houses for the same reason you were," Sophie said. She looked at Julie and Jan. They sat speechless. Mouths open. Sophie continued, "I hadn't intended to tell you about yesterday or the poisoning, but then I realized that in order for you to understand how dangerous my situation is you needed to know it all."

After a few moments of silence, Jan said, "What can **we** do girlfriend?"

Sophie smiled. "Nothing really…just be there. I really don't want you to get mixed up in this. He's dangerous, Jan. Real dangerous."

"Well if you ask me," said Julie, "he probably sees himself as blameless in the failure of your marriage and he's driven by revenge. These control freaks resort to all kind of heinous acts to settle what they see as their scores."

"Speaking of heinous actions…," Sophie said, "In order to illustrate said actions, I need to tell you that Andrew killed two men."

Jan and Julie gasped.

"Who? Who did he kill?" Jan asked.

"Two employees of the Winner Dog restaurant in Jackson," Sophie said.

For once Julie seemed to be at a lost for words. Finally she stammered, "I…I read about that in the paper. It was reported as an attempted robbery. I had no idea…"

"No, it wasn't a robbery," said Sophie. "Andrew was trying to cover up the fact that he'd tried to poison Eileen and me by putting arsenic in our hot dogs. He didn't want to leave any witnesses."

"Arsenic?" exclaimed Julie and Jan.

Gladys said, "Yeah, arsenic. That proves it didn't have nothing to do with my cooking."

For a while they sat silently and watched the flames grow and dance in the fireplace and tried to absorb what Sophie had told them. It was almost impossible to grasp.

Finally Jan said, "Sophie, do you think that Andrew followed you to Seaboard, stalked you, tried to kill you and Eileen, and kill two men because he's mad about you leaving him?"

"No, that's not it. I don't believe that," said Sophie, "and neither does Jeff."

"Then for heaven's sake, Sophie, why is he doing this?" cried Julie.

"I have no idea, Julie," Sophie said simply. "I just don't know and neither does Jeff."

Outside the safety of the den the wind moaned and tree branches began to sway forcefully. Suddenly there was a violent gust and somewhere a tree fell, its roots no longer able to secure it in the ice and snow and wind. The reverberation of the falling tree along with the revelation of Sophie's chilling ordeal caused them to leap from their chairs and shriek with terror.

"Holy cats!" shouted Jan.

"I thought that one had us," cried Julie.

"This is too much!" screamed Sophie. "Just too much! I don't think I can take anymore." And she burst into tears. And they all moved to comfort her.

"Just the wind, Sophie," consoled Gladys. "Looks like we're in for another round of winter weather. Ain't nothing gonna happen with me and Jeff and Melvin round. Trust me."

"And we're here, too," said Julie. "Just let that scoundrel try something. We'll show him a thing or two. He'll not be dealing with timid girls…he'll have to deal with four strong women! Just bring him on."

Sophie laughed realizing that Julie was off again in a fantasy…a fantasy in which every man was an adversary.

Jan hugged Sophie and said, "I wish I'd known sooner."

"He's dangerous, Jan," said Sophie, "and I didn't want to involve you."

"Well you got to remember, the bigger the problem the more you need your friends," Jan said. Gladys nodded. She drew back and added, "Now, as much as I hate to say it, looks like I best stay here in town. Sophie, beings all your beds are full, that just leaves Julie's. Julie?"

Julie's eyes lighted up. "Yes, yes. And we can help with surveillance. Jan, we can take turns watch…"

"We'll see Julie. We'll see," Jan said as she steered Julie toward the door…she gave Sophie a wink, and Sophie returned a knowing smile.

Chapter 22

Sophie went to her room to wait for Jeff. She sat in the chaise beside the large double windows and stared outside at the bleak winter scene. A snow covered flower bed ran along the fence row beside the house. In the summer roses, zinnias, and marigolds provided a wide ribbon of color from one end of the fence to the other. A round stand of colorful holly hawks alive with butterflies and bees would stand stately and erect at the end of the row. Now everything was white and cold and somehow threatening.

Outside the wind whipped and howled around the house like the pitiful cry of a lost animal. Oh, how Sophie longed for spring…to see the end of the snow and ice. She longed to see the end of this nightmare that gripped her every moment and impacted her decisions. She longed to see the end of the nightmare that was Andrew Temple. She longed to see forsythia blooming by the driveway, and she longed to have Jeff with her not because he had to protect her but simply because he wanted to be with her.

Sophie heard a key turn in the front door. An unsettled feeling seized her. She got up, went into the hall, and called down the stairs, "Jeff, is that you?"

Then Jeff's appeared on the stairway. He was running toward her taking two steps at a time. "Sure it's me," he said smiling from ear to ear. "Who were you expecting?" Then he was in the hall and holding her close. For the first time that day she felt safe. He walked her to the bedroom.

"Have you had dinner?" asked Sophie.

"Dinner's not exactly what I have in mind," Jeff said and he kicked the door closed with his heel. He grabbed Sophie, and kissed her hard.

Finally Sophie pushed him away and said, "No...seriously, Jeff. Gladys can't bear to have anyone around who's hungry. She wants everyone to be completely satisfied, and you don't want to get into trouble with Gladys do you?"

"I'll worry about Gladys later...when we're *completely satisfied*," Jeff said. And he eased her onto the bed.

* * *

Sophie and Jeff didn't make Gladys's designated dinner hour, but Gladys said nothing and served them a dinner of fresh green salad, red snapper, scalloped potatoes, and asparagus with hollandaise sauce. Dessert was Sophie's favorite chocolate mousse, and Jeff had two servings.

As Gladys was clearing the table, Jeff looked at Sophie solemnly and said, "I need to talk to you tonight." Gladys turned to leave the dining room in order to give them privacy. "Don't leave Gladys. This involves you too." Gladys returned to the table, set the dishes down, and took a seat beside Sophie.

"We've felt for a long time that Andrew's here for some reason other than revenge toward Sophie. I believe this even stronger since he tried to poison Sophie and might have made another attempt on her life if we hadn't scared him away from the Howard's farm. There's something here he wants. And Sophie, apparently he doesn't need you to be alive to get it."

Sophie turned pale. "But what? Jeff, I already told you I took only personal things when I left Andy. I was in a hurry. I just wanted to get out of there as quickly as possible," Sophie said.

"Tell me again what you brought," Jeff said.

"Clothes and personal items like family jewelry, letters, driver's license, social security card...things like that," she said.

"What did you bring it in?" asked Jeff.

"I told you—suitcases," said Sophie.

"She's telling you the truth, Jeff," said Gladys. "She come home with everything she had in three suitcases and a hatbox. I remember telling Melvin, 'Melvin can you believe that girl's been married ten years and she comes back here with everything she owns in three suitcases and a hatbox'. That's what I said," said Gladys.

"She sure did say that," Melvin's voice said from the kitchen.

Sophie laughed. "Melvin you come on in here. And, Gladys, it wasn't a hatbox. It was an overnight case. In fact it was one I took to college."

"Well whatever," said Gladys. "You was still a pitiful sight."

Then Jeff said, "Gladys, where are those suitcases now?"

"Stored up in the attic, of course," said Gladys.

"You want I should fetch 'em?" asked Melvin.

"Yes, get them, Melvin. And take them to Sophie's room. Sophie, do you still have the clothes and other items you brought with you?" asked Jeff.

"I think I do…no, I'm sure I do," said Sophie.

Jeff thought for a minute. "How much do you need those clothes?"

"What do you mean?"

"I mean we might have to cut them up in order to search them thoroughly. You know pockets, hems, linings," said Jeff.

Sophie looked at Jeff seriously. "Jeff if it helps find what Andrew is after, we can cut them to shreds."

"Good," said Jeff. "Gladys we need several sharp knives and a couple pairs of scissors. Then let's all go upstairs."

By the time they got to Sophie's room, Melvin had moved three matching suitcases and a round overnight case into Sophie's room. Jeff told Sophie to put clothes, shoes, and personal effects that she brought to Seaboard on the bed.

"Melvin and I will start by searching the suitcases," said Jeff.

Jeff and Melvin took the luggage apart. They cut off the leather covering, tore it from the metal cylinders that formed the shape, and shredded the linings. They examined each cylinder to make sure nothing was stuffed inside. They found nothing.

"Okay Sophie, now you and Gladys search the clothes," Jeff said.

"Just what are we looking for?" asked Gladys.

"Anything that's out of place...that doesn't belong there," said Jeff.

Sophie picked up pants to a gray tweed suit and said, "My favorite!" And she ripped out the hem.

Gladys reached for a suede jacket, shook her head, and said, "What a waste." And she tore out the lining.

Two hours later the floor was covered with shards of leather, cloth, and metal that was once luggage. On the bed and on the floor scraps of silk, suede, and fabric lay in heaps. Tossed in a corner shoes and boots without heels or soles were ripped apart. In the bathroom, a lady's electric shaver and an electric toothbrush were broken down and tossed in the trash can. A small digital camera was torn apart and lay on the dressing table beside a string of pearls, a cameo necklace, a ruby ring, and some identification cards Sophie brought with her. Her old driver's license was confiscated when she got her North Carolina license.

Exhausted, Melvin slouched in one of the chair by the fireplace, and Gladys and Sophie sat on the floor. Jeff paced back and forth. "I really thought we were onto something," he muttered.

Finally he went to Sophie, knelt down, and took her hands. He looked at her beseechingly, "Think, Sophie, think. Did you bring anything else?"

Sophie shook her head. "No, Jeff. This is all I've got."

"What about a watch?" Jeff asked.

"No. No watch. Andy gave me a watch once, a Rolex, but I didn't want to take anything that reminded me of him. Jeff please, I'm exhausted, and just look," and her hand swept the room. "All of this is for nothing. I still have to worry about Andy." She covered her face with her hands and began to cry from exhaustion.

Gladys put her arm around Sophie, looked up at Jeff, and said, "Jeff, Sophie don't cry real easy. She's plumb tuckered out. She hasn't been out of sick bed that long you know."

"I'm sorry, Sophie," he said and reached for the cameo locket on the dressing table. The profile was carved from ivory, set on a rectangular piece of onyx, and surrounded by tiny planted stones.

Sophie looked up and wiped tears from her cheeks. "It opens you know, and there's a picture of me inside when I was a child. My grandmother wore it until the day she died. It's just a school picture but it was her favorite."

Jeff opened the locket. A little girl of about six with a toothless smile grinned back at him. Jeff smiled. "I'd forgotten how cute you were," he said and pressed the locket shut…except it didn't catch. Jeff examined it closely and saw that the picture had slipped out of the framework and prevented the catch from fastening.

"The picture's slipping out," Jeff said.

"Let me see it," Sophie held out her hand. "That's happened before."

Jeff handed the cameo locket to Sophie and she moved the small picture around in an effort to fit it back into the frame. The small size of the picture made her attempt awkward and she dropped it on the floor. But when the picture fell Sophie saw something else…something that didn't belong there. Snapped behind where the picture had been was a small rectangular object no longer than a quarter. It was black and had seven tiny copper tabs attached to it.

"Jeff, what is this?" Sophie asked handing the object to him. "I've never seen this before."

Jeff took it and began to examine it. Suddenly his face lit up and he thrust his fists upward, and shouted, "Yes! This is it! This is it! So Andrew Temple, how you like them apples!!!"

They all crowded around Jeff as he held the small object in the palm of his hand. "How'd it get there and what's it for anyhow?" asked Gladys.

"I'm sure Temple hid it there," said Jeff. "It's a digital memory card."

"But what's it for?" asked Sophie as she took it and examined it by turning it over and over in her hand.

"It stores information," said Jeff.

"What kind of information?" Sophie asked.

"Any kind you want…any information you can take a picture of…people places, and things," said Jeff. "You snap a picture and the image is stored on this. When you want to retrieve it, you insert this into a computer and the images come up on the computer screen. You could take a picture of something as large as a battleship at a distance or something as small as the page of the book. It can all be stored right here in this little gizmo. Sophie, where did you keep the locket?"

"I've been keeping it in that little concealed draw in the dressing table.

But you said you wanted to check everything so I took it out," Sophie said.

"Show me," said Jeff, and she walked to the table, felt underneath, and moved a tiny wooden lever forward. A small decorative rose, that appeared to be carved wooden ornamentation, popped out. Inside the rose was a drawer.

Jeff looked astonished. "I've never seen anything like that, "he said.

"Secret doors and secret drawers were common in the Victorian era," Sophie said and slid the drawer shut.

Gladys began to pick up the wreckage. "Melvin fetch me some of them large trash bags," she said. "Well leastwise we don't have to worry about Mr. Andrew Temple no more. **We** got what he's been after. Now there's no reason for him to be a threatening Sophie."

Jeff shook his head. "I wish that were the case, Gladys," he said. "Yes I'm pretty sure we found what Temple wants, but he doesn't **know** we've found it."

Gladys looked at Jeff with alarm. "What you mean?"

"I mean since he doesn't know we've found it, he'll still be trying to get to Sophie to force her to tell him where the locket is," Jeff said plainly. "Or he may want to drive her from the house so he'd be free to search it."

"Couldn't you just leak to the press that we done found what Andrew's looking for?" asked Gladys.

"That wouldn't do it," said Jeff. "Sophie is still a witness albeit unknowingly. He'd still want to silence her."

Suddenly Sophie felt flattened. She went to the bed and sat next to her shredded clothes.

Gladys looked at the room cluttered with good clothes that was now reduced to rubbish. "And all of this was for nothing. What a waste!" she said.

That night Sophie lay awake and listened to the whishing of the sleet. It sounded like sand being thrown against the windows. She also listened to Jeff's hushed voice from the hall as he reported the discovery of the memory card to some higher authority.

Finally he crawled into bed and snuggled Sophie close to him. "Soon Sophie. Soon. We're closing in on him…I can feel it."

"You know what I feel like?" Sophie asked.

"What?"

"I feel like bait," she said.

"No!" Jeff said, and he clasped her to him tightly. "You're not being used as bait. You weren't planted here. You came back here after your divorce of your own accord. And as his wife you were put in the middle of something you never dreamed was going on just to make him appear above suspicion."

"But how long is **this** going to be going on? This stalking?" Sophie asked.

"Not much longer, Sophie," he said. "I really think we've got him cornered."

Chapter 23

"Good morning Sophie," Jan's voice chirped on the phone. "How's the girl this morning?"

"Hi Jan. Tired and frustrated. We were up late last night searching my things and discussing my dilemma," she said. Sophie told her about the discovery of the memory card, but was again careful not to reveal Andrew's occupation as an assassin.

"So what do you think is on that card?" asked Jan.

"We've no idea," said Sophie. "The rub is that he'll probably still stalk me."

"Well, we saw your lights on until the wee hours or the night and knew something was happening. I'll tell Julie about you clothes. She'll be tickled to death. This will give us a reason to go shopping," Jan said mischievously. "Say, we're fixing to go to Roanoke Rapids this morning. Wanna go? Julie would love to be your fashion consultant."

"Great, but not this morning," said Sophie. At that moment Jeff walked into the room. "Gotta go. Jeff just walked in." And she hung up

Jeff kissed Sophie on the neck and began to struggle into his coat. "Where are you off to?" asked Sophie.

"Raleigh's sending some men down to pick up the memory card this morning. I'm meeting them in Jackson," said Jeff.

"Jeff, why didn't you take that over to Jackson last night?" asked Sophie.

"I didn't want to do anything out of the ordinary," said Jeff. "Didn't want to tip Temple off that we have the card in case he's out there

171

watching the house."

Sophie shivered. "That gives me the creeps...to think he's out there. What about your *guys* who are suppose to be watching the house?"

"They can't be everywhere," said Jeff as he zipped the parka. Sophie looked startled. Then Jeff said, "Don't worry. Gladys and Melvin are here and you have the snoop sisters next door. He'd have to be invisible to get pass them."

Sophie laughed. "They saw our lights on all night, you know," Sophie said.

"I'm sure. What are they going to do for drama when this is all over?" he said and walked toward the door. "I'm off." And he was gone.

Sophie showered and washed her hair. She replaced the bathroom towels with fresh ones. She picked up her room, and made the bed. She dressed, stared at her near-empty closet, and shook her head. And she started a list of clothes she needed to buy.

"I should go shopping with Jan and Julie...start replenishing my wardrobe," she thought. She walked to the phone and dialed Julie's number. Ring, ring, ring...then the message machine came on. Sophie hung up. "I'll just catch up with them in Roanoke Rapids," she decided. She already felt reinvigorated. She had a plan...a mission. With Julie's help she'd have an entire new wardrobe by this evening.

She looked out the window hoping to spot a blue pickup or an old Chevelle, and there it was. This time they were in the Chevelle.

"Okay," said Sophie. "Let's take a ride." And she grabbed a parka and headed for the door.

Sophie walked into the kitchen where she was met with frowns and grunts of disapproval.

"Now where in tarnation do you think you're off to?" Gladys demanded her hands on her hips. Melvin said nothing but shook his head in disapproval.

"I'm joining Julie and Jan in Roanoke Rapids. There's no time like the present to start replenishing my wardrobe," she said rebelliously and started for the door.

"Does Jeff know about this?" Gladys asked.

Sophie turned in defiance and said, "My *bodyguards* are outside in that old Chevelle. They'll be following me. And I'll be safe as a clam in a shell."

"You don't answer my question," said Gladys. "Does Jeff know about this?"

"No," Sophie said. "I can still make a *few* decisions for myself." And she turned slamming the door behind her.

Sophie walked to the garage, clicked the remote, and opened the door. Inside was dim and gloomy. Again the light didn't come on.

"Melvin!" she muttered as she walked to the car, opened the door, and slid into the driver's seat. She was surprised when the inside car light failed to come on. "What next?" she said as she fumbled for her key. She clicked on her seat belt, inserted the key, turned it, and the engine fired. She swung her arm onto the back of the passenger seat and swiveled in her seat to look over her shoulder in the back-out position. And there she was face to face with...Andrew Temple.

"Hello, Sophie," Andrew murmured in a sinister voice. Then he grinned malevolently. Sophie shrieked and went limp.

Andrew grabbed her throat and pressed hard in a spot that cut off her flow of air. "Hush, Sophie," he whispered. "Don't make me hurt you again...at least not yet. Understand?" The 'understand' was punctuated by more pressure.

Sophie couldn't breathe but she managed to nod her head anxiously. He released her and said, "You shouldn't have run away, Sophie. We have a lot to talk about...but not here. We have to go somewhere where we can be alone. It was always better when we were alone. Remember?"

Sophie didn't say anything. Andrew grabbed her neck again. "Wasn't it?" Sophie nodded. He released her.

"Now this is what we're going to do," he said slowly. "I want you to back up, go out the driveway, and turn left. And Sophie, don't try to signal Gladys and Melvin...that is unless you want to see them dead. Understand?"

This time Sophie answered quickly, "Yes."

"That's better," Andrew said. "Now easy does it. Back out and head toward the street."

Sophie complied meekly while Andrew lay on the floorboard behind the driver's seat. When Sophie reached the street she looked toward the old Chevelle.

"Forget about your guardians, Sophie, they can't help you now." Sophie whimpered and turned the car to the left.

* * *

Gladys watched Sophie drive pass the kitchen window. Then she spent the next twenty minutes banging around the kitchen and railing about how "hard headed" Sophie was and always had been. She pulled out the vacuum cleaner and stomped out of the room to vacuum the front hall. As she bent to plug in the machine, she glanced across the street where the Chevelle was parked. And there it sat. The old Chevelle had not moved from that spot all morning..

"Melvin," shouted Gladys. "Come here."

Melvin trotted in obediently. "What?"

"Look a here," Gladys said. "There's those no-good bodyguards just a sitting out there...probably asleep. They's suppose to stick with Sophie. Melvin this is serious."

Melvin bent over and was peering through the window. "Sure is serious," he said.

Gladys headed to the telephone. "Where's that emergency number Jeff gave me this morning. I'm gonna call him and he'll tell them what for." She rummaged through a drawer and came up with a small piece of yellow paper. She dialed the number on the paper and waited for the rings.

A strange voice said, "Yes?"

Gladys shouted in her long distance voice, "Yes, yourself. This here is Gladys and I gotta talk to Jeff Sands right now."

"Ah, ahhh," the voice answered.

"Don't you 'ah' me," said Gladys. "If I don't speak to Jeff you're gonna wish I had."

Empty air on the line let Gladys know that the man had covered the phone with his hand. Soon Jeff's said impatiently, "Gladys, this number was supposed to be for emergencies only."

"Well, Jeff," Gladys said in a loud feisty voice, "would you think it's

174

an emergency if I told you that Sophie's taken off? Would you think it's an emergency if I told you that your watchmen are still a sitting out there…probably asleep?"

Jeff said with alarm, "When did she leave?"

Jeff's tone told Gladys she'd been vindicated. "About fifteen—twenty minutes ago," she said.

There was more dead air on the phone. Then Jeff came back. "Let me speak to Melvin," he said.

"He wants to talk to you," Gladys said and handed the phone to Melvin.

Like Gladys, Melvin spoke loud enough for Jeff to hear him all the way in Jackson without a telephone. "Yes?"

Jeff said, "Melvin, I want you to go out to that Chevelle and see what's up? I've been trying to reach them for about five minutes. Call me right back."

"Okay," Melvin shouted and hung up.

It took some doing for Melvin to struggle into his heavy coat, pull on his boots, and put on his knit cap and gloves. Then he slowly, slowly inched his way down the steps, out the gate, and across the street to the rusty Chevelle. The windows of the car were iced over and he only saw blurred shapes propped up inside.

He knocked lightly and said, "Hey." There was no response. "Hey" again. Still no response. He walked to the other side of the car. From this spot he could see that the windshield was shattered, and a dark red—almost black—spray was splattered on the glass. By struggling, Melvin opened the ice crusted door and gawked at the two men sitting upright their eyes staring straight ahead. Each had a red circle in the middle of his forehead. The backs of the seats where their heads lay were soaked in blood.

"Oh, Jesus," whispered Melvin. And he trudged back across the street much faster than he'd come.

Melvin stumbled into the house hardly able to breathe "Gladys! Gladys! Get Jeff back on the telephone. It's bad. Real bad!"

Chapter 24

Jan and Julie sat in Ruby Tuesday and sipped sweet ice tea...except Julie's sweet ice tea was without sugar.

"You can't call it *sweet* ice tea if it doesn't have sugar, Julie," said Jan sounding exasperated.

"I'll not compromise my health just to comply with a Southern tradition," said Julie. "Besides it's not so much about ingredients as about appearances."

"Your *appearances* are phony," argued Jan. "I've always been told that sweet tea was a Southern cocktail with the emphasis on sweet. You just moved up North and bastardized a whole Southern tradition. Shame on you, Julie Hinson."

"Jan Ewing, I'm every bit as much of a Southerner as you. I was born and raised in Seaboard, too," Julie said heatedly. "Besides, I do sweeten...with artificial sweetener."

"Uke!," said Jan. "*Artificial sweetener* is not sugar, Julie."

And then Julie felt a sharp kick under the table. "What in the world...?" Julie snapped. She glared at Jan who had a curious look on her face and was nodding at something outside the window. Julie looked where Jan was focused.

Two men in a black car with government license plates zipped into a parking space designated as handicap parking. They bolted out of the car and headed into the restaurant.

"Somebody wants their morning coffee real bad," said Jan.

"They are nicely dressed," said Julie whose mind always went first to what someone was wearing. They were dressed in dark suits with buttoned jackets, white shirts, and striped ties. They wore short black boots and somber expressions. As they entered the restaurant their eyes anxiously searched the crowd. Then one man's eyes fell on Jan and Julie. He nudged his partner, nodded, and they began walking purposely toward their table.

"They're coming over here," whispered Jan. "Don't look at them. Don't encourage them." And she turned her head and pretended to be concentrating on something outside.

"Just let me handle this, Jan," said Julie. She sat erect, tossed her hair, and crossed her legs. "I know how to handle these urbane types."

The two men stopped at their table. The driver of the car spoke. "Are you Julie Hinson and Jan Ewing?" he asked.

"Who wants to know?" Jan asked with attitude.

"Now, Jan," said Julie. "Must you be so rude…"

The two men reached into their pocket, flipped open a small leather holder, and flashed a badge. "U. S. Marshals, ladies. I'm Tibbet and he's Sherman. Have you ladies seen Sophie Singletary this morning?" He appeared to be number one on the team.

Julie shrieked, "Sophie!!! Oh my God! Something's happened to Sophie!!! I knew it, Jan. I told you we should have insisted…"

"Julie, stifle it!" Jan said forcefully. Then she turned to number one and said, "I talked to Sophie this morning on the telephone. We asked her to come shopping with us, but she declined. What's wrong?"

"Do you know where she would most likely shop?" Number two Marshal finally spoke.

"Well," Julie said superciliously, "Sophie shops at the best…"

Jan interrupted, "Sure we know where Sophie shops, but I'm not answering your question till you answer mine…*what's wrong?*"

Number two looked at number one. Number one said, "Sophie Singletary left the house this morning…ah, ah, without bodyguards. It's essential that we find her as soon as possible. Can you show us where she shops?"

Jan and Julie were already gathering their things, "Now was that so hard? Sure we can show you. Just follow me," Jan said. And she was up and heading for the door. When she was outside she turned, walked back into the restaurant, and spoke to the hostess. "Cancel our order, please," she said. And then she left.

The hostess and a waiter who had watched the whole scenario stood shaking their heads.

"Wasn't that the lady who pulled out in front of that eighteen wheeler and almost caused a pile-up," the waiter asked.

The hostess nodded. "Sure was. It certainly took the law long enough to catch up with her."

* * *

Jeff arrived on the scene of the two murdered operatives in Seaboard. The area around the rusty Chevelle was taped off. A crowd of onlookers was assembled outside the tape, and from nearby windows Jeff saw curtains pulled aside and frightened eyes peered out. The neighbors gawked and speculated about this vicious crime so alien to their quiet town.

As Jeff walked toward the scene old friends hurled questions at him. Questions he couldn't answer. He just shook his head and moved quickly toward the car. Staying outside the tape, Jeff walked around to the side of the car where the door stood open. Even from where he stood, he could see inside the car. The heads of the two men lay back on the seats a large dark stain underneath. Even from that vantage Jeff could see the round holes in their foreheads. How were they taken off guard? These were two of his best surveillance men. Had they, like Sophie, grown to think of Seaboard as being out of harm's way? Had they become too complacent? Or had Temple, the seasoned assassin, been too cunning for even these hardened field operatives? Of course the neighbors would be questioned about any suspicious noises such as gun shots, but Jeff knew that he'd probably never know the answer to all his questions. Jeff reached for his cell and put a rush on a crime scene team. They arrived quickly and Jeff made his way back through the crowd of spectators and to his car. He saw Melvin and Gladys peering through the window. He sped pass the house and headed back to Jackson.

Soon the office was in crisis mode. Immediate response to a missing person was essential. The first few hours were the most critical. And since they were dealing with a man who had already committed four murders, two which were U.S. Marshals, the level of the crisis bar was set real high.

Jeff notified the local sheriff and police about the murders of his two men and sent Jesse over to Seaboard to meet them. Four men had come down from Raleigh to retrieve the memory card, and Jeff recruited two of them to help out with their latest crime in Northampton County while the other two transported the card back to headquarters. Soon four other Marshals showed up from Raleigh to assist in the search.

Jeff sent Buddy to the library, Howard's farm, and to cruise around Jackson in case Sophie had changed her mind and decided to do genealogical research instead of shopping. Buddy even cruised the Winner Dog.

Given that Jackson was such a small town Buddy returned quickly having no luck. Jeff was still hoping that Sophie was somewhere in Roanoke Rapids leisurely browsing the stores. But his hopes were dashed when he received a call from the two Marshals in Roanoke Rapids saying they found Jan and Julie and that they had accompanied them to search all the usual shopping places…the mall stores, restaurants, bookstore…but no Sophie. As Jeff listened to their report, he was also told in no uncertain terms that the two Marshals had their hands full with Jan and Julie and would like to return to Jackson before Jeff had two more 'murders' on his hands. Jesse told them to come on in.

Jeff had called a meeting of the local police, sheriff's men, State Troopers, and Marshals who were not working the scene in Seaboard. Feelings were running high at the death of one of their own. Jeff was feeling the strain of the attempt on Sophie's life, the death of two men he'd known for years, and the terror of losing Sophie again.

Jeff, another Marshal, and two State Troopers were hunched over a county map discussing Northampton County's close proximity to the Virginia State line.

"We'll alert the Virginia…" one of the Troopers was saying when a

Sheriff's deputy rushed up the steps.

"Found her car," he shouted, "parked in the back of old Seaboard High School. We got the scene cordoned off, and two guys are there."

"Any sign of Sophie Singletary?" another deputy asked.

"None," the messenger replied.

"Any bl…any sign of violence?" asked Jeff.

"Don't think so," said the deputy who was breathing hard and waiting wide eyed for further instructions.

"Okay, let's get a crew back over there," said Jeff. And he started for the door.

Chapter 25

When Jeff arrived at the old school a group of onlookers were gathered in a small field behind the school. Jeff was quickly recognized and someone in the crowd shouted, "Hey, what's going on, Jeff?" Jeff raised a hand but didn't reply.

Jeff walked to the yellow tape and peered into the barricaded area. The driver's door and the door behind the driver's seat stood wide open. There were footprints in the dirty snow and slush. They appeared to be prints made by a man and a woman. The footprints were skewed and erratic indicating a struggle most likely took place, and they led to tire tracks of a second car. Jeff was told by one of the local deputies that tracks made by the second car exited the school ground area and were obliterated by traffic. Then Jeff looked back at Sophie's car. There in plain sight on the front passenger's seat lay Sophie's purse.

"Damn, we must have just missed them. He wanted to make damn sure we knew he had her," Jeff said an undercurrent of fear rippling through his body.

"Who found the car?" Jeff asked.

"Those two kids over there," said a deputy pointing to a teenage boy and girl. The girl saw the deputy point. She grinned, jumped up and down, and waved excitedly to Jeff. Jeff nodded and he and Buddy walked toward the couple. The closer Jeff got the more animated the girl became, and the more sullen the boy.

"I'm Jeff Sands," he said. "I'd like to ask you a couple of questions."

The girl's jeans were so tight they appeared to be pasted on. The legs were tucked into fur top snow boots with red tassels that jiggled about her ankles as she bounced eagerly. Her sky blue down parka was unzipped and pulled back to reveal a white knit turtle neck sweater stretched tightly across her ample young breasts. She wore glittery light blue eye shadow, dark blue eye liner, long black lashes, and sparkling pink lipstick. Her blonde hair was in desperate need of a root job. Her boy friend, on the other hand was as lackluster as she was attention-getting. Everything he wore was black—boots, jeans, tee shirt, coat, ski cap, gloves. His complexion was deathly white and the contrast with the black clothes made him appear ethereal.

"Hi, I'm Heather," the girl giggled and glanced back toward a small group of girls that began gathering when they saw Jeff approach Heather.

Jeff looked at the boy. "S'up?" the kid said. He stared at the ground.

"Oh, he's Curtis," Heather said dismissively.

"Okay," said Jeff. "I understand you two are the ones who spotted that car." He nodded toward Sophie's car.

"Yes, we're the *spotters*," Heather said and she looked toward the girls again and giggled. They giggled too.

"Tell me about it," Jeff said.

"Wellll," said Heather drawing her finger to her cheek and staring upward pensively. Finally she said, "Curtis and I were coming from our houses over there. (And she pointed toward some houses on Washington Street beyond the school.) And I saw that car. (And she pointed to Sophie's car.) And I said 'Curtis look at that car'."

Jeff waited patiently. Finally he said, "And?"

"Well Curtis looked but he didn't say anything. We just kept on walking. Then when we got to this side of the car I noticed that the doors were open. And I said 'Curtis, look. The doors are wide open'," she said.

"And Curtis didn't say anything," Jeff guessed.

"That's right," said Heather.

"Did you see anyone on the school grounds or around the building?" Jeff asked.

"No," Heather said. "Not a soul. Of course, I don't go near that old building." Then she leaned toward him and whispered, "Haunted, you know."

Jeff ignored the 'haunted' comment and said, "Did you go up to the car?"

"Are you kidding?" Heather said and she looked shocked at the suggestion that they would have approached the abandoned car.

"I take that as a 'no'?" said Jeff.

"Yes…I mean no. I mean no we didn't go up to the car," Heather said.

"Have you touched anything in the area behind that yellow tape?" Jeff asked pointing to the tape.

"What? You think I'm nuts? And you can take that as a no," Heather said, turned to look at the group of girls again, and snickered. They snickered too.

"Okay Heather, Curtis. Thanks for your help," Jeff said and turned to go.

"Later man," Curtis mumbled. Jeff looked back, and Curtis was still looking at the ground.

Jeff called the Seaboard policeman aside. "You the only policeman in Seaboard?"

"Yep, Dillon's the name," said the policeman. He was a man of about sixty five…probably a retiree looking for an easy job to help him through retirement years. He had a belly that hung over his belt. He wore jeans, a fur lined denim jacket, cowboy boots, and packed a .44 magnum in full sight. His eyes were blood shot, and he hadn't shaved. "I can deputize a couple of boys if you need me too."

"Okay, do that. Want you to go inside the old school and look for signs of anyone having hidden in there," Jeff said.

"Okay," said the policeman. "Any suggestions as to what we should look for?"

"Look for anything that might lead teenagers to think there's ghosts in there," Jeff said and walked away. "Let me know what you find."

"Okay," said the policeman skeptically. Then he walked toward a group of men who were watching the investigation and suggesting ways it could be done better. "Robert, how 'bout you, Frank, and William coming with me?"

The three men joined him eagerly. "What up?" asked Frank.

"I'm gonna deputize you to help me search that old school building," said Dillon pointing to the school. "You are hereby deputized."

"Hot damn," said Robert. "Just like that I'm the law. What are we searching for anyhow?"

They started toward the building. "We're looking for anything that might be mistaken for a ghost," said Dillon shaking his head.

"Hot damn," said William. "We're a team of freaking ghost busters." And they walked away chanting... *who you gonna call—ghost busters?* When they realized that Jeff wasn't smiling, they immediately assumed a more serious attitude.

After close examination of the outside of the school building, the 'ghost busters' realized this wasn't going to be an easy task. All the windows were boarded up, and the doors padlocked. They walked around the building looking for the best way to break in when William called, "Hey, I've found something."

The others joined him below an auditorium window. They could tell that plywood had been loosened and hastily reattached, and then they spotted a ladder lying behind the bushes. Gouges on the brick indicated that the ladder had leaned against the wall.

"We got ourselves evidence of a trespasser," said Dillon.

They leaned the ladder against the side of the building, climbed up, and tore loose the plywood. Then one by one they climbed up and entered what had once been an auditorium. Seats were stripped out. The window curtains and the stage curtain hung in dusty rags. The tiny room at the back that had housed the stage lighting equipment had been broken into and the equipment vandalized. The floor was rotten and many planks were missing. They made their way through the auditorium and into the downstairs hall. The men walked silently, almost reverently as if the place were sacred. The first floor had housed the elementary classes. They moved through the old structure where young students once roamed the long halls filling them with laughter and squeals. They searched every room, behind every coat closet, and restroom. There was no indication that the thick dust that covered everything had been disturbed.

"Let's take it upstairs," said Dillon, and they walked to the corridor that housed the stairwell. "Now watch your step here, boys," he said.

"These steps are rotten and it's a long drop down."

Finally they reached the second floor which had accommodated high school classes. This was a place where teenagers felt they fit in—a home away from home where they shared secrets, dreams, and disappointments. They studied, learned, skipped class, played sports, stole sweethearts, danced, sang, and did all the things that crafted a bond. The men used the same search procedure as they'd used on the first floor searching every classroom, laboratory, and restroom. Then they finally got lucky. They searched a tiny room in the home economics lab between the kitchen and classroom and found it to be uncharacteristically clean. The thick dust they discovered in the rest of the building was absent especially in a corner of the room farthest from the window. And there upon the window sill was a red cellophane strip that might have been torn from a package of crackers or gum.

"Hey, look here," said Robert reaching for the strip.

"Don't! Don't touch a thing," said Dillon as he moved in for a closer look.

"You think *that's* something," said Frank. "Take a look at this," and he pointed to a dusty corner behind the door at the other end of the room. There lay a flashlight battery.

"Hot damn!" exclaimed Robert. "We found ourselves a ghost."

Jeff was called to the school building to view the men's discovery. He felt a wistful tug as he climbed the decrepit stairs of his old high school. Even under such nerve-racking circumstances a flood of memories drew him back to a less complicated chapter in his life. When he reached the small room in the home economics department he looked carefully at the disturbed dust, the red cellophane strip, and the flashlight battery.

"Damn," Jeff said. "Looks like he was here in Seaboard right under our noses. Keep this room secure and wait for the scene people. Hell, if we keep finding crime scenes, we're going to need some serious man power."

Chapter 26

Jan and Julie decided they would return to Seaboard even though they had neither eaten nor shopped. The drive back to Seaboard was uncharacteristically quiet. They had gotten all the way to Gumberry, which was only three miles from Seaboard, before either spoke.

Jan spoke first, "I want to go straight to Sophie's house. I want to check on Gladys and Melvin. I know they're both fit to be tied."

"I agree," said Julie atypically. Julie seldom agreed with anything Jan suggested.

"Might even stay the night if they don't mind," said Jan.

"I was going to suggest that we stay there. Somehow I don't want to be alone," said Julie.

"Me neither," said Jan. "And I don't like this feeling. I don't like it that this creep can come in here and impact so many lives…Sophie, Gladys, Melvin, Jeff, you, me."

"You see," said Julie, "how we are affected by the friends…and husbands…we chose? This is a perfect example of a poor choice in a husband."

"Well, you oughta know. Julie, get off your soap box for awhile, hear? Must everything result in a lecture? I don't think Gladys and Melvin will be comforted by your opinion of the situation," said Jan as she turned right onto Main Street, crossed the railroad, and headed up the hill towards Sophie's house.

Julie and Jan were shocked to see emergency vehicles, law

enforcement vehicles, the cordoned-off crime scene, and a crowd of onlookers that was growing steadily. There was a photographer from the Daily Herald, the Raleigh News and Observer, and the Virginian Pilot. A WAVY-Norfolk TV camera was set up and a spiffy-looking news reporter moved among the crowd asking inane questions that usually started with '…and how did you feel?'

A former classmate of Jan pushed through the crowd and nudged Jan. "Jan, you missed the excitement. Two men were shot to death in that old car. The medical examiner just took them away in one of those zipped-up black bags. Ugh!"

Jan looked toward the window of Sophie's house. She saw Gladys and Melvin staring incredulously at the chaos outside. "Come on Julie," she said and nodded toward Sophie's house.

They pushed their way through the crowd. A reporter realized they were heading toward the house and hurried toward them, microphone held in front of her. She overtook them just as they were going to open the gate.

"Could we have a moment please," the reporter said. "Please." Jan opened the gate and Julie walked in. The reporter continued, "Do you live in the neighborhood? Do you know the two men who were killed? Could you give me your names please?"

"No comment," said Jan. And she banged the gate shut, walked quickly up the path and to the porch dragging Julie by the arm.

Julie said excitedly, "No comment? Why Jan, you sounded just like one of those actresses on a television crime show. Now let' see…who would you be…"

"Shut up, Julie," said Jan and she rang the bell.

"Well, you don't have to be rude," Julie said.

"Yes, I do, Julie. Sometimes I do," said Jan.

Suddenly the door opened. Gladys stood sobbing and wringing a big white handkerchief in her hands. "It's my fault," she wailed. "It's all my fault."

Jan eased her back into the house fearful that the reporter would jump the fence and stick a microphone in poor Gladys's face.

"Come on, Gladys, let's go sit in the den. Tell us what happened," said

Jan and she led Gladys into the den and to the couch.

Gladys sat down and continued to cry uncontrollably. Jan and Julie realized she was traumatized and ask if she wanted a doctor.

"Don't want no doctor," said Gladys.

"Okay then," said Julie. "How about a nice cup of tea?"

"Don't want no tea either," she said. "Need something stronger than tea right now."

"Melvin, get Gladys a drink," said Jan.

Melvin hustled out of the room mumbling that he thought a drink would be 'fitting for him too'. He returned quickly with two juice glasses half full of a brown liquid. He handed one to Gladys and stood holding the other glass aloft. "Here's to my good friend, Jack," he said and took a substantial gulp. Gladys didn't toast. She held the drink in both shaking hands, lifted it to her lips, and drank as whiskey dribbled down the sides of her mouth.

"Feel better?" asked Jan.

Gladys shook her head. "Won't feel better till they find her," said Gladys.

Julie said, "Gladys will you please tell us what happened? All we know is that Sophie is missing. How did this happen?"

Gladys put her face in her hands and shook. They thought she was going to cry again but when she lifted her head she looked at Jan then Julie and said, "Well, this morning Sophie marched into the kitchen and announced she was going to go to Roanoke Rapids to replace all them clothes we cut up last night. You know about cutting up the clothes don't you?" Jan and Julie nodded. "Well, I asked her if Jeff knew she was going to do this and she got mad and told me she could make her own decisions. Then she prissed right out and slammed the door. I should have grabbed her and hog-tied her right there in the kitchen. But no, I was too proud. Wasn't gonna argue with somebody who sassed me. I just plum let my pride get in the way, and you see what's happened?" And another round of tears followed.

"The dead men in the car..." Jan began.

"Her bodyguards," said Gladys. "Melvin's the one who found them dead. Some bodyguards!"

"Don't go speaking ill of the dead like that, Gladys," Melvin scolded. Then he looked at Jan and Julie and said, "I've seen dead people before, mind you, but I ain't never seen ere dead person that's got shot."

"Have you talked to Jeff?" asked Julie.

"Only on the telephone this morning," Gladys said. "I saw him drive by a couple of times, but he didn't even so much as wave," Gladys said indignantly.

"Now Gladys, Jeff's got his hands full right now working his investigation," said Melvin. "He ain't got time to hold our hands."

"You're right, Melvin," Gladys said and she sniffed. "I'd rather him be out a looking for Sophie than wasting time with us."

Julie walked to the window and lifted the curtain. A tow truck was backed up to the Chevelle and the operator was hooking a cable to the car under the watchful eye of a Marshal. After the hook-up, the operator climbed into the truck and slowly towed the Chevelle onto the road in the direction of Jackson. The Marshal followed close behind.

"Well, there goes the car," Julie announced. "I suppose the crowd will disperse now."

Jan, Gladys, and Melvin walked to the window and watched the tow truck and two cars disappear down the road towards Jackson. There were still people milling about and the red and blue emergency lights of a trooper's car still flashed. But dusk was turning into dark, and when night approached, the temperature would drop drastically.

"Neighbors will go inside as soon as it gets too cold for them, but I doubt the reporters will go anywhere, and heaven help us if they connect anyone in this house to what's going on. They'll crawl all over us like ants at a picnic," said Jan.

Julie dropped the curtain and said, "I need to run home and get a few personal items. Jan would you go with me…before it gets too dark?"

Jan said, "Oh, I forgot…Gladys can we stay here tonight? We don't want to be alone, and we want to keep up with the latest about Sophie?"

Gladys said, "You most certainly can stay here. The more people's in this house the better I feel. You wouldn't believe the noises I've heard 'round here when I'm alone. Stay!!! Please stay and I'll get some supper whilst you fetch your things."

189

By the time Jan and Julie returned from next door carrying a couple of small bags Gladys had warmed two quarts of Brunswick stew she'd canned last fall and sliced a loaf of homemade bread.

"These here is slim pickings," she said as she and Melvin brought the stew, sliced bread, bowls, and spoons into the den. "But I wanted to watch the news, and see how them reporters report this thing."

They spooned out bowls of stew, turned on the television to the evening news, and sat anxiously with their eyes glued to the screen. Suddenly a shot of the reporter Jan had encountered earlier that day popped upon the screen.

"Tonight we are reporting from the small town of Seaboard where the bodies of two unknown men were found shot to death in a parked car in the middle of this peaceful North Carolina town. Sources say that the unidentified men were killed gangland-style. (A shot taken earlier of the Chevelle popped up on the screen. The reporter continued to talk over the shot.) The bodies of the victims were discovered by Melvin Brinks who works in the house across the street. (The camera panned to focus on Sophie's house.) We have also learned that the owner of the house shown in this picture is missing. She is Sophie Singletary, age 41, Caucasian, five foot seven, auburn hair, about 135 pounds. (A picture of Sophie flashed on the screen. The viewers gasped.) Ms. Singletary has been missing since 11:00 am this morning when she left home to shop in nearby Roanoke Rapids, North Carolina. Later, her car was discovered abandoned in the back of the old Seaboard High School which is no longer in use. Law enforcement officers would like to question Andrew T. Temple, ex-husband of Ms. Singletary regarding her disappearance. (A picture of Andrew Temple appeared up on the screen.)

"So that's what the dirt bag looks like," said Jan.

Gladys said, "I got a better word than dirt bag...I'd say he's..."

"Now Gladys, watch your tongue. Remember you're a Christian woman," said Melvin

The reporter continued, "When asked if Temple is a suspect in the disappearance of Sophie Singletary or the murder of the two unidentified shooting victims we were told he is a person of interest. (The camera again focused on the reporter.) Stay tuned for more information on this bizarre murder and missing person investigation of Sophie Singletary. This is Cynthia Weeks WAVY—TV, Norfolk reporting live from Seaboard, North Carolina."

"Well, they have connected this house to the crimes," said Jan. "and we're in for a bumpy ride."

Chapter 27

The usually quiet office in Jackson was buzzing with activity. Marshals, Troopers, State Police, Sheriff's men, and local police milled about waiting to hear the plan. Four men from the State Police finally arrived, and Jeff began to brief everyone at the same time.

"Okay, now listen up folks," Jeff shouted. The ruckus quickly faded and all faces turned to Jeff. "Now here's what we got. This office has been keeping Sophie Singletary under close surveillance for about eight weeks. There are two reasons for this surveillance. First reason—she was married to Andrew T. Temple for ten years. Andrew T. Temple is under investigation in the assassination of several high level people in the United States and Europe. Part of his cover was to travel with his innocent-looking wife, Sophie Singletary. **She**, however, was not aware she was part of his schemes. So we planned to use her as a witness against her former husband. Second reason—we knew Temple was stalking her. At first we thought the stalking was an act of revenge because she divorced him. Recently we realized he was looking for something. By keeping an eye on Sophie Singletary, we hoped to capture the fugitive and learn what he was looking for. So these are the reasons why Sophie Singletary was under surveillance. It is important to remember that at this point, Ms. Singletary was not aware of her ex-husband's profession or even that she was under surveillance. Any questions so far?"

There was complete silence. "Good," said Jeff. "The surveillance seemed to be working until several weeks ago. Andrew Temple tried to kill Sophie Singletary and a friend Eileen Brown with a large amount of arsenic put in hotdogs. (There were gasps and the murmuring.) Fortunately, both women survived. However, two restaurant workers were murdered we believe to hide the identity of the person who put the arsenic in the hotdogs. We increased surveillance of Ms. Singletary and revealed to her for the first time her ex-husband's profession and how he used her for cover. We also told her that he was here and that he was the one who tried to poison her and her friend. Finally she was assured she was safe because we had her under surveillance. Well, you see how that worked out," Jeff added regretfully. "So that's why Sophie Singletary was under surveillance. Questions?"

"What kind of information you hoping to get from her as a witness if she didn't even know her husband was killing people?" a tall slim black man wearing a Trooper uniform asked.

"Where he did jobs and when," said Jeff. "Where did she travel with him and when? There's probably lots more, but that's not our job...it's the prosecutor's. Other questions?"

"So, that's why Sophie Singletary was under surveillance in the first place. Now at this point I have to tell you that we conducted a through search of the Singletary house. The search produced what most likely is what Temple is looking for...a memory card. That card has already been sent to Raleigh. However, Temple doesn't know the card has been found. And we believe that as long as he thinks Sophie still has the card, she's safe. The only reason he needs her is to find it." Jeff waited to let this sink in. Then he continued, "Now to today's events. We learned this morning at about eleven a.m. that Sophie Singletary started out to Roanoke Rapids to meet friends and shop. Shortly after that, two of our best surveillance men assigned to Singletary were found shot to death in their vehicle not far from the Singletary home. The killing has Temple's trademark. We immediately dispatched men to Roanoke Rapids to find Sophie's friends who showed them the most likely places to search for her. They didn't find her. Meantime, Sophie Singletary's car was found abandoned with her purse inside in the back of the old Seaboard High School. A search of the abandoned school found evidence that someone had stayed there for at least one night. So that's the update. Any questions?"

There were several questions from men who didn't know the area and they were assured they would be partnered with people who did.

"Okay," said Jeff. "Now our mission is obvious. One—find Sophie Singletary. Two—locate and take Andrew T. Temple, hopefully alive but deadly force if necessary to rescue Sophie Singletary.

"It's now eight o'clock p.m. Sophie has been missing nine hours. We got to get a move on. We have people out there looking already, but now we're going to ratchet up the search. One other very important thing…Andrew Temple is an assassin. He kills people for money and he's good at his job. So watch your backs and watch your partner's too.

"So right now I'm going to turn the briefing over to Trooper Anderson and Sheriff Parker. They know the roads around here and they've come up with some search strategies. Sheriff, Trooper…" and Jeff stepped aside.

Jeff walked over to a corner of the room to listen to the two men. Jesse joined him and said, "How much of that do you believe?"

"What do you mean?" said Jeff.

"Do you really think she's safe as long as he thinks she's got the memory card?" Jesse asked.

Jeff was quiet for awhile. He stared straight ahead with a faraway look in his eye. "I gotta believe it, Jesse. That's what keeps my hope up."

Chapter 28

Sophie was forced to drive on country roads for over two hours. Andrew repeatedly looked back to see if they were being followed. The only talking allowed was when Andrew gave Sophie directions. Every time Sophie tried to speak, he fixed iniquitous eyes on her. Andrew's eyes always achieved complete intimidation. She still saw them in nightmares. His eyes filled her with terror very early in their marriage. Only once had he used actual physical abuse as control...and that was the day she left.

Many of the roads Andrew chose were unfamiliar to Sophie. Most were unpaved and full of potholes. Under the noonday sun, the snow and ice melted just enough to leave the ruts filled with muddy slush that spattered high enough to spray the windows as they jolted along the country roads. Sophie became unnerved and began to cry. Andrew screamed, "Shut up!" and she did, although an occasional sob escaped from deep inside her.

They reached a large cleared plot of land that had been a corn field. Stubs of corn stalks push through the snow a mere corpse of the once tall green plant. In the middle of the field a herd of deer...about eight in number...foraged for snippets of fodder. The car engine frightened the deer and they dashed toward the adjacent pine woods.

Andrew ordered Sophie to turn onto a barely visible trail that crossed the field. At the end of the trail was a large dilapidated barn. Sophie followed his order and the car bounced toward the barn. Intense panic gripped her as they approached the barn. She realized that then she may no longer be needed to drive, Andrew would be free to do whatever he wanted.

They reached the barn and Sophie was told to drive inside. When she pulled into the barn, she saw a second car. The car was a more recent model than the one she had been forced to drive. It was a black Jeep Cherokee.

Sophie immediately began to look around for means of escape. She didn't see a room in which he could lock her. The barn was missing several planks and through the cracks she could see outside. A door hung precariously by one hinge. She felt a surge of hope. She certainly should be able to get out of here. Then when she turned the key and the engine died, Andrew snatched the key. He grabbed her wrists and pulled out plastic restraints. He was so quick…he forced one hand on top of the wheel and the other underneath and wrapped the restraints around her wrists to fasten her hands together. Sophie looked down. She was shackled to the steering wheel. She looked back at him in horror.

"Sophie, you didn't think I'd leave you here unshackled did you? We have much to talk about, my wife." Andrew said menacingly. He reached over, gently brushed a strand of hair from her forehead, and stroked her cheek. Then he suddenly grabbed her throat and began to press.

"Sophie, you have something that belongs to me," he whispered, "and I want it back."

Sophie couldn't breathe. Darkness moved in. Then Andrew released her throat, and she gulped for air.

"Don't play games with me Sophie," he said. "You know you can't win. Now once more…you took something from me Sophie and I want it back. Where is it?"

Sophie breathed heavily. She gasped and tried to swallow but she couldn't. Her throat seemed to be paralyzed. Gradually the muscles in her throat began to work.

"Take your time, Sophie," Andrew said. "We have plenty of time."

After a few seconds Andrew said, "Now…let's try again. You have something of mine, and I want it. Where Sophie? Where is it?"

Still struggling to breathe, she turned to Andrew and said cautiously,

"Andrew, I didn't take anything of yours…" He started to reach for her throat again. "No…please wait," she gasped and took several deep breaths. "Andy, when I left…I tried…tried…very hard not to take anything that belonged to you. Honestly…if I did take something…it might help if you told me what."

"Ahhh. I like it when you call me Andy," he said soothingly. "It resurrects so many tender memories. But we have no time to go there. You do not need to know exactly what is missing. You must only tell me where the object is that contains what I'm looking for."

Sophie knew he was talking about the locket but tried to look confused. "I don't understand," she wheezed and continued to breathe heavily.

"That's better," said Andrew. "I think you want to cooperate. That's smart, Sophie. What I want is inside your grandmother's cameo locket."

Sophie feigned surprise. "Inside my grandmother's locket? How could that be? It is so small."

Andrew became angry. "It is not for you to ask questions. It's for you to give answers. Now where is that cameo locket?" And he raised his hands and moved toward her.

"No..no, please," whimpered Sophie. "I'll tell you."

Andrew sat back in the seat and resumed a condescending tone. "There that's better. Where?"

"The locket is in a drawer of the dressing table in my room," she said quickly.

Andrew's face turned red. His eyes were wild, maniacal. He lunged at Sophie, grabbed her neck, and began to squeeze. Sophie blacked-out momentarily and when she came round Andrew's face was only inches from hers.

Andrew shouted, "You're lying! Did I not tell you we haven't time for lies? Don't you know I won't stand for it? I know that locket is not in your dressing table drawer. I have looked in that drawer. I have looked in all the drawers in your room. I have searched your entire house. I have not found the locket. You keep lying to me Sophie and you're going to die."

"Andrew, Andrew, please listen. Listen," Sophie gasped. "I'm not lying. The locket is in my dressing table drawer…a secret drawer. One you wouldn't find."

Suddenly Andrew relaxed. A grin crossed his face. "A secret drawer? How very Victorian! Victorian…just like you. That's why you were such an excellent choice for a travel companion. You look so innocent…so Victorian. *Now tell me* about the secret drawer, Sophie!"

Sophie swallowed several times to loosen her throat muscles. Then she said, "Underneath the dressing table there is a small wooden lever. If the lever is moved a certain way, a drawer pops out. The drawer looks like a decorative rose when it's closed. I put the locket there, not to hide it but to keep it safe."

Andy reached across the seat. Sophie flinched. He began to gently pat her cheek. "Aw, don't be afraid, Sophie. See how simple that was. All you had to do was tell me where the locket is."

"I didn't know that it was the locket you were looking for," Sophie said.

"True. But now you understand that I mean business," he said as he sat back in the passenger seat. His mood again turned dark. "And if you are lying to me…if the locket is not there…then I'll return and you, my dear, will beg to die."

Andrew turned in the seat and opened the door. "Andrew, wait," said Sophie. "How could you have searched my house? I don't understand." She thought of Gladys and Melvin.

Andrew stopped and faced her again. "Don't you remember, Sophie? Don't you remember you gave me the grand tour of your old home place…twice. I was particularly intrigued by one room. Remember? You told me it was a *secret* room. Actually it was a room in which your ancestor grandfather isolated and treated patients with contagious illnesses. Well, your ancestor grandfather would be pleased to know the room has not outlived its usefulness. I hid there. And when the chance presented itself, I leisurely searched your house."

Sophie was shocked. She thought of Gladys's many complaints about noises she ascribed to ghosts. Sophie looked at Andrew in disbelief.

Andrew laughed. "Don't worry, Sophie. I never spied on you and your lover. By the time Jeff Sands took to your bed, I realized the locket would not be easily found. That's when I decided it would be best if the house were **completely** empty…then I could tear it apart uninterrupted." And

Andrew opened the passenger door and swiveled to get out.

Sophie whispered, "Andrew is that why you tried to poison me? So the house would become vacant and you could search without anyone knowing?"

Andrew turned, bent over, and peered in at her. "Bingo," he said.

"But Eileen?" Sophie asked.

"My dear Sophie, I had to put arsenic in **both** hotdogs. I had no way of knowing which one **you** would eat," he said. And he slammed the door and walked to the other car. He unlocked the trunk and pulled out a package. Inside the package were clothes. He pulled the clothes out and put on a black heavy-weight sweat shirt and pants, a black hooded ski jacket, black socks and black athletic shoes, and black gloves. He snatched a black ski mask and crammed it in his pocket. Then he got into the Cherokee and drove off.

Sophie began to struggle. She tried to free herself from the restraints. She twisted, pulled, and even tried to chew through the plastic. Her wrists were on fire and blood covered her hands. She cut her lip and blood dripped onto her clothes and the seat. She tried to pull the steering wheel loose but only succeeded in injuring her wrists more.

Finally exhausted, Sophie laid her head back on the seat and poured over what she'd learned from Andrew. She shivered at the thoughts of Andrew secreted in her ancestor grandfather's secret room waiting for an opportunity to sneak out and rifle through her personal belongings. She regretted that she'd dismissed Gladys' complaints of strange noises. And Sophie was sorry she'd made light of her fear. She thought of poor Eileen whose only mistake was having lunch with the wrong person. She thought of the surveillance men whose lives she'd made miserable by continuously straying from her routine. Then she was suddenly struck with sickening thoughts. Would Andrew hurt Gladys and Melvin? What would Andrew do when he found the locket and discovered the memory card missing?

Through the cracks in the barn wall Sophie watched the sun dip below the horizon. Soon a curtain of darkness fell and a large full moon rose behind the tall pines its amber light making the trees appear on fire. A wind stirred and banged the barn door that hung precariously on one hinge. And with the wind came the cold...a bitter, teeth cracking, killing cold. She felt helpless, isolated.

Sophie sat up, threw her head back, and screamed, **"Help!!! Help!!!"** But she knew Andrew was clever enough to leave her where no one would hear.

Chapter 29

Jan, Julie, Gladys, and Melvin had not moved from their seats in front of the television.

Cable news networks had picked up the story, and the solemn face of a CNN scene reporter appeared on the screen. "This is Jennifer Eccleston reporting from a small rural town in eastern North Carolina where earlier today the bodies of two men were found shot to death in a car where quiet homes and two churches are located close by. Local, County, State Police, and State Highway Patrolmen are working closely with U. S. Marshals in the investigation. The involvement of so many branches of law enforcement is attributed to the fact that the two murdered victims were themselves U. S. Marshals."

(The camera moved back and forth between the scene reporter and the news desk.)

The anchor asked, "Jennifer, do we know why the two U. S. Marshals were in the small town of…what, what's the name…yes, the small town of Seaboard, North Carolina?"

"No, John we don't have that information yet. In fact, the Marshals haven't given any statement at all," Jennifer said.

John asked, "Wasn't there a kidnapping in Seaboard earlier today too? And is that connected to the murder of the two U. S. Marshals?"

"You're right John, a young woman, Sophie Singletary, went missing this morning at about eleven a.m. (A picture of Sophie appeared briefly on the screen. Then the camera moved back to the reporter.) However, it has not been confirmed that the two incidents are related."

"Seems like too much of a coincidence, Jennifer," said John.

"Well, that's why we're here, John, to find out all we can about these two crimes that have brought law enforcement people from all over the area to such an unlikely place for murder and kidnapping," said Jennifer.

"Keep us posted, Jennifer," John said.

"Sure will," said Jennifer. "This is Jennifer Eccleston reporting live from Seaboard, North Carolina. (And the camera switched to a Geico commercial.)

"Well, I'll tell you one thing," said Jan, "if CNN's on it, they'll uncover everything. They'll not leave a rock unturned."

"CNN...humph! What we need is fair and balanced assessment of this situation," said Julie. "Well, I can tell you..." Julie was suddenly knocked off her soap box by the door bell.

Gladys stood and said, "Oh Lord, there she is now...that CNN reporter. I can't stand it! I just don't think I can stand to have that camera stuck in my face without going all to pieces!"

Jan stood up and eased Gladys back into her chair. "Don't worry, Gladys. I'll handle this." And she started for the door.

Julie called after her, "Why do **you** get to talk to the reporter?"

"Because **I'm** more fair and balanced," Jan said. She threw open the door and screamed, "Travis White and Sam Barnett. Get yourselves in this house right now."

Two men about the same age as Jan stepped inside and quickly closed the door. Jan flung herself into their arms.

Finally Jan called, "Hey y'all, look what the cats drug in."

Jan walked into the den with her arms hooked through the elbows of two rugged, roguish looking men dressed in jeans, sweatshirts, and boots. Travis was a bit taller than Sam and had sandy blonde hair and a hefty build. Although thinner than Travis, Sam's body appeared to be hard and muscular. Sam's hair was cut short, dark, and curly. Both faces showed a fading summer tan. Sam and Travis were North Carolina Alcohol Beverage Control law enforcement officers and spent a lot of time working their territory out on the Outer Banks of North Carolina.

Gladys stood and screamed. "You boys come at just the right time.

I'm fixing to fall completely to pieces."

They rushed to Gladys. Travis hugged her and said, "Don't you worry. Gladys. Sophie's going to be just fine. Why they've got the entire law enforcement community of northeastern North Carolina out there looking for her."

"Yeah," said Sam, "and now we're here. What more help do they need?" Then he grabbed her and squeezed her hard.

Gladys fairly collapsed back into her chair.

"She's plum tuckered out," said Jan. "Julie and I are here for the night, and I hope we can convince her to get some sleep."

"Gladys," said Travis, "You won't be of any help at all if you don't get some rest."

"That's right," agreed Sam. Sam spied the bottle of whiskey on the table and nodded. "Just go to bed with old Jack there," he teased. Gladys looked at him through tears and laughed.

"Now," said Travis, "that's what we're looking for."

No one knew what to say. Fears were confirmed and reassurances made and the room fell into an awkward silent.

Finally Julie said, "Have you heard anything from Jeff? We've heard nothing…at least nothing from him directly. We've just been depending on the television for our information just like forty million other people all over the world. To think that my oldest friend is out there…Lord only knows where…and we have to depend on CNN for information. Now if I had my choice…"

Travis interrupted Julie's spiel. "As a matter of fact, we have talked with Jeff…as we were driving back from Nags Head. He's pulled out all the stops and called in all his IOU's. We asked where we could be the most help and he said here. Told us to make sure you are okay and handle things in Seaboard. He says to tell y'all to hang in there. It's gonna be all right, you know."

"Well, I suppose belated reassurances are better than none at all," Julie petulantly.

At that moment Travis's cell vibrated. He looked at it and walked into the hall to take the call. Sam turned to Julie and said, "Julie, you haven't changed a bit since high school."

Julie looked pleased, smiled, and said, "Why thank you, Sam."

Jan quipped, "Sam might not have meant that as a compliment, Julie."

Travis came back into the room. "That was Eve," he said. Eve was his bride of less than a year. "I'm gonna swing by and see her. Then we need to check in with Dillon."

Sam stood. "We'll be back before y'all turn in. Now don't get all bummed out over what they report on TV. Half of it is speculation."

"Right," Travis agreed. And Sam and Travis walked out into the hall.

Jan followed them into the hall. "Watch those reporters. They're thick as flies out there."

"Any hot ones?" Sam kidded.

Jan closed and locked the door. She turned and looked around the shadowy hall and at the stairway that rose and disappeared into darkness. Suddenly this house that Jan had visited so many times seemed strange and somehow ominous.

* * *

Andrew Temple took the road that ran in front of a country church, Pleasant Grove Church. He found this stretch of the road to be relatively clear of snow. There were a few potholes where the snow had melted and refrozen leaving a slippery situation but the Cherokee handled them well. Soon he took a right onto Buck Howell Road which he found more difficult to navigate. Here there had been little traffic and the road had not been scraped, but Andrew was a skilled driver...he had to be in his profession...so the drive was little challenge. He turned onto a path that ran across a wide field surrounded by tall pine woods. The car bounced and skidded over the path. Several times it got stuck in the snow, but Andrew rocked the car back and forth until it sped out of the rut and into the woods.

Andrew pulled on his ski mask and got out of the car. He recoiled as a blast of freezing wind hit him. He began to jog back through the field and onto the road. It was a three-mile run to Sophie's house on the corner of Main and Church Streets in Seaboard. He'd measured the distance several times and knew just how long it would take him to cover the distance. Three miles was no contest for Andrew. Part of his daily routine included a five-mile run, and he hardly broke a sweat.

The moonlight made it easy to read the road, but it also made Andrew more visible, so he stayed to the shadows. He didn't pass a single vehicle during the entire run. He ran pass the Seaboard Cemetery and then he began to slow. He looked down Church Street at the mob of people and reporters milling around Sophie's house. Andrew was undaunted. He simply cut across yards and used bushes as cover. He crisscrossed the backyards of houses on the same side of the street as Sophie's house and finally ended up at her garage. From this vantage he could see much of the hubbub going on in front of the house, in the church yard across the street, and in neighbors' yards.

Soon he saw an opening and darted across Sophie's backyard. He reached inside his belt, extracted a small metal tool, and used it to quietly unlock her back door. He slipped into the sunroom and listened. Silence. Then he crept into the kitchen and hurried to the back stairs. He listened again. This time he heard voices. He recognized Gladys's voice...and yes, Sophie's friends were here too. Then he heard the voices of two men. He had not heard their voices before. This could be troublesome if he were discovered.

Andrew slowly, quietly climbed the back stairs. Soon he reached the upstairs hall. Now he could clearly hear the voices below, but could only catch snatches of the conversation. He did, however, hear enough to deduce that the two men were law enforcement officers. Andrew decided this situation called for extra caution. He crept across the hall as stealthily as a cat and into Sophie's room. He could smell her scent...a mild, sweet, familiar scent. He rubbed his hand across the soft bedding and was surprised by a feeling of arousal. He quickly withdrew his hand remembering that Sophie laid here with her lover...her lover who was now tracking him like an animal.

The voices downstairs had moved into the hall so Andrew hurried across the room to the dressing table. He saw the decorative rose Sophie claimed to hide a drawer. He reached underneath the table, ran his hand carefully across the underside, and felt for a wooden lever. He found it almost immediately. He gently manipulated the mechanism and immediately the rose popped out. There was the secret drawer and inside laid the cameo locket. Andrew was ecstatic. He reached for the locket, snapped it open, and removed the tiny picture of Sophie. His euphoria was short-lived, however, for there was nothing behind the photograph. A rush of anger surged through him and he would have smashed everything in the room had it not been for the chatter downstairs. He forced himself to remain calm. He would have plenty of time to express his anger when he returned to the old barn.

Andrew calmly snapped the locket closed, placed it back in the secret drawer, and pushed it shut. He stole quietly from the room and into the hall. He heard a door close and footsteps returning to the den. Then he listened as snippets of conversation floated up the stairs. Then Andrew slipped down the back stairs and out the kitchen door remembering to lock it again.

He retraced his route taking care to stay among the shadows. Soon he left the clamor of the reporters behind and reached Buck Howell Road. He began to jog again and with each step he repeated, "That was foolish Sophie, foolish Sophie, foolish Sophie."

* * *

Travis and Sam found Dillon surrounded by reporters. His only comment was 'no comment'. Travis and Sam pulled him aside and asked for a rundown on how he planned to handle surveillance of the house. He told them that the plan was to leave two deputized men parked all night in Sophie's driveway. They'd do intermittent walkabouts. It was agreed that this would probably be sufficient because unfortunately Sophie was no longer in the house. The surveillance team would mostly serve as a buffer for Gladys, Melvin and Sophie's friends by keeping the press at bay.

Travis and Sam said they'd be back in about half an hour and then they'd stay as long as they were needed. Dillon said 'fine' and that he'd wait for them to get back. The crowd was already thinning. Window curtains were dropping and lights were beginning to go off in the houses on Church and Main Streets.

When reporters saw Travis and Sam talking to Dillon, they guessed they were law enforcement and flocked toward them as they started to their car.

"We got nothing," said Travis. "We just got here." And kept moving.

When they got into the car Sam's cell vibrated. He took a look and it was Jeff.

"Hey Jeff," said Sam. Travis was all ears. "Any news?"

"Not yet," said Jeff, "but we've got a lot going on and we're hopeful. How's everything at the house?"

"Gladys's torn up and Jan and Julie are spending the night. Just going to check on Eve and then we'll be back out here for the rest of the night."

"Thanks Sam," said Jeff.

"Sure thing," said Sam and he clicked off.

Chapter 30

Fear and absolute exhaustion caused Sophie to drift sporadically into unconsciousness. She woke up suddenly and looked around bewildered. As reality clicked in a rush of gut-wrenching terror tore through her. This was not one of the nightmares that awakened her so many nights. This was real, and Andrew grabbed her right in her own garage. She'd never been safe from him...and never would be.

Ribbons of moonlight streamed through the cracks in the barn walls, and the wind moaned soulfully as it passed through the pine trees. She tried once more to free herself from the restraints but succeeded only in cutting her wrists more. She had no idea how long Andrew had been gone. Then she heard a car. It was him. She'd never forget the sound of that engine. Sophie's heart raced so fast that she thought it would burst. She began to cry and struggle without regard to the pain from her bleeding wrists.

The car came closer and she could hear a thump as it bounced through the pot holes in the field. Suddenly it sped into the barn, the door flew open, and Andrew tore out. He threw open the front passenger door of the car that served as Sophie's prison and slid in beside her.

Sophie immediately began to shriek hysterically. She sobbed and screamed and thrashed around. Andrew reached over and touched her cheek. She whipped her head about wildly and yelped as if a hot coal had been placed against her face.

Then Andrew spoke and Sophie realized that his voice sounded soft and comforting. Her cries subsided into a mere pitiful whimper.

"Sophie...Sophie, there's no need to be afraid. I am your husband, and even though you lied to me, I forgive you. And to prove my forgiveness, I have a surprise for you."

Sophie screamed, "Andrew, please, I never..."

Andrew barked, "Shut up, Sophie. Don't lie to me anymore! Do you understand?" And he grabbed her by the shoulders and shook her violently.

Sophie stammered, "Yes...yes."

"Now I've grown weary of the games you and your lover play. Your lover took my card and left you holding the bag so to speak. That wasn't very thoughtful of him was it?"

Suddenly Andrew's voice became quiet, soothing. "But no matter...I shall deal with Jeff Sands, US Marshal, and recover my property in good measure. You see, I know just where to find him."

Sophie cried, "He doesn't have it. He doesn't..."

"You're lying to me again Sophie. Have you not learned anything today?" And his face was within inches of Sophie's.

"No...no," sobbed Sophie. "I'm not lying, Andrew. Marshals came from Raleigh and took it back to the District Office."

For a moment Andrew looked anxious. Then his confident facade reappeared. "That's better," Andrew said using his calmer voice. "Raleigh? This does complicate matters somewhat...but it can be worked out."

Andrew looked down at Sophie's hands. "Tch, tch," he said. "Look what you've done to yourself. You're always hurting yourself, Sophie. You should know better than to try to resist me. Now I am going to remove the restraints so we can get into the Cherokee. We are going for a little ride. Won't that be nice?" And Andrew opened a knife and cut the plastic restraints.

Sophie's hands dropped into her lap. They were swollen and she couldn't move her fingers. She gently shook her hands and when circulate began to return, she rubbed them gently.

Andrew reached inside his sweatshirt and pulled out a sheet of paper. He leaned toward Sophie, handed her the paper, and said, "See Sophie, this will make you happy. You've wanted this for a long time, and being an obliging husband, I've always tried to give you what you want. See here…" That was as much as he got to say.

Sophie threw her hands up and slapped the paper away. Adrenalin set in. She threw herself on him and flailed about wildly. She scratched and kicked and hit him savagely. One kick landed in his groin and he yelped in agony. She screamed and cried and went for his eyes and nose. But Sophie's burst of energy was short-lived. Her ordeal had left her spent. Andrew quickly recovered after being caught off guard and his fist made solid contact with Sophie's nose. There was the sound of bone cracking and blood spurted everywhere. Sophie welcomed the darkness as she slipped into unconsciousness.

* * *

From Main Street in Seaboard Travis looked toward Sophie's den window. It was one thirty and lights were still burning. He nudged Sam, nodded toward the house, and said, "What say we try to get them to turn in? The stress and staying up all night is not good for Gladys and Melvin."

"I agree," said Sam, and they walked toward Sophie's house.

As they crossed the street, a couple of reporters approached them.

"Anything new?" an eager young man not much over twenty asked.

"Not a thing," said Travis and kept walking. The young reporter looked disappointed, turned, and walked back toward a group of news people huddled together in the lee of a van.

"Got to be a better way to make a living," said Sam.

"Sure, like our job…chasing bootleggers on the Outer Banks," said Travis.

They mounted the steps and rang the bell. They heard hurrying footsteps and then a voice said, "Who's there?"

"Pizza man," said Sam.

The door flew open and Jan said, "Well, it's about time. Come on in. What's the news?"

"No more than you've heard on TV I'm sure," said Sam. "Jeff says sit tight and he'll keep us informed of any new developments."

Travis walked to the center of the group, took an authoritarian stance, and commanded, "Okay, lights out!" The TV watchers glared at him.

"Right," said Sam. "We've got enough to think about without having to worry about y'all. So upstairs. We promise to wake you if anything new comes up."

They all stood and walked slowly to the front hall, stopped, and looked up at the long dark stairway.

"I won't sleep a wink," said Gladys, "what with all the weird noises inside this house and the hullabaloo outside."

"Well try," Travis said firmly. "You're okay, and we're not going anywhere." And Travis and Sam watched as the four of them plodded wearily up the steps.

* * *

Jeff stood between Jesse and a State Policeman. They were bent over a table intently studying a map. The map showed a section of Northampton County comprised mostly of small farms...that meant lots of houses and out buildings. Some of the farms were in operation but others were abandoned leaving buildings to fall into serious disrepair. Since this area of the county was sparsely populated it would be easy to do a door to door. Jeff cautioned, however, that care should be taken when waking up a farmer who might be armed with a shotgun in the middle of the night.

Suddenly a shout exploded from the first floor. "Jeff, Jeff, we got something." And Buddy was running up the steps. "A car's been found in an abandoned barn on a deserted farm. This may be it, Jeff."

Jeff was already tearing down the steps toward the parking lot. "Tell me what you know," he said to Buddy who had to race to keep up with him.

"Got a call from a woman who lives next to a vacant farm. Said her two boys were out tracking deer...she wouldn't say hunting 'cause it's not deer season. She just said tracking."

Jeff burst out the door, into the parking lot, and headed for his car.

"Buddy, get to it," Jeff yelled.

"She said her boys saw a car parked up under an abandoned barn the next farm over. Boys claim they didn't go up to it, but…but…"

"Get to it, damn it, Buddy!" screamed Jeff.

Buddy blurted out rapidly, "They claim not to have gone up to the car, but then they said they saw blood."

Jeff froze. Blood. He went to the passenger's side, opened the door, and said, "You drive. You know where to go. Call for back-up, and Buddy, warn everybody to be careful not to disturb existing tire tracks."

"Right," said Buddy, and he lifted his phone and called in the order.

They drove in silence. Buddy occasionally glanced surreptitiously at Jeff not daring to intrude on his thoughts. They saw the lights from squad cars long before they reached the farm house. When they pulled up Jeff was scrambling out of the car before it came to a complete stop.

"What's the mother's name?" asked Jeff.

"Lewis. Mrs. Lewis is all I know," said Buddy

The farm house was a one story structure with a small porch and a storm door. From, behind the storm door two wide-eyed boys about ten and twelve years old peered out at the chaos in their front yard. Jeff supposed that they were as much frightened as curious. A woman who looked to be about forty five stood on the porch talking with a deputy. She'd thrown a heavy car coat over her bathrobe and her hair was screwed up in small pink curlers. She held a filter-tipped cigarette in her hand and waved it about animatedly as she talked. Jeff assumed she was the mother. There was a keyed up man in the corner of the yard talking with a State Trooper. Jeff assumed he was the boys' father. The tenor of the group changed immediately when Jeff stepped out of the car, walked purposely to the porch, and spoke to the woman. "Are you Mrs. Lewis?"

"Yes," she said hesitantly and clutching her coat more tightly.

"I'm Jeff Sands, United States Marshal Service. Thank you for calling," he said. Mrs. Lewis relaxed. "Do you think your sons could show us what they've found?"

"Sure," she said. "Sure. Eddie, Aaron, get out here." Then she turned back to Jeff and smiled. "Let me know if there's anything else I can do."

212

Eddie and Aaron opened the storm door and walked toward Jeff hesitantly. "Hi guys," Jeff said smiling. "Understand you ran across something a little scary."

The trepidation on the boys' faces vanished as they realized they weren't going to be chewed out.

"Yes sir," said one of the boys. The other boy just nodded.

"What's your name?" Jeff asked.

"Eddie's my name," he said.

"And your's?" Jeff asked nodding toward the other boy.

"He's Aaron," said Eddie.

"Can you talk Aaron?" asked Jeff.

"He don't have much to say," said Eddie.

"I see," said Jeff. "Well, I'd like you to show us what you found this morning."

"Okay," Eddie excitedly. "Can we ride in a State Trooper car?"

"Sure," said Jeff, and he motioned to a Trooper standing nearby.

The Trooper walked over and Jeff said, "These guys are gonna show us where they found a car this morning. They want to ride in your patrol car."

"No problem," said the Trooper. "Let's go." And he and the two boys walked toward the patrol car. Eddie and Aaron looked back and smiled proudly at their mom.

The patrol car started across the field the other cars following closely behind. Jeff could see the two boys bouncing up and down with excitement as they pointed toward the abandoned barn. The patrol car stopped just short of the entrance to the barn. Jeff was out like a shot. The front doors to the patrol car swung open and Eddie and Aaron jumped out and scampered toward the barn door.

Jeff rushed ahead and grabbed the two. "Whoa partners," he said. "Can't go in there."

"Why not?" asked Aaron. "We done been in there once."

Jeff cocked an eyebrow and looked sternly at the boys. "Thought you didn't go inside."

Eddie frowned at Aaron and said, "See? That's why he don't say much...if'n he does he always lets the cat out of the bag."

A deputy stepped up and walked the boys away from the barn. Jeff and Buddy stepped cautiously toward the barn opening. The old door flapped restlessly on its one hinge as if defying them to enter. Inside they could see the silhouette of a car. They pulled out plastic gloves, snapped them on, and walked cautiously toward the car. When they got to the car they saw that both front doors were open. Jeff pointed to footprints in the mud that went around the car and over the tire prints of a second car. Buddy nodded. Jeff pulled out a flashlight and Buddy followed. With dread they reached the deserted car and pointed the flashlight beams inside. Jeff gasped and recoiled in horror. Blood was on the driver's seat, the floor, and spattered on the window.

"Jeff," whispered Buddy, "I'm...I'm...so...so sorry."

Jeff swallowed hard and breathed deeply. "Damn it Buddy, we just missed them again."

But Buddy didn't hear Jeff. Buddy had walked to the passenger side of the car, leaned in, and stared at something on the floor. "Hey Jeff," he said, "Take a look at this."

Jeff rushed around the car and bent over beside Buddy. He pointed his flashlight beam into the car and focused on something white on the floor.

"Okay, let's see what we've got. Take it out carefully, carefully," Jeff cautioned.

Buddy reached in and picked up a piece of crumpled, mud-smeared, blood stained paper on the floor. He unfolded it carefully. It was a list of names. Beside the names were telephone numbers.

Jeff and Buddy scrutinized the paper carefully. "What the hell..." Jeff asked.

Then Buddy exclaimed, "Hey Jeff, you know what this is? This is a list of the cemeteries and graveyards that Eileen printed off for Sophie. Remember? I picked up a copy from the library trash can and brought it over to the office."

Jeff remembered. "Right! And if you were able to pick up a discarded copy then so could Temple." Jeff was heading to the door. "Tape this off and get a crew out here. And let's get out of here. Maybe now we've got a hit."

Chapter 31

Sophie moved in and out of consciousness stirred only by the rough drive. At some point she became aware that her hands were again in restraints. The car slowed and turned and the ride suddenly became unbelievably rugged. Unable to stabilize herself, Sophie was tossed against the door and then back against Andrew.

After what seemed to be an eternity, they came to an abrupt stop. Sophie heard Andrew's door click open and then slam shut. She heard his footsteps as he walked around the car and opened the passenger door. He mercilessly grabbed her by her wrists, pulled her across the seat, and outside the car. Sophie couldn't stand and she collapsed onto the snow and slush.

"Get up, Sophie," demanded Andrew. And he grabbed the restraints and pulled up on them in an effort to force her to stand, but Sophie immediately crumbled to the ground again.

"Must you make me carry you?" she heard him say. His voice sounded distant like an echo in a cave. Then he pulled her up, lifted her, and trudged through the snow.

Sophie forced her eyes open and looked up at the sky. A few clouds sailed lazily across the sky and then a star. A very bright star hung just above the fading moon.

"Morning star? Could that be the morning star?" Sophie wondered. Cold. She had never felt so cold. The wind stung her eyes and cheeks and blurred her vision.

Finally Andrew stopped walking and dropped Sophie on the snow. He swore as he lifted a metal bar that served as a barricade and grappled with a door. He kicked snow aside in order to pull the door outward. Finally the wind grabbed the door and flung it open. Then he leaned over, lifted Sophie, and carried her inside.

The air inside smelled stale and musty like mold. The cold was clammy and wet. Andrew sat Sophie down on something hard and damp. She began to fall over and he stopped her and sat her upright again.

"Not yet, Sophie," he said. "You must see what I have done for you." Then he moved away, and stepped back toward the door. She heard a match strike, and a flame flickered. Sophie blinked hard against the sudden light. Soon she could focus and she looked around in horror. The floor was dirt. There were no windows, and she was sitting on a gravestone.

"What? Where?" she stammered. Sophie turned abruptly, and found herself looking squarely at a moss-infested gravestone. The words carved into the marble obelisk read, *Willis Singletary, Beloved Son and Brother, 1843-1864, Private-Confederate Army.* Sophie's wordless, quivering lips conveyed her horror

The ceiling was so low that Andrew had to bend over in order to walk to Sophie. He hunched in front of her, took her bloody wrists, and said softly. "I've always tried to give you what you wanted my dear, and then I learned that what you wanted most was to find the grave house of your ancestor uncle. Humph! To me it seemed like a foolish thing to wish for, but then family was never important to me. However, I wanted **you** to have what was important to you. So here you are, my dear." And he swept his arm around the grave house.

"Andrew...how?" moaned Sophie. She was so weak that she thought she might lose consciousness again.

"I'm a resourceful person. You know that. When I found a list of cemeteries in the library trash can, and I knew you were searching for Willis Singletary...well, the deduction was obvious."

He stood upright as much as was possible and said, "And now, my dear Sophie, I must leave you."

"No, please..." Sophie begged. "So cold...cold." She was shaking uncontrollably.

"Ah, yes. The temperature is supposed to drop very low. Very low. I have heard that freezing to death is actually not an unpleasant way to die. I understand one becomes very drowsy, falls asleep, and then peacefully departs this life. Not a bad way to die."

Andrew moved toward the door. "Goodbye Sophie. You're a foolish woman. I could have given you anything...everything." He extinguished the candle and opened the door.

For just a moment Sophie caught a glimpse outside. The full moon had moved to the horizon giving way to the glow of first light. Then the door banged shut and Sophie could hear the sound of a metal barricade dropping in place. The darkness was overpowering. She dared not move from her place on the gravestone lest she be swallowed up in the dark abyss.

* * *

Jeff pulled a number of searchers from the field and ordered them back to Jackson for an update. Back at the office things had really ratcheted up. A visual of the paper found in the abandoned car was projected on a screen. Copies of the paper were made and distributed to the officers. An elderly funeral director who was thought to be an authority on old local cemeteries was talking with Jeff. Occasionally a red check was placed beside the name of one of the cemeteries on the visual.

Finally Jeff faced the group and said in a loud voice, "Okay listen up folks. (The room fell silent) We think we've caught ourselves a break. We found this list of old county cemeteries in the abandoned car at the barn. We know it's a copy of a list given to Sophie Singletary by Eileen Brown, the librarian. Sophie was looking for cemeteries that might contain grave houses in hopes of finding the grave of an ancestor. Notice the red check marks and mark your sheets accordingly. (Pause) Okay Buddy...next. (And a picture of a grave house flashed on the screen.)

"Now this gentleman up here is Mr. Edward Brownell, retired funeral director. He is an authority on old cemeteries. (Mr. Brownell nodded.) Mr. Brownell has identified the cemeteries and graveyards on this list that he thinks are most likely to have grave houses. We've checked them in red. (Jeff points to the screen and the grave house pictures.) And this is a grave house…and this…and this. (The picture on the screen goes from one picture to the next.)

"Okay, now look at your sheet. Who knows the location of any of the cemeteries or graveyards we've checked on the list? (Hands went up.) Alright y'all move over to that table and tell Buddy which cemetery or graveyard you can locate and he'll pair you up with someone who needs help finding them. (People start to move and talk.)

"Hey, wait up a minute! Hear this like you've never heard anything in your life. (Silence) I don't want some overly-enthusiastic searcher to shoot Andrew Temple. Why don't I want the son-of-a-bitch shot? It's sure not because I don't want him hurt…it's because we don't have Sophie Singletary yet, and **we** don't know where she is. **But** Andrew Temple knows. So pass the word…**Alive**…I want him **alive**."

Chapter 32

A deputy sheriff paired up with Jeff and Buddy. He not only knew the location of the old Baskin family cemetery, but he had hunted for rabbits there when he was a kid and claimed to have seen several grave houses there.

Buddy drove. They pulled out of the parking lot and headed east. In the gray winter sky the sun appeared on the horizon its dazzling glow muted by heavy gray clouds. Road maintenance had become predictable...sun softens ice and snow; scrape roads; night falls and refreeze...then begins all over again.

Buddy found the drive to the Baskin family cemetery more challenging than he'd anticipated. The car slipped and skidded over secondary paved roads that eventually led onto unpaved roads that were little more than trails.

Finally they reached yet another abandoned farm house surrounded by rotting out buildings. Broken fence posts lay on the ground and rusty tangled barbed wire could be seen just below the snow. Buddy was directed to turn onto a path filled with ruts and debris. Broken beer bottles protruded out of the dirty snow and fast food cartons and soda cans were scattered about

"Are you sure there's a cemetery back here?" asked Jeff as Buddy swerved to miss a broken beer bottle.

"I'm sure," said their guide as he leaned into the front seat. "Know these parts like the back of my hand."

Soon an old cemetery came into view. It was surrounded by a thick stand of pine trees. Old gravestones were toppled and broken. Faded plastic wreaths and broken vases lay near unkempt graves. Trash was strewn everywhere and black plastic garbage bags lay in a heap at the back of the cemetery. And then they saw them. There, near the garbage heap were stone grave houses…about fifteen in number. Two of the houses were missing roofs and one was so badly vandalized that it appeared to be little more than rubble.

The three men got out of the car. Buddy clicked to lock the doors and pocketed the key. They began to walk around. They moved about the cemetery silently as if in respect for the old place. By checking a few dates on gravestones they concluded that this cemetery could have been used as a burial place for Confederate soldiers.

They began to walk back toward the grave houses. Holes, trash, broken gravestones, and other debris made the trek difficult. They had to concentrate on every step. Thankfully sunlight was appearing more brightly now as it rose above the tree line. Suddenly Buddy caught a glimpse of something that seemed out of place. A glimmer of light bounced off something shiny…something like metal. Metal here should be rusted. He stopped, shaded his eyes with his hand, and focused in the direction of the light. He couldn't believe his eyes.

"Jeff!" he almost whispered.

Jeff and the deputy stopped and turned toward Buddy. Then they looked in the direction Buddy pointed.

"It's a car, Jeff," Buddy said. "What's a car doing out here?"

Jeff was stunned. "Why didn't we see car tracks when we drove in?"

The deputy said, "There's more than one entrance to these places. I just brought you in the way I know best."

Unbeknown to them, as they stared at the out-of-place car, Andrew Temple stared at them from the limb of a tall tree just inside the woods. Andrew was staring at them through the scope of a Winchester Model 70 rifle, and he had a bead on Jeff.

Suddenly there was a sharp crack of a rifle shot and as if in slow motion, Jeff floated to the ground.

"Down! Down! Take cover," Buddy shouted to the deputy and he pointed in the direction of the shot. He took out his phone and called "Back up! Back up! Baskin Family Cemetery. Man down. It's Jeff. Repeat Jeff is down. There's more than one entrance to the cemetery. Repeat. More than one entrance."

Buddy crawled toward Jeff using the gravestones as cover while the deputy fired in the direction of Temple's shot. Buddy reached Jeff who was lying deathly still.

"Jeff, Jeff, can you hear me?" Buddy reached out and gently shook Jeff's shoulder. "Jeff, I called for back-up. They'll be here real quick."

Jeff stirred and emitted a low groan. He was breathing hard.

"Where'd he get you?" Buddy asked.

"Chest. Got me in the chest. Just knocked the wind out of me…had on my vest," Jeff said.

Buddy breathed an audible sigh of relief. "Lie still for a few seconds and get your breath back. We got him pinned down."

Jeff rolled over. "We don't have him pinned down, Buddy. He was gone a second after he fired that shot."

"So what do we do?" Buddy asked.

Jeff raised his head. "One thing we've gotta do is keep him from getting to his vehicle. If he gets out of here, we're back to square one," Jeff said and added, "Think I'm okay, now. Radio again, give description of the vehicle, and remind them that we still don't have Sophie."

Buddy was immediately on the phone. At that point the deputy scurried up.

"Thought they got you, Jeff," he said. "Sure glad to see you're okay."

"Yeah. Okay, here's what we do. We're gonna keep him in the cemetery until backup gets here. I'm going to try to get to his car," Jeff said. "Cover me."

Jeff started across the cemetery…sometimes darting from one gravestone to another and sometimes crawling through the snow and mud. There had been no sign of Andrew since he fired at Jeff. Jeff was only a few feet from the car but it was an open area that provided no cover. This meant he'd have to run for it. Jeff stooped and looked around. No sign of Andrew Temple. He stood in a crouching position and dashed for the car. He worked his way around to the driver's side of the car and secreted himself in a snowy clump of underbrush where he could keep the car under surveillance.

In a distance Jeff could hear the approach of law enforcement vehicles. They came closer and closer. Where was Temple? Surely he hadn't fled on foot. The nearest town was miles away, and the nearest house almost as far. But Jeff knew how resourceful Temple was. He was trained in survival. He'd slipped by so many law enforcement people in the past that he could certainly find his way out of this. The sirens sounded like they were just beyond the path that led to the cemetery.

"Come on. Come on, Temple," thought Jeff. "You know you want out of this. Come get your damn car."

As if in response to Jeff's thought, Jeff saw a movement in some underbrush to his left. Then an arm extended and pushed aside the branches of the bushes. Then a foot appeared and finally a body… a body of the man Jeff knew as Andrew Temple.

"Hold it right there, Temple," said Jeff with his gun aimed at Temple. "Dropped that damn rifle or I'll kill you right here on the spot."

Andrew grinned and lowered his rifle. "Ah, Sophie's lover. I'm Sophie's husband. Are you sure you want to kill me right now? You don't know where Sophie is, do you?" Then they heard louder sirens, car doors slam, and shouting.

Temple quickly raised his rifle and fired. Jeff saw it coming, rolled onto the ground, raised his gun, and fired. Jeff was on his feet instantly, raced to Andrew, and kicked away his rifle. Andrew groaned as he lay on the ground holding his knee. Jeff could hear voices and footsteps pounding in his direction. When they reached Jeff, a Marshal picked up the rifle and a deputy cuffed Andrew.

Jeff looked down at Andrew and said, "Yeah, I'm the lover, but you're not her husband, you son-of a bitch. Now where is she?"

Andrew simply looked up at Jeff and grinned, "Now that's for me to know and for you to find out, Marshal."

Hate surged through Jeff and without thinking he raised his booted foot and kicked Andrew squarely in the face. Andrew pitched backwards, turned his head, and buried his face in the snow. Slowly the white snow began to turn bright red. Everyone stared in amazement.

Finally Buddy stepped up, faced the group, and shouted, "Anybody see what happened here?"

Someone in the back of the crowd yelled, "Did something happen?"

Jeff composed himself and said, "Okay, let's tear this place apart. We're looking at the grave houses. The name is Singletary. We're looking for the grave house of Willis Singletary. Died in 1864. So have at it."

Then Jeff turned and looked down at Andrew Temple. "And get this dirt bag outta my sight before I do something I'll regret."

* * *

At first the cold was brutal, but then Sophie became resigned to it…just as she had become resigned to the adversities of her marriage to Andrew. She'd conditioned herself over ten years of their lives together to accept whatever Andrew demanded. Now he demanded her to die…die in the grave house of her ancestor. Sophie had no doubt she would die. Andrew demanded it.

Sophie discounted the sounds she heard…the voices, the gun fire, car engines. The noises were not real. These were noises she'd hoped for, and now her strong hope was being realized. These were merely subliminal sounds that one hears before slipping into that deadly level of unconsciousness. She would ignore the noises and will herself to drift into peacefulness. That was not really the metallic sound of a bar being lifted from the door barrier. That was not really the rush of more cold air from outside. That was not really Jeff's voice calling her name. These noises existed only in the echoes of her mind. But still she wanted to respond…especially to the sound of Jeff's voice. She tried to speak but no words came. Then Sophie felt arms strong arms wrap around her. Who?

"No," Sophie screamed. "Please…" She cowered as a hand touched her.

"Sophie, it's me. Jeff. Can I have some damned light in here?" The voice was real. It was Jeff.

Harsh light from flashlight beams filled the tomb, and Sophie recoiled at the brightness. She felt a tug on her wrists and she yelped. "No, Jeff. It hurts."

"Son of a…get me a knife or something to get these damned things off," Jeff yelled.

Sophie writhed in pain as Jeff struggled to get the restraints off. Finally he tossed the restraints aside and said, "Let's get you out of here." And he reached and tried to help her stand. Her knees buckled.

"No, Jeff," I can't," she groaned.

"That's okay. We'll get you." And he nodded to some men.

"We got a stretcher out there yet?" Jeff shouted before attempting to lift her.

"It's all ready, Jeff," someone called.

"Okay, Sophie," he murmured as he bent over her. "Take it easy. You'll soon be out of here."

Getting Sophie out of the grave house was not a simple undertaking. The low ceiling forced the men to crouch at the same time they were lifting and moving her. It wasn't until they had Sophie outside in the morning sunlight that they saw the full extent of her injuries. Her wrists were cut, swollen, and coated with dried blood. Her face was caked with blood, she had two black eyes, and her nose bowed to one side. Jeff backed away in horror.

Suddenly he exploded. "Where is he? Where the hell is the bastard? Where'd you put him?" And he swung around and pushed his way into the crowd of officers.

Buddy and another Deputy Marshal moved quickly to restrain him. Others moved in to offer assistance. Jeff was like a wild man.

Jeff could hear shouting—"Jeff! Jeff! Don't…He ain't worth it, Jeff…Don't for her sake…She needs you, man…Don't do anything stupid cause of that ass…."

Jeff finally stopped struggling. Tears ran down his cheeks. Then he turned back toward Sophie. She was being lifted into the ambulance.

"Hey, wait. I'm going," he said. "Buddy you take over…" And he ran and jumped into the back of the ambulance. The door slammed shut, the siren wailed, and they were off to Halifax Medical Center.

A second ambulance pulled in and Andrew T. Temple was loaded into that one. The two Marshals who had come from Raleigh climbed in with the cuffed patient.

Buddy turned to one of the Marshals and said, "Y'all better get

Andrew Temple on back to Raleigh as soon as possible."

"Right. See what you mean," said the Marshal, and he slammed the door. Buddy slapped the side of the vehicle and it took off across the field with its siren wailing.

Chapter 33

Sam and Travis awoke stiff and grouchy from a night spent sleeping in recliners. The sun was trying to force its rays through stubborn drab clouds. The house was unusually quiet, and there was no smell of coffee.

"What time is it?" Sam asked without opening his eyes.

Travis forced his eyes open, focused on the mantle clock, and answered, "Six thirty."

"Gotta have coffee," Sam mumbled.

Travis sat up with difficulty, grasped the arms of his chair, and pushed himself up. "I'll get it," he said.

He trudged towards the kitchen and began to fill the drip coffee pot with water. He was searching the cabinets for the coffee can when Gladys walked down the back stairs.

"What you looking for?" she asked.

"Coffee," said Travis.

"Sit here," she said pulling a chair from under the kitchen table. "I'm the coffee maker around here." Travis sat.

Gladys measured the coffee into the filter basket, slipped it in place, and clicked the switch.

"Don't suppose you heard anything?" she asked.

"No," said Travis. "You'll be the first to know."

"Well I better be," she said cocking a stern eye at him.

The aroma of the brewing coffee served as an alarm clock for the rest of the house. Soon the 'walking dead' as Sam called them appeared in the kitchen and dining room. Gladys served juice, coffee, and coffee cake she had in the freezer. No one spoke. Never before had this crowd gotten together and remained so quiet.

After a while Travis said, "This is like a wake."

Gladys looked horrified. "Travis White, don't you be using that word in this house. Why there's no telling what kind of repercussions it could have."

Suddenly Travis's phone vibrated. He grabbed for it and said, "Yeah." Then he relaxed, shook his head, and said, "Good morning to you too Eve." Then he stood and walked into the hall to finish the conversation.

"Hope that doesn't happen often," said Jan.

"Are the reporters still out there?" Julie asked sleepily.

"Yep," said Sam. "Wonder how **they** slept?" He rubbed his aching back.

"Well, I'm not gonna feed them. If I do, they'll never go away," Gladys said.

Travis walked back in. "Eve said 'hi'. She's been watching WAVY—TV all night. It's big news over in Norfolk too."

Melvin walked into the dining room and laid two newspapers on the table. "It's in the Virginian Pilot and the Daily Herald front page."

Gladys pushed the papers aside. "I don't want to read that stuff until we get Sophie back home." And she began to cry.

Travis's phone vibrated again. This time he walked into the hall immediately.

Jan reached over and patted Gladys's arm. "Gladys, you've got to hold it together. We all have to else we won't be any help to Sophie when she gets home."

"I know. I know," Gladys said. "But I let her down once when I didn't fight her marriage to that evil Andrew Temple. I just couldn't take it if I let her down again."

Julie sat up straight and Jan knew she was preparing to pontificate.

"Julie, this is not the time or the place," Jan mumbled.

Of course Julie ignored her. "Gladys, what you are doing is assuming responsibility for another person's choices. Sophie made the decision to marry Andrew Temple...not you. Her decision...her responsibility."

Then she sat back with a smug look on her face.

"You trying to say that all this is Sophie's fault?" Gladys said angrily. "Why you don't know…"

Gladys rebuttal was cut short when Travis entered the room. "They've found her," he announced.

Gladys's arms flew up in the air and she cried, "Thanks be to God. Oh, thank you Jesus." Then she began to weep silently.

"Where is she?" Sam asked already on his feet.

"Halifax Medical Center," said Travis

"Let's go," said Sam.

"Let's go, Julie," said Jan. "We'll meet y'all over there." And Jan and Julie ran out of the room to dress.

"She's in the hospital?" shrieked Gladys. "Why the hospital? Why not home?"

Travis said, "She's hurt, Gladys. They needed to check her out."

"Well, let's go! Let's go get her," Gladys ordered.

Gladys rushed into the kitchen, grabbed her coat and pocketbook off the hook, and shouted, "Melvin, unplug the coffee pot and let's get out of here."

Travis and Sam looked at each other, shook their heads, and followed Gladys.

* * *

Jeff rode with Sophie in the ambulance. On the ride to the hospital she slipped in and out of consciousness. She stirred and cried in terror neither recognizing Jeff nor where she was.

When they arrived at the hospital Sophie was immediately wheeled into the emergency room, and Jeff was left alone in the waiting room to relive the events of the last two days that had almost snatched Sophie from his life forever. Suppose he hadn't found her? Could he stand to lose her again? Would she blame him for not protecting her? Could she trust him again? Could she trust any man again? Could she trust any person again? Any person…there were others who were worried sick about her too. That's when he reached for his cell and called Travis.

Just as he clicked off his phone, the emergency room doctor approached Jeff. He looked suspiciously at the disheveled, muddy man standing before him.

"Are you Jeff Sands, US Marshal?" he asked.

"Yes," said Jeff, and he realized how dry his mouth was.

The doctor extended his hand and said, "I'm Dr. Sandlin the emergency room doctor. Let's sit down."

Jeff followed the doctor to two straight back chairs with cold plastic green seats. They sat. Jeff could only say, "How is she?"

"She's going to be okay...physically," said the doctor.

Jeff breathed a sigh of relief.

"As you know, this was a brutal assault. Not all her scars will be physical. She was in shock when you brought her in and she was suffering from hypothermia. There was some cardiac arthythmia due to the warming process. She has a broken nose and two black eyes. There are multiple scrapes and cuts from the restraints. Now that we have her stabilized, she is no longer in danger. She was not sexually assaulted. However, we want to keep her a few days for observation. Ahhh...are you the Marshal in charge or are you her, ah...ah, significant other? Excuse my ineptness but I don't know how to phrase *that* today."

"I'm both," said Jeff. "She has no family."

"I see," said the doctor. "At any rate, she has asked for you and you may see her as soon as she's settled in her room. Second floor, 201." Doctor Sandlin stood, shook hands, and walked toward the doctor's lounge.

Jeff pushed the elevator button. The light indicated the elevator was on third floor. Then the light moved to fourth floor. Then...Jeff looked for the stairs and took them two at a time. When he reached the second floor he threw open the door and stood looking down a long empty hall. He began checking room numbers. Three doors down he found number 201. The door was open but a curtain was closed around the bed. He heard voices.

"Alright, honey," said a syrupy high pitched woman's voice. "Now we're just going to slip you over to your bed real fast and easy. Won't take a sec." Then the tenor of her voice changed dramatically. "Okay, Cecil. You ready? One, two, three." (Then sweet again) There you are, sweetie, all comfy."

As Jeff stood waiting, a male nurse with a disgusted look on his face walked out of the room.

The voice inside continued, "Now this is your buzzer, darling. You just push this little red tip, and I'll be in like a flash."

The curtain swung open and a tall, heavy Amazon type nurse stepped out. Jeff wondered if she could actually move 'like a flash'.

She frowned at Jeff. "You the boyfriend?" she demanded.

"I'm with the United States Marshal Service. Here to see Sophie Singletary," Jeff said in an effort to exert authority.

"You're the boyfriend," the nurse said totally unimpressed with his introduction. She eyed him sternly. "You can go in but I don't want her upset, and no hanky-panky. I'll be right outside." She walked to her desk, turned, and glared back at him.

Jeff crept cautiously into the room. Sophie was lying there as white as the pillow on which she lay. An IV bottle hung above her bed and fluids dripped through a tube and down to her arm. Five wires were connected to her chest and linked to a monitor that gave continuous readings of heart rhythm, blood pressure, and pulse on a screen beside the bed. Both of her eyes were black and almost closed. Two wooden objects that looked like ice cream sticks protruded from her nose which was covered with white bandages. Her hands and wrists were bandaged up to her elbows. She turned when she heard him approach and began to cry. Jeff rushed to her and carefully laid his face on her cheek. He began to cover her cheeks and neck with gentle kisses.

"Sophie, Sophie, I don't know what to say. I feel so...so helpless. I couldn't get to you. Oh God, if anything had..."

Sophie tried to lift a bandaged hand to touch his face but didn't have the strength. Her hand fell limply back onto the bed. "Jeff, please don't...don't blame yourself. Andrew is evil, Jeff. So very, very evil. He's gotten worse...so much worse. He's...he's...mad."

Jeff eased away and looked into her eyes. "He's gone Sophie. We got him and he's been taken away. And he'll be put away forever. You're okay. Everything's okay."

He moved his chair close to the bed and laid his head on the pillow beside her. They lay there quietly, peacefully.

Finally Sophie muttered, "Jeff...Jeff, I miss being close to you."

"Hey, it's only been two days," he said jokingly.

"Two days of hell," she mumbled. "just...just look at me."

He sat up and gave her a scrutinizing look. "Well, you do look a little like a raccoon," he said.

"You!" Sophie murmured hoarsely and smiled weakly.

Jeff shook his head and looked thoughtful. "I never thought I'd see you like this again."

"You mean with black eyes and bandages?" she said.

"No, I never thought I'd see you able to joke again. Better be careful though. Nurse 'Ratchet' warned me against any hanky-panky."

"Hanky-panky?" Sophie said unbelievingly.

At that moment there was a commotion in the hall. Sophie jumped and she looked frightened. Jeff realized Sophie's recuperation was going to take a while.

"It's okay. Be right back," Jeff said, and walked toward the door.

As Jeff parted the curtain, Cecil, the male nurse, walked through the door.

"You the US Marshal?" he asked.

"Yes, what's the problem?" Jeff said.

"We got a woman out here says she's going to take Ms. Singletary home. She sure is causing a row."

"Gladys!" said Jeff.

When Jeff walked into the hall there was a stand-off between Nurse 'Ratchet' and Gladys. Travis and Sam were cowering by the elevator looking on in disbelief.

"I don't pay no attention to visiting hours," Gladys was saying. "I'm not here to visit. I'm here to take her home where she belongs."

"No patient leaves my hall without doctor's orders. Do you have such orders?" Nurse 'Ratchet' said.

"I'll show you orders," said Gladys and she stepped up to the nurse.

Jeff leapt into the fray. "Hey, hey you two," he said stepping between them and holding up his hands in a stop position. "Take it easy. What's the problem?"

Gladys shot Jeff an angry look and shouted, "Jeff Sands, you stay out of this. I'm gonna take Sophie home. You know I'm the one who takes care of her. The only time I didn't is when she married that monster and see what's happened."

"Ms. Singletary is not going anywhere without proper authorization," said the nurse. "If you don't leave immediately, I'm going to call security."

"I'll show you proper authorization..." said Gladys.

"Whoa! Hold on Gladys," shouted Jeff. "You don't realize how sick Sophie is. When you see her you'll realized she can't go home yet. Now you take a deep breath and settle down and we'll go in to see her."

Nurse 'Ratchet' started to object but Jeff shook his head and gave her a stern look. Gladys calmed down.

"Okay then," said Jeff. "Let's go see Sophie. She looks pretty rough, Gladys. If you get upset, she'll get upset." Gladys glared at Jeff.

Jeff led Gladys into Sophie's room and slowly pulled aside the curtain. Gladys walked in, went to Sophie's bed, and looked at her with a probing eye. She walked to the IV bottle and checked the drip. She stared intently at the monitor beside the bed. She glared at the wooden sticks protruding from Sophie's nose, and checked her bandages. Then she looked Sophie directly in the eye and said emphatically, "Well Sophie, we got our work cut out for us. But I'll take care of everything...as usual."

Then Gladys removed her coat, set her purse on a cart, and sat down. "I'm not going anywhere."

Suddenly Jeff felt dog-tired. Although Gladys was probably going to cause the hospital a lot of trouble, he knew that Sophie was going to be taken care of. He suddenly hurt in places he'd not realized before. Sleep. If he could just sleep. He looked at Sophie, and then he looked at Gladys. Yes sleep.

Jeff walked to the bed, bent down, and kissed Sophie on the forehead. "I think I'll go and let you rest. Gladys is here and everything's going to be okay."

Sophie's eyes were fluttering. The strong sedative was taking effect. "Yes...okay," she said in a slurred soft voice.

Chapter 34

Jeff fell asleep as soon as he tumbled into Sam's Cherokee. He did not notice that the news crews had now taken up their watch in the hospital parking lot. He did not see Jan and Julie push through the crowd and run in the emergency room door. He didn't wake up until the Cherokee pulled up to the back door of Sophie's house.

"Jeff. Jeff, wake up. We're here. You need some help getting inside?" Travis asked.

Jeff woke with a start. "No, no. I can make it. Thanks for the ride." And he stumbled from the Cherokee to the back door.

He took the back stairs because they were closer. He trudged up the steps, walked to the bedroom and fell into the bed. The pillow smelled like Sophie. He missed her so much it hurt. He clutched the pillow tightly and quickly fell asleep.

The next day he was awakened by the ring of his cell phone. He jerked up and fumbled to get it out of his pocket. Sophie? Could something have happened?

He finally got his cell out and said, "Jeff Sands here."

"Jeff, how good to hear you're okay," said the cheery voice of Arlis Bryant, Jeff's superior in Raleigh.

"Thank you," said Jeff. "I'm still a little groggy. Just got some much-needed sleep."

"Well, you deserve it," Bryant said. "I am just calling to congratulation you on a job well done, Jeff. You apprehended our fugitive and he's locked up, and you rescued our witness. Well done, Jeff. Well done."

Jeff could just see him now…feet on his desk and waving a cigar as he spoke.

"Thank you. I'm relieved that it turned out as well as it did," Jeff said.

"Now how's Ms. Singletary doing?" Bryant's voice had taken on a concerned edge.

And Jeff gave Bryant a brief report of Sophie's injuries.

"Shame! Damned shame!" exclaimed Bryant. "Temple's a mad man, Jeff. I tell you a mad man!"

"That's what Sophie said," said Jeff.

"Well, she's safe now, thanks to you and your team," Bryant said. "Why don't you take some time off? Rest, relax. You deserve it. Besides you probably want to spend some time with Ms. Singletary."

Jeff was relieved that Bryant appeared to accept his relationship with Sophie.

"Thanks," said Jeff. "Need to wrap up some paper work then I plan to do that."

"Good!" said Bryant. And he hung up.

Jeff looked at the clock on the mantle. One thirty. He went into the bathroom, showered, and shaved. He put on fresh clothes and started downstairs. Then he stopped abruptly. No car! He had his cell out just as he reached the downstairs hall. He glanced outside and saw that his car was parked in front. Buddy! Buddy must have brought it over.

When he arrived at the hospital parking lot he saw a hospital administrator standing before a television camera briefing the reporters on Sophie's condition. Jeff slipped through the crowd and into the reception area. He didn't bother with the elevator this time but went straight to the steps. When he opened the second floor door he saw Melvin stretched out on a couch sound asleep. He'd been there all night. Ahead a doctor was talking to Nurse 'Ratchet'. Jeff recognized the doctor as the one who treated Sophie when she was poisoned. He in returned recognized Jeff and hurried toward him.

"Doc, is anything wrong?" asked Jeff anxiously.

"With Sophie? No. No," he said shaking his head. "But we are having a little trouble with Gladys. She won't let the nurses attend to Sophie at all. She orders them out of the room. She's even threatened to go to the kitchen to…let's see how did she put it…give cooking lessons. I've had nurses threaten to quit and an orderly who already has. I tell you, Jeff, we've got a problem."

"Whew!" said Jeff in exasperation. "What'll we do? I'm not sure I can handle Gladys. Sometimes she intimidates the hell out of me."

"Me too," said the doctor as they walked toward Sophie's room. "Fortunately I had am opportunity to observe Gladys's nursing skills when she cared for Sophie during the poisoning episode. If Gladys will just cooperate a little longer…say till five o'clock…then I'll release Sophie in her care."

Jeff breathed a sigh of relief. "Thanks Doc. Maybe I can get her to calm down till then."

But as they reached Sophie's room, a young nurse ran out of the door in tears.

"Oh boy!" said Jeff as he pulled the curtain back.

The doctor entered the room first. "Good morning, Sophie," he said cheerfully without acknowledging Gladys. He walked to Sophie's bed and began to examine her injuries. He looked at her eyes, in her eyes, and checked her nose. He examined a small lesion on her forehead that had required some stitches. He listened to her heart and lungs.

Then he said, "Did you sleep last night?"

"Yes," said Sophie. "I was given a sedative."

"That's fine. What you need right now is rest."

Jeff moved to Sophie's side and took her bandaged hand. He was following the doctor's lead as far as Gladys was concerned. Gladys held fast to her nurse's training and deferred to the doctor. So far she'd not said anything. The doctor pulled a chair up to the bed.

"Sophie, it'll take a while for all your injuries to heal, but I see you receive good care." He nodded toward Gladys. "So, I'm letting you go home today. Now I want you to stay until around five o'clock to make sure you remain stabilized then you can go home."

Gladys spoke for the first time. "I don't see why she has to stay here till five o'clock."

"Well, I do," the doctor said decisively, "so five o'clock it is."

Jeff spoke up. "Besides Gladys, there's no food in the house, and the bed is unmade. Sheets. You know you gotta change sheets."

Sophie realized what was going on and spoke up weakly, "Gladys do you think I could have some of your chicken vegetable soup when I get home?"

Gladys looked from one to the other. "Okay," she acquiesced, "I'll go on home and get things ready."

Gladys gathered her things and headed for the door. Then she turned to Jeff and said, "How's she getting home anyhow?"

"Ambulance. She'll be coming home in an ambulance," Jeff said.

Gladys marched into the hall with new purpose. She called to Melvin who was still waiting in the reception room, "Come on Melvin. We got work to do. Somebody's got to do it."

* * *

Gladys arrived home to find the table cleared, dishes washed, and the kitchen cleaned. The carpet in the dining room, hall, and den had been vacuumed. Upstairs the sheets on the beds in which Jan and Julie slept had been stripped and replace with clean fresh ones. There was a note from Jan and Julie offering to help in any way—any time. Gladys huffed that she 'didn't need no more help…thank you very much'.

At five o'clock attendants slipped Sophie down to the emergency room exit and into an ambulance. The ambulance traveled without siren and Jeff followed. He had instructed the ambulance to drive to the back of the house.

When they reached Gumberry only three miles away Jeff called to let Gladys know they were almost home and they would come in the back. When they arrived Gladys and Melvin were standing in the backyard. Gladys immediately took over directing the attendants into the house, up the front stairs, and into Sophie's room.

The room smelled like lemon Pledge. Sophie's freshly-made bed was turned down revealing clean crisp white sheets. Another pair of sheets, a pillow, and a blanket lay on the chaise. Apparently this was where Gladys thought Jeff should sleep. Fresh flowers were on the desk and a fire in the fireplace.

Sophie smiled. "There were times when I thought I'd never see this room again."

The attendants gently lifted her onto the bed although she insisted she could do it herself.

"You see, Jeff," said Gladys, "that's what we got to watch out for…her wanting to do things before she's able."

The attendants left and Gladys went downstairs to get chicken vegetable soup for Sophie and Jeff.

Jeff nodded toward the chaise. "Gladys has relegated me to the chaise."

Sophie laughed. "Well, she doesn't want any hanky-panky going on in here."

Chapter 35

Over the next three weeks changes took place in the old Victorian house on Main Street. Sophie no longer made trips to the library nor searched for grave houses in family cemeteries. The stitches on her forehead were removed and she no longer had bandages on her wrists and arms. The dressing was removed from her nose and 'ice cream sticks' no longer protruded from her nostrils. Her black eyes were now a yellowish-green color. Consequently Sophie wouldn't go on shopping trips or out to lunch with Jan and Julie.

Jan and Julie came over to play a few hands of bridge with Sophie and Jeff. Sophie and Jeff read to each other, listened to music, and watched television. Jeff didn't use the sheet, pillow, and blanket that Gladys had suggestively placed on the chaise, and finally she took them away and placed them in the linen closet.

Soon Sophie went downstairs for meals, and Gladys prepared enough food for an army. "You'll never get well if you eat like a bird," she said.

One afternoon Sophie lay on her bed lost in thought. During such moments Jeff didn't intrude. He realized she had a lot to sort through.

Finally she said, "Jeff, will you do something for me?"

He walked across the room, sat on the bed, and took her hand. Then in an exaggerated fashion he said, "Anything. Just tell me what you want. You want the moon? I'll get you the moon…"

Sophie laughed and jerked her hand away. "You sound like Jimmy Stewart. No, seriously. I'd like you to undertake a home project."

"Like laying tile in the upstairs bathroom?" he joked. "I'll have to measure you know."

"Jeff, stop. I want you to get rid of the secret room off of my great, great grandfather's office," she said as she ticked off the 'greats' on her fingers.

"You mean board it up?" Jeff asked.

"No I mean tear it down. I'd like to combine the office and that room into a large library. We could put in recessed book shelves and maybe a reading bench where the room is," she said.

"You've given this some thought haven't you?" said Jeff.

"I have. I keep thinking about how Andrew hid in that room waiting for an opportunity to search the house. I don't want that connection anymore."

Jeff nodded his head thoughtfully. "I think it's a great idea. We'll draw up some plans and then I'll go to Lowe's and check on materials. Yeah, this is a good idea. Give us something to do together."

At that moment Gladys walked in carrying a tray of sandwiches, deviled eggs, assortment of pickles, and a pot of cocoa.

"What y'all gonna do together?" she said with a wicked smile.

Sophie laughed. "We're going to tear down the secret room and turn it and the office into a library."

Gladys set the tray on a table. "Well thank heavens," said Gladys. "I'll be glad to get rid of that place seeings it's a perfect place for evil ghosts to occupy."

Sophie shook her head. "Gladys, I told you the noises you heard were probably Andrew waiting to search the house."

"Don't make no difference. You don't know that **all** the noises were made by Andrew Temple," Gladys said and walked out indignantly.

* * *

It didn't take Jeff, Melvin, and a make-shift crew very long to dismantle the walls that enclosed the secret room and convert the two rooms into one space. From a catalog Sophie chose factory-made bookshelves that *required some assembling*. The project moved quickly and to Gladys' relief she'd soon be able to 'clean up the mess'.

Sophie found strength and single-mindedness in their undertaking. She sorted through boxes of books that Melvin and Jeff brought down from the attic while Jeff and Melvin studies directions for assembling the bookshelves they'd ordered. Gladys happily complained about the mess, and all the while smooth jazz played softly in the background.

One afternoon their work was interrupted when Jan and Julie dropped by. Jan was holding several brown dead-looking branches.

"Hey, look what I brought you," she said handing the branches to Sophie.

Jeff walked over and examined the branches skeptically. "What in the...?"

Sophie's eyes lit up. "It's forsythia branches, and look they're covered with buds."

"Oh," said Jeff. He looked closely at the seemingly dead branches and he saw they were covered with tiny bumps that looked as if they might burst.

Sophie said, "If I put these in water in a warm sunny spot, the buds will open early and there will be tiny yellow flowers. We can enjoy an early springtime." And she went to find a vase.

Julie began to inspect the shelves Jeff and Melvin were assembling. "Is this wood real cherry or has it just been stained?" Of course she didn't wait for an answer...Julie never waited for an answer. She continued, "I certainly hope it's real cherry. Stained woods are usually soft woods, you know, and soft woods absorb dirt and liquid which results in permanent stains. It's best to go with the good materials first."

Of course no one listened to Julie and Sophie returned with the forsythia branches in a tall vase of water.

"I'll set this in the window where they will get sunlight," she said admiring the arrangement.

Jeff's cell rang. He looked at the phone and walked into the hall to answer.

Jan said, "Jeff not working?"

"He took three weeks off," said Sophie. Julie and Jan looked edgy.

Sophie smiled and said, "But look what we've done in three weeks," she said sweeping her hand around the room.

"It looks great!" said Jan and she walked over to Sophie, took her by the hands, and looked at her closely. "And you look great too!" And she hugged her tightly.

They heard Jeff click his phone shut and walk upstairs.

"Come on, Julie," said Jan. "We got places to go and things to do." Then she turned to Sophie and said, "And soon you'll be coming with us, Missy."

Sophie picked up the vase of forsythia branches and walked with Jan and Julie to the door. As soon as the door closed Sophie rushed upstairs. She set the vase of forsythia in the window, turned, and fixed her eyes on the bed. Jeff's bag was open on the bed and clothes were inside. Jeff walked out of the bathroom with a small leather case in his hand and saw Sophie staring at the bag.

He walked across the room and put the leather pouch containing toilet articles in the bag with his clothes. He turned to Sophie and took her hands.

"That was Arlis Bryant. I have to go to Raleigh. I have a new assignment," Jeff said simply.

"Whew! When he said three weeks, he meant three weeks didn't he?" Sophie said.

Jeff sat on the bed and pulled her down to sit beside him. "Sophie, we knew this was going to happen. I have to go back to work."

Sophie sighed. "I know. I know," she said resignedly. "It's just...it's just that I'll miss you so much."

He drew her to him and held her tightly. "This won't be for long. I just have to go the western part of the state to escort a fugitive back to Raleigh."

Sophie pushed away, smiled, and said, "Thought you couldn't talk about you job."

Jeff grinned. "Well just this time," he said. Then his voice took on a serious note. "Sophie, I love you," he said.

Sophie smiled brightly. "I love you too Jeff. You, know that's the first time we've said that to each other since...since..."

"Since I dumped you or you dumped me," he said.

"Oh please, let's not go there," she said.

Jeff laughed and stood up. "Gotta go. And I **will** be back soon."

Jeff zipped the bag, threw the strap over his shoulder, leaned in, and kissed her lovingly, longingly. Finally he pulled away and looked at her tenderly. His eyes turned to the vase of forsythia branches.

"I'll be back, Sophie. I'll be back before that forsythia blooms," he said and then he was gone.

THE END

CPSIA information can be obtained at www.ICGtesting.com
Printed in the USA
LVOW051931180712

290617LV00008B/22/P